Dear Reader,

#Koreanfood is trending. TikTok and Instagram feeds are filled with bibimbap bowls, fiery stews, and kimchi. I never dreamed the "funky" foods from my childhood would one day become popular.

Contrary to type, my Korean immigrant mom is a terrible cook (sorry, Umma!). Her specialty, "breakfast salad," is a mishmash of minari grown in her garden, freezer-burned leftovers, filet mignon that's covered in cocktail napkin schmutz because it's been smuggled home from a wedding . . . you get the picture. Umma fled North Korea during the War; from South Korea she immigrated to Argentina, then to the United States. Umma cooks not for pleasure or taste, but *survival*.

I tried to escape Umma's "refugee-style" cooking by devouring Western cookbooks and binge-watching the Food Network. I was well into adulthood before I realized the truth: those stunning dishes were a fantasy. It was impossible to reproduce their picture-perfect results. I've now embraced Umma's approach to leftovers (sans the wedding steak). Each night I coax culturally confused bits and bobs into a cohesive meal. My husband, bless his heart, calls my cooking "jazz."

What's Eating Jackie Oh? is inspired by two things: my love of cooking with leftovers and the fears and frustrations of the AAPI community in the recent spate of anti-Asian violence. In my *New York Times* op-ed, "I'm Done Being Your Model Minority," I called for action. As "model minorities," we're expected to work hard, heads down, without complaint. AAPIs have been so invisible, we're hyper-visible as targets. The violence continues, long post-Covid. We, and our allies, *must speak out against the hate.*

Jackie Oh is like many teens I've heard from since my op-ed went viral. She fears for her family and herself. What's the point of the American dream—straight As, Ivy League, etc.—if you'll still get pushed around (literally and figuratively)? And what about *anti*-model minorities, like her incarcerated—and shunned—brother? Jackie turns to cooking as her therapy. From repurposing leftovers at her grandparents' Manhattan deli, Melty's, to competing on the TV cooking show *Burn Off!*, food feels like a problem Jackie can actually solve in a world that makes zero sense.

    I hope *What's Eating Jackie Oh?* will make you 🫠 😭 🤭. All the feels. Jackie Oh's journey of discovering her identity both on *and* off the plate will tug at your heartstrings—while giving you the munchies. 😋

많이 먹어!
Eat up!

ALSO BY PATRICIA PARK

*Imposter Syndrome and Other Confessions
of Alejandra Kim*

Re Jane

WHAT's EATING
Jackie Oh?

PATRICIA PARK

CROWN
New York

Text copyright © 2024 by Patricia Park
Jacket art copyright © 2024 by Jessica Cruickshank

All rights reserved. Published in the United States by Crown Books for Young Readers,
an imprint of Random House Children's Books, a division of
Penguin Random House LLC, New York.

Crown and the colophon are registered trademarks of Penguin Random House LLC.

Visit us on the Web! GetUnderlined.com

Educators and librarians, for a variety of teaching tools,
visit us at RHTeachersLibrarians.com

Library of Congress Cataloging-in-Publication Data
Datadatadata tk

The text of this book is set in 11.5-point Bembo MT Std.
Interior design by Michelle Crowe

Printed in the United States of America
10 9 8 7 6 5 4 3 2 1
First Edition

THIS BOOK IS DEDICATED TO
MY NEPHEWS, GAGE AND LUCAS.

Part I

NOT YOUR MODEL MINORITY

I'm not one of those TI-84 Plus, Princeton Review, Barron's, Kaplan, Khan, Kumon, hagwon, AP-everything Asian kids with the turtle backpacks crawling all over the 7 train. I used to be. But I'm done with all that.

I just haven't told my parents yet.

Umma went to Bronx Science, like me, and Appa went to Stuyvesant. Unlike me, they were straight A students who went on to Harvard and Yale Law School (Umma), and Carnegie Mellon and Columbia Business School (Appa). That my dad's not a double-Ivy like my mom is kind of a sore spot, and even though he fronts like it isn't, I can tell Appa's still carrying that ginormous chip on his shoulder. But then again, Umma "only" went to Science instead of Stuy—so I guess their "educational disparity" sort of evens out.

These are the things my parents care about. Potato, potahto.

They'd seriously lose it if they found out I was flunking out of Science.

OKAY, "FLUNK" IS A STRONG word. Really, I'm just barely passing one class: world history (70%), and I'm doing "mediocre" (90.1%) in my other classes. My gripe with world history is that there's got to be more to life than memorizing pointless historical facts about someone else's past, when—shouldn't I be concentrating on my future?

Also, Mr. Doumann keeps confusing me for Jennifer Oh, because to him we're All the Same. Most of my teachers are "woke" or whatever, but Mr. D is a relic from the past—not unlike the very subject he teaches. The DOE should just fire him already, but probably can't (because tenure, teacher's union, pension, etc.). I don't tell Umma and Appa about Mr. Doumann because they'll have no sympathy: *Stop making excuses. Tough it out.* The same things they used to tell my older brother ("Oppa" to me, Justin to the outside world).

For us Ohs, to be anything less than perfect means you're already a failure. Just ask Oppa.

BACK WHEN I USED TO drink the model minority Kool-Aid, I was all about the Ivy Leagues, too. I thought that was what you were *supposed* to do. The purpose of life was to study hard, get into Harvard/Princeton/Yale, land a corporate job with a sweet 401k, and make babies that would study hard, get into Harvard/Princeton/Yale, etc., and continue your whole miserable corporate life cycle.

My parents are workaholics, which they'd probably take as the compliment it isn't. *Things cost money* is Appa's favorite catchphrase. He works in private equity and has a closetful of suits that I'm constantly picking up and dropping off at the dry cleaners, and I only see his shadow darting into the apartment when he comes home from work, long after I'm already in bed.

Umma's up for managing partner at Leviathan, White & Gross LLP. According to Appa, the promotion is hers to lose. "Your mom's put in the 'sweat equity,'" and the other candidate's always blowing off work for—Appa curls his fingers into sarcastic air quotes—"self-care days," leaving Umma to pick up the slack. Umma's never been more keyed up and stressed out about this potential promotion. Mostly I try to stay out of her way.

Study hard, get into an Ivy, land a corporate job, make babies. Repeat. These are the Oh Family Core Values.

In other words, it's our American dream.

WHEN I TURNED ONE YEAR old, I grabbed a dollar bill and my fate was sealed—I'd be financially successful for the rest of my life. Instead of all the other objects (fates) my infant self *could* have reached for during my doljabi ceremony: pencil (scholar), calculator (accountant), paintbrush (artist), golf ball (LPGA pro), iPhone (the next Steve Jobs), and so on.

"Pay up!" Halmoni, ever the hustler, had placed bets with her friends. "My granddaughter's going to be *rich!*"

Apparently she told Haraboji to pay up, too. My grandfather fished for his wallet and grumbled, "알았어." *Fine/Got it/*

Capisce. (My Korean's not great, so that's my lost-in-translation translation.)

Haraboji had bet on the bowl of rice—because he wanted me to never go hungry in life.

H&H ARE MY BEDROCK. MY grandparents basically raised me in the kitchen of Melty's, their deli in Midtown. Apparently Umma took the bare minimum maternity leave because it wasn't a good look to take longer than that. She'd drop me off at Melty's each morning on her way to the office. I'd cry and cry, and Halmoni would shush me: "Jackie-ya, you want Umma lose her job? Then how she gonna pay your food? Toys? College? Be good girl, stop crying."

Eventually, I learned to stop crying.

Eventually, I learned to stop depending on my mother at all.

As soon as I was old enough to hold a knife, I was put to work. Which I'm pretty sure is a DOH violation, as well as a Child Services one.

It's the immigrant way.

Umma, whose idea of "cooking" is pressing a button to order delivery, insisted on negotiating my pay at Melty's because "I'll not have you repeat my exploited childhood in that kitchen."

But I'd work at Melty's for free. Cooking's my passion. Which I know sounds like some BS you'd write on a college application—*my passions include Ultimate frisbee, AP Physics, and cleaning hamster cages at the animal shelter!!*—but I'm actually for real.

I think it's what I want to do for the rest of my life.

BAYSIDE

On Fridays after hagwon—that's Korean for "the school you go to after school because regular school isn't enough"—I head to H&H's house in Bayside for *Burn Off!* Yes, my Friday night jam is watching a cooking show with my grandparents and their dog.

Don't judge.

We're sitting at the kitchen table, eating candied kelp. Bingsu, the jindo, sits alert at Haraboji's feet. She's too dignified to lie down and beg for scraps. Her foxlike are ears perked up, like an attack could come from anywhere at any time.

Dogs are funny like that. They are their own people.

Host Dennis appears on the TV screen in his usual toga and laurels. He's so white, he's orange—if that makes any sense—like he's been steeped in Tang. His eyes are the same shade as chlorine pool water. Halmoni is in love with him.

He starts his opening spiel: "Ladies, gentlemen, countrymen! Lend me your ears! Coming to you *hot* from Kitchen Coliseum, it's *Burn Off!*"

Host Dennis smiles his bleachy grin. When he's not hosting *Burn Off!*, he's flashing his pearls in all those toothpaste ads. Halmoni claps and swoons, and Haraboji and I exchange an eyeroll.

The camera pans to a Roman gladiator blowing on a long Viking horn. It's completely culturally inaccurate. I say this as someone flunking world history.

Speaking of which, my last exam is still crammed in the bottom of my backpack. I don't want to think about it. Just like how I don't want to think about the world history exam is in two weeks, and I'm so not prepared. I fix my attention back to the screen.

Host Dennis goes, "Today's contestants will slice. They'll dice. They'll fight to the finish! But only one chef will win the crown of—"

The crowd finishes for him: "*Burn Off!* champion!"

The TV fritzes out.

"이놈 . . . !" Haraboji grunts, which is Korean for *You little misbehaving bastard!* He slaps the side of the TV: nothing. It's so old, H&H should have curbed it last millennium. Bingsu snarls at the "misbehaving" TV because she always has Haraboji's back. He's her favorite. Bingsu likes Halmoni okay, and she and I just coexist.

The TV comes back to life.

"—secret ingredients are! Zucchini! Toasted sesame seeds! Red wine vinegar! Prime rib! Strawberry lollipops! And . . . chocolate-covered ants!" says Host Dennis. "Chefs, you get thirty-seven minutes to complete your dish! So cook off or—"

"*Burn Off!*" we shout along with the TV audience.

As the TV contestants scurry around the kitchen, my brain is organizing the ingredients, trying to coax them into cohesion. I could see searing off the prime rib with a sesame seed crust, then finishing it in the oven to roast. Sautéed zucchini with a splash of vinegar, like the hobak bokkeum Halmoni made last week. I'd melt down the chocolate-coated ants, forget about the chocolate (because a chocolate mole sauce is too obvious), fish out the ants, and deep-fry them for a frizzled crunchy topping for the meat. But the strawberry lollipops . . .

Halmoni is scribbling the ingredients on the back of an old receipt. "Jackie-ya," she says, "what you think? Most difficult part is chocolate-covered ants."

I laugh. "Seriously, Halmoni? And *not* the lollipops?"

"Easy," she says. "Lollipop instead of kiwi or sugar for beef marinade to make meat tender. Use grater. But chocolate? Make no sense for the dinner."

Then *both* my grandparents give me a look like, *Duh*.

"That's actually pretty brilliant," I say, marveling at how they cracked the riddle of the candy.

I tell them my menu ideas, but Haraboji shakes his head. "No," he says. "Sesame already toasted. Gonna burn and turn bitter, you try to do like that."

Now *I* shake my head. "Haraboji, are you sure? I swear I tried baked sesame from a Middle Eastern bakery—"

"You not believe your own Haraboji? Let's go."

He hits pause on the remote and gets up from the table. Never mind that H&H just put in a fourteen-hour day at Melty's. It is *on*.

7

We round up the *Burn Off!* ingredients or the closest approximations of. We don't have "American" zucchini, but we have hobak—Korean green squash, which is as thick as my forearm. We have the sesame and rice wine vinegar. No prime rib, but sirloin in the freezer. Grape-flavored hard candy. And chocolate-covered . . . chocolate. We make do.

And with that, the three of us are cooking—each of us making our own interpretation of the secret ingredients. I make my sesame rib. Halmoni makes grape candy-and-soy-marinated galbi, and Haraboji does beef-and-zucchini shish kebabs. We sit down to our smorgasbord, rounded out with leftover pizza from Nino's on Springfield, kimchi, and a jar of kosher dill pickles—which for some reason H&H have an endless supply of.

And it turns out, Haraboji is right. My sesame crust is bitter and burnt.

"Telling you so," Haraboji says, and Halmoni howls at my mistake because there is no mercy in our family.

IT MIGHT SEEM KIND OF random, how we started watching *Burn Off!* But it's the one show the three of us agree on. H&H's English isn't great, so American TV shows are hard for them to follow. My Korean isn't great, so Korean TV is hard for *me* to follow. And H&H are into those Joseon dynasty K-dramas—the ones where they speak in Ye Olde Korean, which even *Korean* Korean people need subtitles for.

One day we were flipping through the channels, and we landed on this bizarre cooking show. The kitchen set was decorated with marbled columns and ivy. The host, wearing a toga and laurels, announced different challenges: *Make an entrée with six secret ingredients in thirty-seven minutes! A beef dish for less than twenty dollars! A dessert using only a fry pan and mallet!*

It was a show I didn't have to translate into English, and they didn't have to translate into Korean. Food is like the universal language.

Haraboji and I are the true believers—we're in it for the cooking—but Halmoni's favorite part of *Burn Off!* is Host Dennis. Which Haraboji pretends makes him jealous, but I think makes him *actually* jealous.

People once ran a cover story on Host Dennis, his husband, their beautiful children, and their McMansion in Malibu. I don't have the heart to tell Halmoni he's off the market.

Haraboji likes Judge Johnny, who brings a down-home, slapsticky element with catchphrases like *You got to eat it to mean it!* My favorite is Judge Stone McMann, who takes a cerebral approach to his food. I own all the cookbooks in his McMann's Authoritative Cookery series. And 55 percent of Burnees are American men ages twenty-one to forty-nine who tune in just for Judge Kelly Sharpe because she's a gorgeous hard-ass who once appeared on the cover of *Maxim* wearing nothing but a bikini-apron thingy.

What can I say? We all got *burnt*.

Umma and Appa have no idea what goes on in my weekends in Bayside.

***

H&H AND I EAT DINNER and heckle the contestants on TV:

"You forgot the lollipop!"

"Turn on the ice cream maker!"

"Get your steaks off the grill!"

Our running commentary is punctuated by H&H's heckles about my eating and weight:

"Jackie-ya, slow down!" Halmoni tuts. "Too fast eating makes you fat."

"Okay, Halmoni."

"Because Korea, no such thing fat people. Like looking at space alien."

"Okay, Haraboji."

"Because we poor country back then. Now Korea rich, because Samsung and K-pop."

"Okay, Halmoni."

"First time I see fat person, American GI. Haraboji think, '와! 역시 미국이 부자 나라 이구나!'"

Wow! Beautiful-Country (aka America) *sure must be a rich country!*

"Okay, Haraboji."

"GI give us Hershey's chocolate bar." Halmoni smiles, as if remembering that faraway moment. "Best day my life."

"Better than the day you meet me?" Haraboji asks her teasingly.

Halmoni looks me dead in the eyes. "Better."

HOST DENNIS MAKES HIS ROUNDS, sticking his mic in each contestant's face and giving them the third degree while the poor chefs are trying to cook. Chef Janice is going Emilia-Romagna style with her dish. Chef Bryce, Normandy. When Host Dennis gets to the last station, it looks like it was hit by a tornado, then a hurricane, then a typhoon: spilled sauces and upside-down pots and pans, false starts every which way.

"Chef Dave," Host Dennis asks, "tell us about your dish!"

The camera zooms in on the ingredients at his workstation: garam masala, Shaoxing wine, rambutan, natto, and kimchi.

Chef Dave doesn't have a clue.

"Absolutely, Dennis—big fan, by the way!" he says, smiling big. "I'm really embracing the Asian direction of my dish. Because once you go Asian—"

A loud, brassy GONGGGG!!! sound effect rings out over the speakers. The studio audience laughs.

I wince. But to my horror, H&H start laughing, too.

"That's *so* offensive!" I say.

"What?" H&H don't get it.

"They're being racist, with that gong," I say.

"Why you take everything so serious?" Haraboji says. "They just having fun."

I say, "Did any of the other chefs go, 'I'm really embracing *European* flavors?' No, they're each cooking a specific region of a specific country! Western Europe's only"—I glance at my phone for the stat—"*three percent* of the world's population. Meanwhile Chef Dave's got, like, four billion people's food sitting on his counter."

I list the ingredients: Garam masala is from Northern India but is also used in Pakistan, Nepal, Sri Lanka, Bangladesh.

Shaoxing wine's from the Zhejiang region of China. Rambutan is native to Malaysia, Thailand, Myanmar, Sri Lanka, Indonesia, Singapore, and the Philippines. Natto's from Japan, and kimchi's Korean, so—why's Chef Dave mixing the colonizer with the colonized?

"Jackie-ya, what you expect?" Halmoni says. "This America. Asian people not famous like Europe people."

"But they can't even get our countries straight," I say. "We're all just 'an Asian direction' to them."

They still don't get it. I hear their obsequious laughter with the customers at Melty's. Customers who are looking down at them *right to their faces.* The bar is so low for them.

But H&H just want to watch the rest of *Burn Off!* in peace. So I let them.

When Chef "Asian direction" Dave gets the win—with a "hot pot" that makes no kind of sense—Haraboji says, "See, Jackie-ya? Now Chef Dave gonna teach American people our food not so scary."

What I hate more than what he says is the *way* he says it. Like we should be most grateful for this Small Win for Asiankind.

I USUALLY SLEEP LIKE A baby at H&H's. Tonight I toss; I turn. The pink flowered blanket, which was probably the same blanket Umma had when this was her room, is thick and dap-dap-hae, like I'm being smothered. Outside the window, garbage cans rattle and roll. Queens wildlife. Umma's old posters—Erasure and Depeche Mode, stuff she still rages to when she's having what she calls one of her "han" moments—are giving me the stink eye in the dark from across the room. Oppa's old letters are in a shoebox stowed under the bed since I can't keep them at home.

I can't quiet my mind. I might fail history. Which means I'll sabotage my GPA, which means I won't get into a good college, which means I'll be a failure in life, according to my parents. And I'm only fifteen.

So I do what I always do when I'm stressed or anxious: I start thinking about food.

Recipe-making is my mental happy place. Maybe other people get the same kicks from crosswords or the Rubik's cube. Kind of like how Umma's addicted to sudoku puzzles.

I think about all the other things I could have made with those same *Burn Off!* ingredients.

I make it through four dishes.

Then I drift off to sleep.

MELTY'S

It's five a.m. the next morning at Melty's, and we're prepping for service. Eggs are hardboiled and chilling in an ice bath. Oatmeal bubbles on the front boiler. Home fries roast in the Blodgett. Beef bone broth and minestrone simmer on the back burners. And pastrami and turkey meatloaf are baking in the oven. Our prep list is still a million miles long.

We're a little behind schedule because H&H's car stalled on the LIE. Then H&H got into another minifight about getting a new car versus throwing good money after bad to fix the old one. They went on like this by the side of the service road until the car miraculously resuscitated itself, and Haraboji shot Halmoni a *told you so!* look.

On weekdays, the customers are construction and office workers who know what they want and needed it yesterday. But Saturdays at Melty's is Amateur Hour. Tourists making their Midtown Manhattan pilgrimage gawk forever at the menu—*Madison*

Avenue wrap or the Lexington panino? Augh!—order, then change their minds halfway through prep.

That's why I can't wait for sophomore year to end already. Because then I'll get to work at Melty's full time, just like I did last summer, and cook for primetime.

Ratón, Segundo, and I are on veg prep. Their real names are Manuel and Miguel, resp., but for whatever reason they just go by Mouse and Number Two.

We're recapping last night's *Burn Off!* Segundo thinks Chef Dave is like the Messi of the kitchen, but Ratón and I think that's foul talk.

"Chef Dave should have gotten burnt already!" I say. "He literally dumped everything into a pot and called it a day."

"I would have made tempura zucchini," Ratón says. "So obvious."

"Nah. They burn the other guy who made that," Segundo says, waving him off. "What about la Jackie?"

Ratón and Segundo call me "La Jackie," which I don't know if it's supposed to be a compliment or insult or maybe both.

"I would've—"

I'm interrupted by a series of thuds coming down the basement steps.

"Ah, Min Produce!" Haraboji says. Except it's not Mr. Min with the produce order, but his son Stephen.

"안녕하세요, 사장님!" *Good morning, Boss!* Stephen greets Haraboji, dropping into a big bow because he's a kiss-ass like

15

that. "¿Qué pasa?" he says as he fist-bumps Segundo and Ratón, who call him "el Guapo."

I'm *The Jackie,* and Stephen's *The Handsome.*

Stephen Min is the year ahead of me, but at Stuy. He gives me his usual side-eye. You know how some guys, usually the hot ones, size up girls like our only purpose is their eye-candy? That's Stephen Min. Except to him I'm more like eye-broccoli.

This isn't false modesty; I'm not "pretty" by Korean standards. Halmoni's brutally honest about my shortcomings: My eyes are monolids, my nose is a boiled mandu—*dumpling*—and my legs are mu, *giant white radishes.* And Umma always harps on my bad posture and worse clothes: *Dress for the job you want, not the job you have!* The Banana Republican outfits she buys me each birthday and Christmas are shoved in the back of my closet, and every day I just wear dark, baggy T-shirts and jeans I don't mind getting food splattered on.

(I don't know *what* they were thinking when they named me after Jacqueline O.)

Stephen drops his hand truck, loaded with crates, with a reverberating *thump.* "Yo," he shouts in my general direction. "Where do you want this?"

"You're late," I say. We were expecting the delivery a half hour ago.

"*You* try driving local all the way from Hunts Point." Hunts Point Market is in the Bronx, where all the wholesalers get their produce.

"Ever heard of the FDR, Stephen?"

"Ever heard of 'commercial vehicles are not permitted on the FDR so you have to drive down Lex with a million potholes,' *Jacqueline O.*?" He says my name all sarcastic.

"It's just *Jackie.*"

Guys like Stephen Min are what my best friend, KT, aka Kaitlyn Tseng, and I call Lowest Common Denominators. LCDs are conventionally attractive enough to appeal to the masses. But to me, that's basic and boring, like spaghetti. Yeah, spaghetti's a crowd-pleaser, but where's the interestingness in spaghetti?

Stephen catches me looking at him, which is even more infuriating because he probably thinks I'm checking him out. So I deaden my eyes into a glare and jerk my head in the direction of the walk-in. He wheels off.

Haraboji shimmies by me with a cauldron of hot water, and mutters, "Be nice, Jackie-ya."

After Stephen finishes unloading the produce, he asks Haraboji how business is doing.

"응, 그냥 . . . ," Haraboji answers, which is kind of like a noncommittal *Oh, you know, just, whatever.*

Stephen nods sympathetically. "Covid 때문에 많은 장사들이 망했죠. 너무 안타까워요."

I catch the first part—*Covid caused a lot of businesses to fail*—but the second part is the equivalent of SAT vocabulary. Stephen's Korean is way better than mine—his dad's like *from* Korea, whereas my parents were born here.

Haraboji nods back. "인생이 그렇지, 뭐." *That's life.*

Halmoni comes downstairs. She works front of house

because arthritis keeps her from the kitchen. She only cooks at home now. Her fingers are permanently curled over, like she's still cradling the hilt of a phantom knife.

"Stevie-ya! Did you eat?" she calls out in Korean. "Jackie-ya!" Halmoni jerks her head at me, like I'm Stephen's personal servant.

So I have to stop what I'm doing, which is peeling ten dozen hard-boiled eggs, and ladle up breakfast for Stephen. Halmoni fawns all over handsome boys, like they're kings to be waited on. She does the same thing with Appa, and she used to do it with Oppa—always piling food onto their plates while ignoring Umma and me.

Stephen Min takes a bite from the bowl I unceremoniously hand him. "It's pretty bland."

"It's *oatmeal*."

"Let me get an egg with that," he says, about to reach for my pile of freshly peeled hard-boileds with his grubby hands.

"Stop!" I say. "Here." I fish one out with a spoon and plop it onto his oatmeal.

Stephen Min pulls a tube of red pepper paste from his jeans pocket and squirts it all over his breakfast. I have never seen anyone eating oatmeal with an egg, let alone with *gochujang*. Who packs their own heat, in squeeze-bottle form?

"You should serve juk," Stephen says, mouth full. "With a jammy egg, sesame oil, and gochujang self-serve. Toppings bar with roasted myulchi, gim flakes, candied garlic, the works. If I was some corporate sellout on my way to work, I'd totally order that sh—"

"Well, you're not, and we don't, so."

"I'm just saying." Stephen tosses his now empty bowl in the trash. He wolfed that down in seconds flat. "Think about it."

After Stephen Min leaves, Segundo and Ratón give me amused looks.

"¿Qué?" I say.

"Nada, nada," they say, laughing to themselves.

"¡Vamos, chicos!" says Haraboji, and we all get back to work.

IN THE WALK-IN BOX, I survey yesterday's leftovers.

Clarification—they aren't *leftovers* leftovers. The food is still good to serve. But that's the way of the food business—Wednesday's pot roast is Thursday's chili con carne. Friday's roast chicken becomes . . . and therein lies the conundrum. A dozen rotisserie chickens are staring back at me in the walk-in, waiting to be transformed.

One of my food heroes, Anita Lo—she subbed in for Judge Kelly while she was on maternity leave—is as obsessed with leftovers as I am. Each time you cook something, you have to think of how you'll transform its afterlife. In the food world, there's no such thing as Uranium-238, with its half-life of 4.5 billion years. Every product has an expiration date.

The gears start turning. The obvious solution is to repurpose the chicken into chicken noodle soup. But the obvious solution is almost never the most creative one. My mind grabs the chicken, tearing the meat from the bones. Brown the meat to get a nice sear and set it aside. Pour cooking wine to scrape up the brown bits in the pan, then soy sauce and sugar that bubbles into a sauce. Fold back in the browned chicken meat, along with the potatoes, mushrooms, onions, carrots, and scallions. A heap of spicy gochugaru flakes because spicy makes everything better. Simmer over low heat, so the whole dish cooks up into a nice stewed meat. It's not so much a soup as it is a jus, which is some fancy French word for meat-juice reduction. Spoon it over rice, and—

"Chicken noodle soup," Haraboji announces without discussion, then he goes to fill a cauldron with water for the chicken stock. Taking the cleaver, he whacks the bones of the chicken. His biceps bulge. Haraboji's pushing eighty, but he can break down whole chickens faster than most people open a can of Campbell's.

"But we always do chicken noodle," I say.

"Because customers like," Haraboji says.

"Why don't we switch it up for once?" I say. "What about . . . jjimdak for today's lunch special?"

I brace myself for the reaction. I *never* propose Korean food for Melty's leftovers, but something about Stephen Min's oatmeal-gochujang-egg-and-juk bar idea must have wormed into my head.

Of course Haraboji immediately vetoes it. "*Jjimdak?* Customers not going to like, Jackie-ya. Funny smell, they get upset. Then they never come back."

"But what about the cro-knish? And the soy sauce?"

Last year, we were staring down roast pork and knish leftovers, and I off-roaded it. I diced and fried the pork, mixed it with the mashed-up knish, and added parsley, cheese, soy sauce, and Worcestershire. I bound the mixture with an egg, rolled the patties in panko crumbs, and dropped them into the fryer. I was inspired by Judge Stone's ham croquette recipe in *Bon Appétit*.

H&H initially vetoed the soy sauce—*why you make weird mix like that?*—but eventually they agreed it added an unexpected savory depth.

The name "cro-knish" doesn't exactly roll off the tongue, but they always sell out.

"Cro-knish still *their* food," Haraboji says. "Jjimdak *our* food."

He has a point—to a point. But H&H are so afraid to veer off the tried-and-true. Last week during *Burn Off!*, Haraboji made a genius budae jjigae—aka "army stew"—from hot dogs and mac 'n' cheese. But it's like all of his creative energy disappears the second he starts making food for The Man.

"But last night, when we were watching *Burn Off!*, you said—"

Haraboji interrupts me. "That's Fantasy Fun Time, Jackie-ya. Now is Business Time."

"But—"

Halmoni comes down the stairs to grab receipt paper for the register, so I enlist her help. "This is *not* Fantasy Fun Time," I argue. "What else are you going to do with the chicken? It's too hot for chicken noodle soup, anyway, and we always have leftovers of the leftovers."

Especially after Covid. Business has been hurting since so many now work from home.

"Can't we try out jjimdak?" I plead. "Just this once?"

Halmoni and Haraboji exchange a look.

"Chicken noodle soup," Halmoni says.

And with that, H&H end the discussion.

Service begins; the grill is slammed. Breakfast turns to lunch in no time flat. Halmoni's at the register. Segundo's on salads, and Ratón and I are working short-order. Haraboji is expediting: "Five Madison! Three Lex! One pastrami provolone horseradish no pickles! One BLT all the way! One medium-rare cheddar with mushrooms! One well-done pepper jack with bacon! Four cro-knish!"

"Yes, chef!" Ratón and I answer back, and get to work.

Orders fly at us, and I pivot and do-si-do from the griddle to the burners to the deep fryer to the cutting board and back. It's intense, but I've never felt more focused than in the literal heat of the moment.

In the kitchen, I'm in my zone.

VALLEY OF ASHES

Umma picks me up from Melty's at the end of the day. Lately she's been doing that a lot—picking me up to take me home. It was cute when I was, like, eight; now it's just kind of annoying, like I'm on surveillance.

She's wearing her fresh-from-the-office clothes, even though I'm pretty sure she's the only one in her office who actually goes in on a Saturday.

Umma greets H&H. "Josie-ya, watguna." *You're here,* Halmoni says, then frowns.

"What's wrong with your face? So old and tired-looking! The hanyak I sent you, why don't you eat it? Dr. Hong charges gold prices for it, but what do you care, always throwing money into the garbage. What's the point of working until your bones fall out and you look like *that*!" Halmoni jabs a finger at Umma's *so old and tired-looking* face. "Aigo-ya, how many times do I tell you, sell your apartment—so small! so expensive!—and come live with us in Bayside? Justin-Appa won't have to do a thing.

He can just lie there and eat rice cakes all day. Okay, maybe once a week he helps Appa put the garbage can out. *Ung?* And don't forget to put the cinder block on top. Those raccoons, so smart now, they know how to open lids and everything! What a mess they made at Mrs. Bae's house. You remember the Baes, right? The daughter, Harvard MBA. Such a good girl, she takes her parents to all their doctors' appointments. Always so happy and smiling, it makes people enjoy looking at her. Not like *your* face!"

(I swear this all sounds way less harsh in Korean.)

Halmoni strikes her chest with her fist.

"Josie-ya! If you don't take care of yourself now, then your problems will be a thousand times worse when you're my age! Why don't you listen to your umma, *ung*?"

Umma looks like she was over it two paragraphs ago. "Okay, okay, Umma."

She mostly talks back to H&H in English. Umma doesn't speak in Korean if she can help it.

Next Halmoni's pushing chicken noodle soup—yes, there were leftovers of the leftovers—on Umma.

"It's too salty, so make sure you water it down. You know American customers, everything has to be salty-salty or else they complain on the internet." Halmoni clucks. "You need to eat hot things if you don't want to be sick, Josie-ya!"

Haraboji gets in on the act, too. He's piling bagels and kaiser rolls into a bag. Umma tries to protest, but he says, "Not for you" and winks at me. "For Jackie."

The compromise is taking home *only* two bags of leftovers, which I know only Appa and I will eat. Umma doesn't touch Melty's food.

"How's business? The same?" she asks.

Haraboji gives an *Eh, what are you going to do?* shrug.

"Well, maybe it's time to give it a rest," Umma says. "Jackie, get your things and let's go."

I grab my bag, hug H&H goodbye, fist-bump Segundo and Ratón, and follow Umma out the door.

It's only once we're on the 7 train heading home that I realize Umma didn't even hug her parents goodbye—and neither did they.

THE 7 CROSSES INTO QUEENS, toward home to Long Island City. Once upon a time, LIC was an industrial wasteland of factories and street workers; now it's overpriced high-rises, cafés, craft breweries, and the i-bankers who love them. LIC is the Midtown Tunnel and Fifty-Ninth Street Bridge spitting out taxis and exhaust, and candy-cane Con Ed smokestacks and the glaring neon Pepsi-Cola sign.

Our building is even called "The Gatsby," which I'm pretty sure would make F. Scott Fitzgerald barf all over his wingtips.

Umma's starting the third-degree about Chwaego Hagwon. "So? How did it go?"

What she means is *What did you get on your practice PSAT?*

Hagwon yesterday was boring and a little judgy because

the 1600 kids were giving me patronizing side-eyes for scoring lower than them.

"Fine."

She still looks at me expectantly, so I tell her a score fifty points higher than I actually got.

"Jackie. That's not your best effort." Umma's shaking her head. "How many times have we gone over this? You have to practice, practice, practice the questions until it's like muscle memory."

I'm just relieved she didn't ask for proof.

"And school," she continues. "Did you get your history test back yet? It's supposed to be prep for your final, right?"

I can practically see her busting out her calendar, counting back the days. I don't say anything at first. But my face must tell it all because Umma holds out her hand.

I have no choice but to fish out my 70% from my bookbag.

I can't unsee the horror flashing across Umma's face.

Appa does this thing where he throws out random stats to prove his point. So I jump in with "Three-quarters is *great* by most metrics. If the subway ran seventy-five percent of the time *on time,* New Yorkers would throw a frigging parade! If Americans saved a whopping seventy-five percent of their income, would interest rates be—"

"You're closer to two-thirds than three-quarters," Umma snaps. "If you don't know that, then *that's* a problem."

"Why? Because I'm Asian?" I'm stalling, distracting from the central argument—one of her usual tactics. "That's so racist, Umma!"

That gets people's attention on the train. Well, the

English-speaking half. Fifty percent of the passengers start glaring at Umma.

Umma glares back at them. For a five-foot-one woman, my mother can be pretty intimidating.

"Nice try, Jackie," Umma fumes. "You started the class with a ninety-five percent. Now, you're failing? Colleges will *see* that!"

"I'm not *failing*—"

"Your final exam's coming up. Colleges will see that score as a reflection of your effort. Tell me, Jackie. Are you even *trying?*"

"That's not 'positive reinforcement,' Umma," I say. "It's hurting my self-esteem."

It's our stop. Umma lets out a sarcastic tut as we step off the train. " 'Self-esteem,' " she says, air-quoting, "is what mediocre people say to make themselves feel better about not trying their best."

"Ouch."

Umma's only getting started. Her lecture continues all the way out of Court Square station, down Twenty-Third, and up the elevator to the nineteenth floor.

"Do you know who I ran into on the elevator this morning? The Seos. You know their daughter Camelia, she's graduating from Stuy.—97.5 GPA and 1580 on the SATs, fourteen AP classes, captain of the track team—and she only got into Georgetown. *Off the waitlist!* Forget Harvard. It is so much harder for us, Jackie. When are you going to get it through your head? Don't laugh, this isn't a joke. This is your *future.* You're competing against everyone who looks like you. You have to be **extra**ordinary for them to consider you ordinary. *This* is our reality."

KT texts me:

u tell ur mom yet

affirmative

eee how's she taking it

she's giving me OPPROBRIUM

that was on my vocab list last week

same!

but isn't OPPROBRIUM more like public
shaming
like if they dragged u into the town
square for the crime of
exposing too much ankle
& put u in a pillory
maybe u mean VITUPERATION
EXCORIATION
CONDEMNATION
...

Now KT's just showing off.

I guess that's why she's a debate champion, and her dream
is Harvard.

She's pretty much the daughter Umma never had.

"Jackie! Put that phone away."

"Sorry."

I *put that phone away.*

Umma continues, "When I was a junior associate, do you think I wanted to get up at four-thirty every morning to put in an eighteen-hour workday? Do you think, if I said, 'No, I'm just going to sleep in and relax,' I'd get where I am today? In the running for managing partner at Leviathan? The highest-rated law firm in over ten territories?"

It's a rhetorical question, so I don't answer it.

"Would your father be where he is today? Would you and your—" She stops herself. "Would *you* be where you are today?"

Umma sweeps her arm around our apartment: floor-to-ceiling windows that open to a 95 percent view of condo construction sites and, across the toxic sludge of the East River, a 5 percent view of the Manhattan skyline. Her fingertips graze the slab marble countertops and Viking stove and EuroCave wine fridge, before sweeping to the living room with the giant flatscreen and entertainment system and the white leather sofa that sits crisp and cold in the living room.

So small, so expensive. Umma and Appa worked *until their bones fell out* to afford this apartment. But it still feels cold and sterile—not at all like a real home.

Not at all like H&H's house in Bayside. It's cozier with well-loved (and well-worn) Kenmore appliances and a beat-up couch across the junky TV set that Haraboji keeps smacking to make the staticky fuzz go away. Their house with its comforting smells of ginger and garlic, dwenjang and kimchi fermenting in the basement, and all the other "funky" foods my grandparents would *never* dare cook for the customers at Melty's.

Their Bayside house also smells like pas—which is this icy-hot pad you stick on your shoulders and back when you're in pain. Halmoni and Haraboji are always slapping pas onto each other's backs, which, to me, is the epitome of growing old together.

"We had a deal, Jackie," Umma reminds me. "And you violated the terms."

Dread hits my gut. She's right. The "terms" of our "deal sheet" were my parents would only let me work at Melty's as long as I kept my grades up. They didn't want me working there in the first place, but—I'm bad at sports, and worse at extracurriculars. So maybe they figured "budding entrepreneur" sounded better than leaving a blank under "After-School Activities" on my college apps?

I start making all the promises. "I'll get my grades up!" I say, beg. "I've already started reviewing for the final, you should see my notes! And I'm on track to—"

Umma crosses her arms. "Show me."

". . ."

Umma marches toward my room.

"It's called *boundaries!*" I call out after her, but what's the point when she owns everything in our house, including the house.

All over my desk are dog-eared cookbooks, spread open and heavily annotated with highlighters, pens, and Post-its. Before I can stop her, Umma finds my world history textbook, buried under a mountain of laundry. It hasn't been cracked open in a minute.

A very long minute.

The only Post-its are flapping from chapters one to three, after my first 95%.

"You just lied to me, Jackie." Umma looks at me, cold.

I say nothing because we both know she's right.

She opens her mouth to speak, but I already know what's happening next. The words come hurling at me, the ones to which I have no answer:

"Do you want to end up like your brother?"

JUSTIN OPPA

Oppa is as good as dead to my parents—even though he's not. The *too long; didn't read* version is my brother got kicked out (school, home), fell in with a bad crowd, and is now serving time at a medium-security correctional facility Upstate. In other words: he's a kkangpae—a *gangster* and/or *garbage human being.*

We don't visit Oppa. I suspect his biggest disappointment to my parents, bigger than his armed robbery charge—because by then Appa had already disowned him—was the fact that Oppa didn't get into Stuy/Science/Tech, Townsend Harris, or even Cardozo. And the failure to get into a good high school was the slippery slope to wrack and ruin. Oppa was never "book smart," and that he didn't apply himself was tantamount to a crime to Umma and Appa.

I'm almost the same age Oppa was—sixteen—when he was first sent to Rikers Island. Ironically enough, I can't visit him in prison by myself because I'm too young to visit an inmate without an adult, yet sixteen is not too young for an inmate to be incarcerated *as* an adult—at least back when Oppa was put away.

The system doesn't even try to make sense.

OPPA DIDN'T SEEM LIKE A kkangpae to me. He was always smiling and looking happy—at least when our dad wasn't around. Oppa would take me to get Mister Softee; he'd tell me I'm smart and to keep up the good grades. I loved it when he called me "lil 똥생." 동생 means *younger sibling,* and 똥생 is . . . *poop sibling*?

Whatever, it was our thing.

What I remember of him, which isn't much—he's seven years older than me—were the epic fights with our parents. Oppa would bring home report cards that looked like the keyboard got stuck on the F key. *Why are you so lazy and unmotivated?* Appa would boom. *You want for nothing!*

Some days, Oppa would shout back. But most days, he'd sit there and take it. Like he'd internalized those Fs as a measure of his self-worth.

Of course, I was too young to understand any of that back then.

I barely do now.

OPPA WAS IN AND OUT of schools—dropping out or getting kicked out, or maybe some combination of both. What I do remember most was picking him up from his last school, Valley Forge Military Academy. It's hard to describe the look on Appa's face as we pulled up to the parking lot, where Oppa was waiting for us, duffel bag at his feet. It wasn't just straight-up anger. It was beyond that, like *Surprise, surprise. I didn't expect any less of you.*

Oppa could see it all over his face, too.

They got into it about something—a teacher, or maybe another student.

Oppa arguing: "They look down on us. They think we have no power!"

Appa, arguing back: "Do you want to keep playing the victim? Or do you want to be productive and *go places*?"

Oppa whipped his head toward me. "Watch out, 똥생. You have to be perfect if you want to survive in this family."

Then he hoisted his duffel bag over his shoulder and walked away.

I didn't see Oppa again until he was arrested.

IT WAS A BOTCHED LIQUOR store "stick 'em up." Oppa didn't pull the gun on Kim Sung-gap, but he was still one of the guilty and charged trio.

At sixteen years old, he'd be prosecuted as an adult and sentenced to ten years in prison.

* * *

THE CRIME WAS IN ALL the Korean-language newspapers, TV, radio. H&H couldn't go to H-Mart without someone shooting them a dirty look. They stopped going to church, where it was worse.

We don't have any pictures up of Oppa in the house. Umma and Appa mostly act like he never existed. After he was sent to prison, we stopped going to church too, and my parents fell out with a lot of their friends. Even our extended family kind of looks down on us because they think it's Umma and Appa's fault, and even H&H's, that Oppa became a bad apple. Maybe they're afraid of "catching" bad apple syndrome.

Why did Oppa do it? It made no sense to me. For years, I've turned the question over in my head. If he was really hurting for money, he could have gone to our parents. Or H&H.

Did Oppa hate our family so much that he'd rather risk jail time than ask Umma and Appa for help?

It's been seven years—no, longer, because he was kicked out of the house even before that.

Some days, I don't even remember what his face looks like. The pixels come in all blurry.

EVEN THOUGH I'M NOT ALLOWED to go visit my brother—from Rikers, he was sentenced to a prison called Placid Falls in practically Canada—I still write to him. And Oppa writes me back. He sends his letters to me c/o H&H, so I don't ruffle any parental feathers. Usually I just write light, silly stuff, and he writes light, silly stuff back. Because things are heavy enough.

Our letters are on a four-to-one ratio because Oppa has a limit on how many he gets to send out each month. Sometimes it's longer, like if the prison's in lockdown.

That's okay. I know he'd write more if he could. Plus, I know writing isn't his favorite thing, so each letter means that much more.

After my fight with Umma, I sit down and write Oppa a letter.

Dear Oppa,

Umma is driving me nuts! Can you believe she actually raided my room today? Looking for "evidence." They're flipping out over a 70% on my last exam! It's all because I can't stand Mr. Doumann. They're on my case about Mr. D's final exam next month. And now Umma and Appa won't let me work at Melty's? I swear, I . . .

I crumple the letter. It just sounds like I'm complaining about our parents worrying about me. About not getting to cook. About . . . being free. Which are all luxuries Oppa doesn't even have.

I start again.

Dear 오빠,

We all miss you. Last week during Burn Off! time, Haraboji made budaejjigae, with chicken bone broth, seared Spam, and leftover hash browns. I think next time I want to kick up the heat a little, to cut through the richness of the broth. Maybe two tablespoons of gochugaru instead of one. But then I'm going to have to up the sugar to counteract it, and I dunno, I don't want it to get too cloying . . .

What'd you think of Chef Janice getting booted off of Burn Off! this week? That vegetable terrine looked LIT! She got ~~robbed~~ She should have won, if you ask me. But Judge Stone was totally on the money when he hated all over the Texas guy's eggplant. I bet Texas forgot to salt the eggplant first, to leech out the water and make it tender . . .

Oppa loves *Burn Off!* time. He loves hearing about all the random dishes H&H and I make. He works in the kitchen at Placid Falls, so he tries to get creative, too—to the extent he's allowed. Sometimes I feel a little guilty about all the rich food we're making that he doesn't get to eat. Oppa says *Burn Off!* is popular with the guys at Placid Falls, but it's hard to get a good seat to watch it. He leaves it at that.

I don't tell him about world history, my big fight with Umma and Appa, or any of it.

OPPA'S LETTER WILL EVENTUALLY COME back to me:

> Man! What I wouldnt give to have some of that jjigae.
>
> Dont forget a sour note too J. Maybe add some kimchi juice? You got to balance out da sweet + heat. Same w food same w life.
>
> They now got gochujang in the kitchen here. Right??? Crazy. They dont sell shin ramen in the commissary only that American brand crap. But maybe Ill try to make some Budae a la Placid Falls.
>
> Keep up your grades 똥생. Dont end up like me lol.
>
> Be good. Send my love to H&H and the rents.

Oppa ends every line of his letter like that. And I always tell him I will, but I never do.

But I think we both know I'm lying.

BRONX SCIENCE

Umma and Appa put me on "probation." It's what happens right after you get a "verbal warning" and before you get fired. Normal parents would just call it "grounded," but that's not on-brand for Umma and Appa.

I will also no longer be working at Melty's for the rest of the school year, effective immediately. I'm to come straight home from school, except on hagwon days. And absolutely no TV, which means no *Burn Off!* But the real kicker is this: If I don't ace—and I mean *ace*—world history, I can kiss my summer of working at Melty's goodbye.

I CALL H&H TO BREAK the news to them and to apologize for letting them down, and they just laugh in my face.

"Let you down?" Halmoni scoffs in Korean. "You let yourself down! What kind of student throws away her studies like that? For a smart girl, you're so foolish."

"Jackie-ya," Haraboji says, also in Korean. "Don't waste this good opportunity."

Back in Korea, Haraboji studied literature. Halmoni once told me he dreamed of becoming a poet. His dream didn't survive immigration.

"You want to work this hard forever?" Halmoni says. "Cooking is what you do when you have no other choice. Look at my varicose veins; for forty years, I can never wear a skirt, it's humiliating. Look at my arthritis. You want to end up like me? Business is slow, we don't need you, anyway. Goodbye, Jackie-ya. Don't come back."

"IT'S SO UNFAIR," I COMPLAIN to KT the next day at school. "My parents even put a tracker on my phone! That's such a violation of my civil liberties."

I'm kind of scrounging for sympathy points, but KT says, "*A violation of your civil liberties?* Hyperbolize much?" She gives me a no-nonsense look. "At least they didn't take your phone away."

I grumble incoherently.

We're sitting on our usual graffitied bench, at the far end of campus, near the back entrance where the truancy cops wait to pounce on you for cutting class. The scheduling gods have granted KT and me two back-to-back periods together—lunch, then world history with Mr. Doumann. But then they've cursed us with fourth period lunch, which means we're eating cafeteria hockey pucks at 10:25 in the morning.

Except I don't do cafeteria food. I bring my own lunch.

Today it's quiche Lorraine with pâte brisée, aka short-crust pastry. I offer KT the first bite, but she says, "I'm good" and goes back to her lunch.

KT eats the same thing every day: white rice, black beans, and defrosted spinach, flavored with a stingy splash of soy. I don't know how she doesn't get palate fatigue.

"This recipe's from Judge Stone's new French cookbook," I tell KT.

"That's that short bald guy on TV you're obsessed with?"

"Don't hate," I warn. "You never know when *Burn Off!* might be a literal debate topic."

"Dubious," KT says. "You *do* know it's not like *Jeopardy!*, right?"

KT and I used to be "best" friends, but now we're kind of settling into just . . . "regular" friends. You know how freshman year you don't know anyone, so you make fast friends with the first person you meet in your first class? But as the months go by, you realize you don't actually have much in common, and you start to wonder if you'd still be friends with that person if you hadn't met that fateful first day of freshman year, when you bonded in double-period Honors Bio over mitochondria and Golgi bodies?

That's what it's been feeling like with KT.

But it's kind of awkward to talk about, so.

And if I'm the only one who thinks it's kind of awkward, then it'll make things *more* awkward.

"You think the final's going to be cumulative," KT asks, "or just new material since the midterm?"

At first I think KT's referring to the final for *Burn Off!*, but then I realize she's talking about world.

"Why are you already stressing already? That's next month's problem," I say. "I don't even know what I'm having for lunch tomorrow."

That's a lie. I plan out all my meals five days in advance, timed to Melty's leftovers. You should see my spreadsheets. But not like I'm going to volunteer that to KT.

"I've been reviewing all the chapters since the *start* of the year, just in case. But I don't know." KT opens her textbook and starts leafing through her pages.

I point to my quiche. "Judge Stone says the key to the pâte brisée is cold butter and ice water. The dough has to be super cold, or else it just gets warm and gummy and you can't work with it *at all*."

I messed up four other versions of the pâte brisée. You don't even want to know how much butter gave up its life for my mistakes. But fifth time's a charm, I guess.

"Jackie, can we, like, not talk about food all the time?"

"Uh . . . okay."

KT goes back to her textbook, and I start scrolling through my phone. It's another pop-up for *McMann's Authoritative Guide to French Cookery.* The search gods know what's up. If I'm being totally honest, yeah, I was too busy reading his cookbook when I should have been studying for history. I probably would have gotten at least fifteen points higher if I hadn't "goofed off."

In his autobiography, *Rebel Without a Restaurant*, Judge Stone dropped out of high school. So did Bobby Flay. Anthony

Bourdain dropped out of Vassar College. Rachael Ray dropped out of Pace. *The* James Beard was expelled from Reed—though he was kicked out for being queer.

The point is, plenty of successful people "made it" without achieving the Ivy League American Dream.

"KT," I ask, "don't you ever think there's more to life than just studying and stuff? Like . . . what's the point?"

"What's the point?" KT repeats. "Uh, to get into a good college, so you can get a good job, so you can buy a house and food so your family doesn't, like, starve?"

"Yeah, but. What if school's overrated?" I say. "Maybe I should just drop out now and cook full time. History's such a joke. I'm already flunking anyway, ha ha."

KT frowns. "Jackie, you okay?"

When I don't immediately answer, her frown deepens. "What's with you lately?"

What *isn't* with me lately? Grades. College. Umma and Appa. Oppa. *Covid.*

I SPENT ALL OF COVID in New York. We weren't one of those families with a spare house in the country to flee to, so we stayed put. H&H closed Melty's because offices were shut down, construction was shut down, tourism was kaput; there were no customers. Midtown was a ghost town.

Little by little, I started to hear the stories: First a man on the train getting sprayed with a cleaning product; another getting spit on; another getting pushed to the ground. The fact that the NYPD didn't label them as hate crimes made me dismiss things at first. *Don't confuse causation with correlation,* as my Chwaego Hagwon math teacher always says.

Then there were full-on attacks: a woman shoved to her death on the subway tracks in Times Square. Another getting followed into her apartment and stabbed to death. Another assaulted in an elevator bank after one hundred twenty-five blows.

All of the victims were Asian. All of the attacks were unprovoked.

It. Wouldn't. Stop.

It was happening all over the country. In Georgia, six Asian women were shot in a massage parlor, and the police said the killer was "having a bad day."

I nearly lost it.

It was just people like us, minding their own business, getting attacked for being in the wrong place at the wrong time. With the wrong skin.

About a year into Covid, I was heading to a dentist appointment. I was sitting in one of the end seats on the subway, scrolling through the playlist on my phone. The car was empty.

A guy came in through the side doors from another car and stood right next to me in the doorway, unmasked. I was a little nervous, but I had my poker face on under my mask, because only amateurs show their nerves on the New York City subway.

The guy unzipped and started *peeing,* right there in front of me. His urine pooled by my shoes, but I had to front like nothing was happening. It took all I had not to run screaming for the door. I kept my face and body still until it was all over.

As he zipped up, he said, "What are you looking at, C—?"

The C-word. I froze; there was so much ugliness and hate in the man's face.

And it was all my fault, for stupidly staring down at my phone instead of keeping my head on a swivel.

I now never sit on the end seats.

And I never look down at my phone when I'm alone on the subway.

I got shook.

SOMETIMES I THINK ABOUT THOSE victims. Didn't they all have dreams, too? Some were immigrants who sacrificed everything to try to make it in this country. It's like, what's the point of working your butt off, just so you can get shoved into the tracks someday—just for being Asian?

So, yeah. That's been eating at me lately.

On top of everything else.

And maybe that's one of the reasons why I love cooking so much. Being in the kitchen helps me shut out all the scary nonsense from the outside world.

Cooking is my therapy.

UMMA AND APPA DON'T GET it, and I don't think H&H do, either. They all act like Melty's is their tragic endgame.

Oppa would get it, but—

Not like I can just pick up the phone and go, *Hey.*

Sometimes, I think about telling KT all this.

But the expression on her face right now—a mix of pity, concern, horror—tells me everything I need to know: she won't get it.

There's a reason why I've never told her, or anyone else at school, about Oppa. I don't need to be judged any more than I already am.

So I say: "What if I added a toasted panko crumble to my quiche? You know, like crumb cake but savory? There's a textural element that's missing . . ."

KT rolls her eyes and goes right back to her textbook.

THE NEXT PERIOD, MR. DOUMANN ANNOUNCES that our final exam will be a survey of the *whole* year. The class groans, except KT. She looks pretty pleased with herself—I'm groping for the SAT word that means the same thing—and for some reason the look on her face makes me irksome. Irked? Whatever.

I have great short-term memory. I think it comes from working short-order at Melty's, where the tickets fly at you fast and furious. So it means I can pull an all-nighter and cram for a test, but forty-eight hours later, all the facts I memorized vanish, erased whiteboard-like, from my head.

Especially facts from last semester that haven't made it from RAM to ROM.

At the end of class, I hand Mr. Doumann back my signed 70%. That's his class policy for any test under an 80%.

"Oh, Ms. Oh?" he says. "You know I add or subtract five

points from your final grade based on overall progress, right?" He taps on my 70%. "Keep that in mind, Jennifer."

My name is literally right there on the exam in his hand.

"I'm *Jacqueline*?"

"Right, right. So many J names with you p—"

He catches himself.

I swear to God Mr. D was about to say, *you people.* He's pretty dumb, but not dumb enough not to risk losing his NYC pension.

92ND STREET Y

Tonight 7pm!

Stone McMann of *Burn Off!* will appear
at 92nd Street Y to promote his new book,
McMann's Authoritative Guide to French Cookery!

In-Person and Streaming

Register Here

The search gods/stalkers must know what's up, because Judge Stone's appearance keeps popping up on my phone. Umma and Appa are working late tonight, like they always do. And even though I know I shouldn't—

I click the link.

After homework and reviewing two chapters of world, I make dinner of lardons and chanterelles over rice, and a pea shoot-and-ramps side salad/banchan in soy sauce vinaigrette. I run the kitchen exhaust and open all the windows, so I won't get "caught" by Umma and Appa later. (They'd left me money for takeout so I wouldn't waste time in the kitchen.)

Seriously. Other kids hide smoking or drugs; I hide all trace evidence of *cooking*.

When it's time, I log on to the talk:

VOICE-OVER:

Stone McMann made his start in the culinary world as the inaugural "food investigator" for *am-NewYork*. His talents then flourished at *The New York Times*, where he penned the award-winning food column "To Go Boldly Where No Food Has Gone Before (Never, for the Love of God, *To Boldly Go . . .*)". The author of six cookbooks in the James Beard Award-winning Global Culinary Arts series and the NBCC Award-winning memoir *Rebel Without a Restaurant*, in development for a TV adaptation with Chop Chop Productions, McMann joined the ranks of *Burn Off!*, where he brings his signature sharp wit to the Judges' Table. McMann has since left the *Times* to start a digital media/food laboratory collaborative, Icebox Plums, launching next year.

Please join me in welcoming Stone McMann!

JUDGE STONE (late forties, balding, urbane; dressed in smart casual, right down to the pocket square in his left breast pocket) steps onto the stage:

I've been a rebel without a restaurant for as long as I don't remember. Prenativity, in fact, since Mom's idea of "fine dining" was the McDonald's on Steel Creek Road. We didn't even have a *kitchen* growing up in Appalachian Riviera Estates, which, by the way, was the finest RV park this side of the Allegheny River. All we had was a hotplate my brother and I called "Shocky." "Life, liberty" . . . I'm pretty sure "cook-top" was right up there as a constitutional right.

"Don't Yinz go cooking up nothing fancy, hear?" was always Mom's warning before leaving the house for, well, whatever it was she did all day. She'd nod at the pile of laundry and add, "Them shirts n'at need ironed."

Shocky, by the way, was also our iron.

With Mom gone, we had carte blanche to go *fancy*. Earl and I would raid the cupboards for Corn Pops, Cheetos, Fritos, Tab, Crystal Light . . . We didn't even have sugar, as such. All we had were the packets of Domino and Equal that come free with your coffee. Same with our salt and pepper and ketchup and mayo and creamer.

I see those horrified looks on your faces. Yinz Upper East Siders think my childhood was the culinary equivalent of Kosovo. Fear not; our Dickensian tale of woe has its happy ending. Which is more than I can say for our dear little friend Pip.

Scarcity, they say, breeds invention, and boy—invent we did. Other kids were out back cooking up coke, and we were . . . also cooking up Coke. Which is how I first wrote the recipe for "Chipped Ham with Coca-Cola and Cardamom (Never, for the Love of God, Pepsi)" that put me on the map—I still receive your letters thanking me for liberating you from the fetters of the Thanksgiving turkey—but what you may not know is that the early prototype of that recipe was the innards of a ham sandwich I smuggled out of the cafeteria, and I suffered through *three more periods of class* with that ham jammed into my jeans pocket.

Ham-Butt is a nickname I may never live down.

Our Virgil, guiding us through the l'inferno gastronomico that was Appalachian Riviera—where you couldn't find a wheel of brie should your life depend upon it, forget about sambal oelek—was Julia Child. Kids these days, you know how they're obsessed with fantasy and sci-fi? Wizards and dragons and unicorns n'at mind-rot junk my ex-wife insists on feeding our kids on *her* days with them. Don't get me started.

You know what my fantasy books were? *Mastering the Art of French Cooking. Larousse Gastronomique.* It doesn't get more escapist than that.

Chiffonade, mirepoix, vichyssoise, soupçon . . .

These words were as foreign and fantastical to me as Vulcan or Elven or Orkish.

It is with that spirit—that which was once foreign has now become the familiar, the foundational, the *indispensable*—that I present to you my new cookbook: *McMann's Authoritative Guide to French Cookery,* from McMann's Global Culinary Arts series. Some—many—might argue that French cooking has gone the way of the brontosaurus—which, I would argue, is the most *elegant* of the extinctosauri. And yet, and yet. Still we cling to those fossilized bones of our earliest origins on this land, *borne back ceaselessly to the past.*

If there's one message, one memento mori I may impart with you all tonight, it is this: *French cookery is here to stay.* Yes, it's hard; French techniques require concentration and precision. Classics are intimidating for a reason. Ask any high schooler forced to read *Moby Dick.* Not me, for obvious reasons. It is a *truth universally known* that I was the only high school dropout on the *Times* payroll.

But classics are classics for a reason. They stand the test of time. They *endure*—fossils and all.

Now let's get real for a moment or three. You're not here to hear me talk about food. You're here to *taste* my food. And so, without further ado, I present my quiche Lorraine, in tartlet form. The recipe is on page 378 of *McMann's Authoritative Guide to French Cookery*, a presigned copy of which was included with your in-person ticket. Linus and Augusta are coming around now with the plates. Thank you, Linus and Augusta.

Bon appétit!

I'm *electrified*. During the Q&A, I raise my virtual hand before I lose my nerve.

Judge Stone answers the live questions. There's a kid in the front row with a ponytail who asks about molecular gastronomy. Judge Stone's badass response? "Just cook good food. Period."

I can't believe I actually get called on. My camera's off, but my voice comes out in a warble. "Judge Stone, do you have any, um . . . advice for a young chef?"

When Judge Stone doesn't immediately answer, I wonder if there's a problem with the feed, or maybe it's that my question was too weirdly open-ended? My English teacher, Ms. Rose, is always on our case to ask *focused* discussion questions.

I tumble forward with "Like, what if your parents think it's the Ivy Leagues or bust, but all you want to do is grow up and work the line in a hot, cramped, stressful kitchen, even if it means you have to skip all the Thanksgivings and Christmases and New Years and weddings, and you can barely afford the rent on your crappy apartment, and you don't even have time to *shower*, but you don't care because, because . . . you love it so much?"

I'm breathless from the rush of adrenaline from public speaking and my embarrassment for being TMI. I'd die if I actually had to do this on stage.

Judge Stone laughs. The audience laughs; titters of *Aw!* ripple through the crowd like they think I'm cute.

It's more of a *laugh at* than a *laugh with*.

"Well, firstly, if I weren't rubbish at school, I wouldn't be here right now," Judge Stone starts. "I'd be a doctor in Squirrel Hill."

A couple more people titter. (Probably whoever gets the reference.)

"No, but to seriously answer your question."

Judge Stone leans forward in his seat, drops his elbows to his knees. "What will you regret more: going for your passion and failing, or never trying for it at all? Do you want to be the chump who spent the rest of his life wondering, *What if?*"

CHOP CHOP

I become the dutiful daughter-drone Umma and Appa always dreamed of. I start cramming a year's worth of world for the final. I plow through mountains of schoolwork, then Chwaego Hagwon homework; some nights I don't put myself to bed until two a.m. Then we're all up at five a.m. so Umma and Appa can check over my work before they leave for work and I leave for school. Lather, rinse, repeat.

But I can't stop thinking about Judge Stone's advice. *What will you regret more?* I'm being dutiful, yeah, but I feel like I'm just going through the motions.

Mr. Doumann gives us a pop quiz, and I only get one answer out of five wrong. Which is still "only" an 80%, but that's an improvement. "Not bad, Jennifer Oh," Mr. D says, and I just let it go.

KT ASKS ME IF I want to study together for our final. I say okay, but then she checks her calendar, and between her debate practices and tournaments, and my hagwon schedule, we can't find a free date.

It doesn't matter. I know her offer was half-hearted, and we're both kind of relieved a study session won't work out.

I DON'T EVEN GET TO see H&H, because of the tracker. I argued to Umma and Appa that it was cruel to keep a child *from their own grandparents—the same grandparents, by the way, who helped* raise *said child!*—but they're like, too bad.

So now, after hagwon, instead of going to H&H's in Bayside, either Umma and Appa come to pick me up or they order a taxi to take me straight home.

I keep writing Oppa every week. But I don't have *Burn Off!*, Melty's, or H&H to talk about. And it's not like I can write complaining about Umma and Appa. So I just report back on old stuff.

My letters are sim-sim-hae—like they're boring and lacking in flavor.

I miss Melty's so much. I miss the thrill and rush of the fire of the grill, the chaos of the kitchen. Even the calluses on my hands are growing soft, and the burn scars start to fade.

A MONTH INTO MY "PROBATION," it's Friday night, and Umma, Appa, and I are eating takeout burrito bowls. It's a rare night when we're all home together for dinner.

When I was little, I used to live for these moments: dinner together as a family. I'd save up all my stories from the week and blurt them out at the table. Even Oppa would shyly show Umma and Appa his drawings and comics.

But every five seconds, our parents' phones would ping with work calls. There were *always* work calls interrupting our dinner, and Umma and Appa would get up from the table and put on their "good" voices: tight, respectful, and ending in the word "yes."

When they'd come back to the table, they were distracted. Even as a kid, you can tell when someone's only listening to you with half an ear. They were harder on Oppa than on me, correcting his spelling and grammar of his comics, until he stopped showing them at all.

Over dinner, we're all on our phones. There's no talking. The only sounds are tapping and chewing. Compare and contrast that to dinners at H&H's, which are loud smorgasbords where we're all talking over each other, spoons and chopsticks clanging, and Bingsu looking up at us like, *You humans need to RELAX IT DOWN.*

My phone pings, breaking the dead silence.

Free tom for study sesh

Umma looks up from her phone suspiciously.

"Who's that?" she asks, but then loosens her face when she sees it's KT. "Kaitlyn is a driven girl," she says. "She's a good influence on you."

So I milk it.

"Speaking of which, KT wants to study together tomorrow for our world history final. But since I'm grounded . . ."

Umma and Appa exchange a *Should we renegotiate the terms of Jackie's probation?* look.

"Want me to leave the room while you guys deliberate?" I ask.

"Very funny, Jackie," Appa says.

Umma and Appa shoot looks of parental telepathy across the dinner table. I want to take KT up on her study offer because I recognize an olive branch when I see it. And I know if I don't say yes, our friendship would do the slow fade over the summer. Come junior year, we'd be those used-to-be friends that nod awkwardly at each other in the hallways but never actually say "hi," let alone hang out.

This study sesh feels like it might be the last stab at friendship, if you will.

Finally, Umma and Appa decide they'll make an "exception" because it's "study-related" and I've "displayed good behavior" while on probation. In other words, they'll allow it.

Plus, they can still track my every move.

THE NEXT MORNING I'M ON the 7 train heading to the Lions, aka the New York Public Library (main branch) to meet KT. I'm running early. Halmoni texts me:

Justin letter here. I mail you?

No!

I text back.

> On my way into the city
>
> I'll stop by Meltys

Halmoni texts back:

> I dont want trouble your umma!

But then I go underground and I lose her.

STEPHEN MIN IS LEAVING MELTY'S just as I'm arriving. He gives me his usual side-eye. "Where've *you* been, Jacqueline Oh?" he says. "A busload of tourists just pulled up."

The grill is slammed, so there's no time for chitchat. It's just Haraboji and Ratón working the grill.

Halmoni runs over to me. "No, no!" she says, because she can read my mind. "I don't want your Umma yelling me. You go straight back to library."

"But you guys need help!" I say. "Where's Segundo?"

"Not your problem." Halmoni hands me Oppa's letter and goes back to the register. But the line of customers snakes past the grill, and they're antsy and huffy because they needed their food *yesterday.* I'm worried but also relieved that business is finally picking up. What am I going to do, stand there and twiddle my thumbs?

I jump in.

We process the first rush of orders, including an order for a cro-knish from a young woman customer. She gives me a funny look when I hand her the platter, and she takes it to the window table.

Not one minute later, she comes back to us, holding her food. I'm immediately on alert. Customers only come back when they have complaints.

"Uh, this thing?" she asks. "What's, like, in it?"

This thing? "It's a cro-knish," I explain. "We sautéed up some ham with onions and garlic, and . . ."

As I launch into the recipe, my mind immediately shoots to the worst-case scenario. This woman got food poisoning. She had an allergic reaction. Or even worse of the worst: She thinks my dish sucked.

The customer points at Halmoni. "May I speak with your mother?"

"Uh . . ." I don't correct her, and I can't stop her from walking over to my grandmother.

Halmoni spots the situation and jumps into damage-control mode.

"So sorry, miss!" she says, dinging open the register. "You want, we give full refund."

"No, no!" The woman stops her. "This food is *delicious*! I can't believe your daughter made this! She's a *very* talented chef."

Halmoni looks relieved, then—suspicious.

"How old is she?" the woman asks.

Halmoni hesitates. I'm anxious, too. Is this customer going to bust me for being underage? Technically I don't have working papers. "Are you in high school?"

That seems safe. I nod.

"That's *amazing*?" she says. "I've actually seen you around here before, but I must keep *missing* you? I'm Meg from Chop Chop? You'd be *amazing* for this new TV opportunity for teen chefs? Come to our meet-and-greet next Wednesday, you'd be like, a *total* shoo-in? Here's the permissions form and my card?"

Meg from Chop Chop is one of those people who speak regular sentences in question marks.

Halmoni stares down at the card and papers Meg places on the counter. She's putting the pieces together faster than I can process.

"Chop Chop?" Halmoni says incredulously. "That means—"

"Yup?" Meg nods. "Okay, bye?"

IT IS ONLY WHEN MEG leaves that I realize two things:

(1) Chop Chop Productions is the name of the credits that roll up at the end of *Burn Off!*

(2) The meet-and-greet is the same day as my world history final.

THE LIONS

"In 2700 BC, the War against Elam led by the Sumerian king Emmebaragesi was for the purpose of . . . ?"

KT and I are sitting on the front steps of the Lions, and she's waiting for my answer. It's there, somewhere, under the piles of random facts I've stared at for the past two hours.

But all I can think about is *Burn Off!*

I'm not one of those people who dreams of being on TV. I'm serious. I don't ham it up for the spotlight. You know those people. Like this one girl from hagwon who's always putting on a British accent like she's ready to bust out Shakespeare. It's so annoying.

But, I can't keep the mind-reel from imagining myself on *Burn Off!* If I win, I'd get

- A "stage"—French for "internship"—with Judge Stone at Icebox Plums. *Stage,* btw, is pronounced *staghj*—not *stage* rhymes with *wage* (which, by the way, you don't get on a *stage*).

- An all-expenses-paid food tour of France for two, *including* dinner at the exclusive three Michelin–starred restaurant, Le Flâneur (the reservations list is booked up one year out).
- A guaranteed spot and full scholarship to the CIA, aka Culinary Institute of America.

Total value of prizes: over $150,000.

Which means I don't need Umma and Appa's permission to go to culinary school. If I win, this will prove to them I'm serious about cooking.

Do you want to be the chump who spent the rest of his life wondering, what if?

I can't *not* take this chance.

AFTER CHOP CHOP MEG LEFT Melty's, Halmoni and I studied the info sheets. For "meet-and-greet" next Wednesday at eight-thirty a.m., I'd have to bring in a signature dish, demonstrate basic cooking skills (chopping, boiling, frying), and have a "chat" with the judges.

"You think Host Dennis be there?" Halmoni asked excitedly, then she went, "No, no, no! You on probation. Your umma never gonna let you miss school."

"I'd only be missing gym and art and lunch," I said quickly. "Oh, and English, but I'm turning in my final paper next week." Then I switched into beggar mode: "This is a once-in-a-lifetime opportunity, Halmoni!"

Eventually Halmoni, and Haraboji, gave in. Because even they understood this was too big to say no to. Halmoni agreed to be my chaperone, and we sent off the release form.

And we're all keeping this a secret from Umma.

I didn't mention my world history final to H&H.

Which isn't until 11:11 a.m.

I can make this work.

I can *so* make this work.

"Jackie, should I repeat the question?" KT goes, bringing me back to reality.

"I'm buffering," I say. "It's to . . ."

She knows when to call it. "It was to preserve and protect the waterways leading back to ancient Mesopotamia."

I close my textbook and massage my temples. "Maybe we should take a break," I suggest.

"We're already taking a break, Jackie." KT waves her arm. "You wanted some fresh air, so here we are."

She sighs. I know when I am trying the bleep out of her patience.

"I'm kind of OD-ing on the whole war-and-destruction thing," I say. "I get it: History is all about big people oppressing the little people. Hello, the reason for every single person fleeing to the United States! I just don't understand why we have to memorize every useless factoid about what some rando

Mesopotamian said and did to another rando Mesopotamian. It's called Google."

"Jackie—"

"How's any of this"—I gesture to our textbooks and notebooks—"going to help us in real life?"

"You mean, how's it going to help you with your *Burn Off!* audition."

KT says it flatly, with none of the OMG-you-might-be-on-TV! energy. Her tone is as flavorless as her school lunch.

"It's a *meet-and-greet,*" I correct KT.

"You're not really going to go through with it." But she can read the answer all over my face. "Seriously, Jackie? Mr. D will never let you make up the final. If you don't show up, you'll fail the class!"

"The *Burn Off!* thing will take, what, an hour, tops?" I say. "I'll totally make it back in time."

"And what if you don't?" KT argues. "I mean . . . it's kind of a long shot, right?"

A long shot? "Gee, thanks for the vote of confidence, KT."

I thought friends were supposed to support their friends. Especially their *best* friends.

Or, former.

I think KT senses a fight because she just says, "Let's go back to studying, shall we?"

And we do. Except KT does, and I start jotting down ideas for my signature dish for the *Burn Off!* judges.

"Think it's too hot for stew?" I ask after a while. "Stew travels well, but, I don't know. I'm kind of thinking boeuf bourguignon, but I'd have to buy, like, two bottles of red wine, and there's *no* way I can convince my parents to—"

"Jackie! Ohmigod, just like, stop!" KT cries. "World history might be a joke to you, but it's not for me. Some of us can't *afford* to play around with food all day, okay?"

Play around with food? This really sets me off.

"Is that all you think of me? Cooking isn't just some hobby for me, KT! It's my passion!"

"Lucky you."

Luck? Like she could be any more sarcastic. What's luck have to do with the fact that I've busted my butt in the kitchen? Cooking didn't just come to me. I don't just slice 'n' bake, Duncan dump-a-box-in-a-pan Hines all day. I'm not basic.

"What do *you* know about food, KT," I scoff, "with your same old, same old rice 'n' beans! Seriously, who eats like that? You wouldn't know flavor if it smacked you in the face!"

Whenever I'd tease KT about her boring lunches in the past, it was all in good fun. But . . . today's different. She turns red, then hisses: *"Stone McMann says I should make this quiche with cream patisserie!"*

"You never make quiche with crème pat!" I hiss back.

Neither of us says anything for a while. The M1, M2, M3, and M4s groan exhaust down Fifth Avenue. Tourists lollygag on the sidewalks. Office workers dart around them. Pigeons peck at leftover crusts.

Then KT asks, "Why'd you bother saying yes to studying today, Jackie?"

"Because—"

Because it felt like the last stab of friendship. Because I thought it was worth it.

"Never mind," I say instead.

KT starts gathering her things, shoving books into her bag. "I have a ton of *actual* studying to do. And Cat Nats this weekend. So."

I grab my things, too. "Don't let me stop you."

KT hoists her bag over her shoulder and marches back up to the library. I head down the stairs.

We go our separate ways.

I'M HEADING DOWN TO THE subway when Umma texts me:

How's your study session going?

Me, lying:

Great! Just wrapped up.

Come to my office. I'm finishing up work.
We'll head home together.

But Umma's *finishing up work* means I sit around in a conference room for an hour while she dashes off a hundred emails.

Plus I don't want to ride an awkward and/or lecture-filled subway ride home with Umma.

I'll just meet you at home.

And I ignore the rest of her texts as I go underground.

IT'S ONLY WHEN I GET home that I realize I forgot to give KT the treat I nabbed for her from Melty's. Black-and-white cookies, crushed in the bottom of my bookbag.

TIMES SQUARE

So much depends upon a quiche Lorraine.

. . . That's been triple-wrapped in tinfoil and placed in an insulated cardboard box I jerry-rigged with more foil, a hot-water bottle, and those hand-warmer packet thingies they sell at Duane Reade. You can eat quiche cold, but it tastes better warm.

Halmoni and I are on line for the *Burn Off!* meet-and-greet, and I'm cradling that quiche more preciously than Gollum in the cave with the ring while the gawking tourists and tourist-scammers jostle and bodycheck us outside the Marriott in the middle of Times Square.

She still has no idea I'm cutting my history final.

I know I'm technically making my own grandmother an "accessory," which I feel terrible about, but apparently not so terrible that I didn't *not* ask her. Is this a slippery slope to other worser crimes?

I shouldn't joke like that.

H&H vetoed my quiche idea. Haraboji thought I should make something more Lowest Common Denominator for my signature dish, like lasagna or meatloaf. "Make what American people like," he said.

But I knew that if Judge Stone was going to be tasting my dish, I'd have to pull out all the stops. Quiche Lorraine would show off my mastery of difficult classic French techniques. I followed Judge Stone's recipe to a tee, but just like I told KT, I still wasn't happy with the filling. So I tweaked it, reducing the milk and cream in favor of an eggier "custard," and I spent half my paycheck on the thick slab bacon and block of Gruyère.

For the last week and a half, I did nothing but practice this dish after school, and I aired out the apartment so Umma and Appa wouldn't catch me violating probation when they got home. I distributed my practice quiches to people in our building, getting their feedback and taking notes. It took so many tries to get it right.

One of those red-jacketed, double-decker tour bus pamphlet-pushers shoves into me—which sends me tripping into the brown ponytailed kid in front of me.

"Watch it!" I shout, but the pamphlet-pusher doesn't care; he's on to the next thing.

New Yorkers aren't shy about letting you know you're In Their Way.

Brown Ponytail whips around to face me.

"My bad," I tell him, then "sorry." I jerk my thumb in Red Jacket's direction.

"No worries." He turns back to his dad. "As I was saying, I'm unimpressed by the Pacojet. Look at what it did to the texture of my goose liver sorbet."

"River, remember what Daniel says," the dad says. "You want some of the fat crystals to maintain suspension, for bursts of richness."

"Daniel and I disagree on that. The Pacotized mouthfeel was wrong."

Halmoni and I exchange an uneasy look. I think she understood as little of that English as I did.

Then from behind us, we hear, "Remember what Coach Serge always says: 'Chin down, wide eyes to the screen!' Got it, Becca?"

"I *know*, Mom."

"Becca" is a model-tall, model-thin girl with perfect sheets of black hair. She sees me gawking and is all *"What?"*

"Nothing," I say, and go back to minding my own business.

Except I can't. *You'd be a total shoo-in!* I thought Chop Chop Meg singled me out as primo *Burn Off!* chef material. I thought I was *special*. Which I know sounds totally snowflakey.

I had no idea this was an open casting call.

I'm feeling all kinds of queasy.

Halmoni does reconnaissance. She strolls down the line of competitors, fronting like she's a Korean granny who doesn't understand a lick of English. I pull out my phone, but then I remember I shut it down right when I got to the Marriott. How else was I going to shake Umma and Appa off my track?

Later, I'll explain to them I wanted to avoid all distractions before the big exam.

Right before I went off the grid, when I got out at Times Square, Umma texted me:

💪💪💪💪🖖

Good luck today on final, Jackie! I hope your hard work pays off!

And an accidental "Live Long and Prosper" because Umma is terrible at emojis.

I texted back a quick Thx! then slid the power off.

If there were an emoji for "Bad and Shameful Daughter," that'd be me. Stabbed all over with guilt, dread, and guilt again. I'm lying to my parents. I don't even want to *think* about the looks on their faces when I bring my report card home.

With my first-ever F.

Because I have no phone, I have no watch, which means I have no idea what time it is in relation to fifth period, and whether I can still make it in time for the final.

The line of other meet-and-greeters doesn't budge. One of Appa's favorite expressions (he has many, and they're all econ-related) is *Forget the sunk costs, focus on the marginal*. I think it means to stop throwing good money after bad.

Maybe KT was right: I'm a long shot. Why am I bothering? If I leave now, I might make it to school in time. I've studied well enough that I think I'd get an 80 to 85%, which is still subpar to Umma and Appa, but at least I wouldn't fail the class. I wouldn't have to repeat sophomore year social studies while I'm taking junior year social studies—which is basically bonkers.

Judge Stone said the choice is either going for your passion and failing or never going for it at all.

If I could just get some face time with him, I know he'll see my *Burn Off!* potential.

So I stay.

Halmoni is back with her spy report: "That girl there"— she nods in the direction of a kid with a messy blond bun— "her father owns a restaurant with two Michelin stars. And that boy there"—she points to another kid in a crop top—"he's in new mafia movie. Plays dead son inside Lamborghini."

"This is not helping, Halmoni!" I say.

"Jackie-ya, why quiche?" Halmoni says, in the tone that barely covers her exasperation with me for not taking her advice. She uses that tone a lot. "이왕이면 김밥이나 잡채라도 만들지 그래!" *While you were at it, you should've made kimbap or japchae or something!*

이왕이면. *While you were at it.* Or maybe it means more like, *If you were going to go through all the trouble, then* . . .

At first I think Halmoni suggests kimbap and japchae because they're better for transport.

Then I think she's telling me I should have used this opportunity to sneak in some propaganda for Korean food being chwaego—number one.

But now I get what she's putting down.

"You don't think I stand a chance," I say.

". . ."

Halmoni hedges her words. She's never one for tact. Which means she's *really* about to bring it on: "너 같은 애를 고르겠냐?" *Would they really choose a kid like you?*

I'm not going to let Halmoni's negativity worm its way into my dream.

"Halmoni," I argue, "they're looking for a 'diverse cast.' They even said it on the info sheet!"

We are looking for a talented and diverse cast of budding teen chefs . . . I'm reaching for my phone to show her the email proof, but—nope.

"They just say like that," Halmoni says dismissively.

"You've seen me cook, Halmoni. You've tasted my food. I'm *good.*" I jiggle my quiche, as if proving my point.

"그건 그렇지만 . . ." *That's true and all, but . . .*

My own grandmother gives me the same fake placating smile she gives to Melty's customers. It's a smile that fronts like, *Yes, you're 100 percent right!* but in actuality she's thinking, *You're 100 percent wrong!*

Then she switches back to English, as if that's supposed to make me feel better. "Maybe they just choose one of each: one yellow, one brown, one black, like they picking M&M candy—"

"Halmoni!" I interrupt in Korean. "You not say like that in public!"

"—but has to be *most beautiful* yellow, brown, black M&M," she continues, ignoring my warning. Halmoni ticks the colors off her fingers, then switches again to Korean: "You're too young to understand, Jackie. American people, they say nice words to your face, but behind your back it's a completely different story. Korean people don't do that. We tell the truth to your face, even if it hurts, so you don't make a babo of yourself in public."

Halmoni looks me dead in the eye as she says it.

"So you think I'm just here, making a complete babo of myself," I say.

Halmoni's nonanswer tells me her answer.

"Wow. Thanks, Halmoni."

She nudges me forward. "Line moving, let's go!"

I say the same words KT said to me last weekend at the Lions: "Why'd you bother saying yes to coming to this meet-and-greet in the first place?"

Halmoni considers my question, then lets out a schoolgirl giggle.

"Because I want selfie with Host Dennis."

MEET-AND-GREET

Host Dennis is even cheesier in real life—and I mean that quite literally. He looks like someone sprayed him with Cheetos dust. His huge, marble-blue eyes are loose in their sockets, like they'll pop out any second. And his whole head bobbles, like the figurine of Derek Jeter that Appa keeps on the dash.

But Halmoni doesn't look the least bit disappointed. She's sitting on the sidelines, biting her lip in silent fangirl mode.

Host Dennis introduces himself, and we shake hands. For a second, I worry he might actually leave some of that orange residue on my fingers. (He doesn't.)

"So! Tell us about yourself"—Host Dennis consults his clipboard—"ha ha, Jacqueline Oh!" The "ha ha" is accompanied by a look: *You sure are nothing like the real Jacqueline O!*

I get that look a lot.

I mumble my stats: *Fifteen years old . . . sophomore . . . from Queens . . . love cooking . . .*

I can't concentrate because the *Burn Off!* judges are sitting at a long table and, well, judging me. Judges Stone, Kelly, and Johnny are there, in the flesh.

I can't get over how different/same they all look IRL, if that makes any sense. Judge Stone, who seems so imposing on screen, is actually small and reedy, with narrow shoulders but also, weirdly, a dad-bod paunch.

Judge Johnny's larger than life. He looks younger now than he does on TV, his skin smooth and wrinkle-free. His swollen ankles spill out over his lime-green Crocs. If you're wondering why I'm checking out his ankles, it's because I can see the judges' legs and feet peeking from the other side of the table.

Judge Kelly, at first, looks identical to her TV self—tiny yet toned, with perfectly sculpted arms, hair and makeup flawless. I still can't shake the image of her on the cover of *Maxim*.

But on closer look, she's much older than she seems. On screen, she looks like she's in her twenties. IRL, she's probably closer to Umma's age.

I kind of respect that. But it's also frustrating. Judge Kelly looks like she's been up since five in the morning doing yoga and Pilates and spin, then hair and makeup and wardrobe. Is *this* what it takes to be a woman chef? It's not enough to chop and slice and cook; you have to be ready to strip down for the cover of a men's magazine?

The other judges kind of look like they just rolled out of bed. It seems unfair.

Before I was ushered into the judges' room, a flurry of

producers and handlers and assistants (no sign of "Meg" who scouted me; apparently she doesn't work here anymore) pointed cameras at me and did a series of tests. They pinned my number—I'm Contestant 4893—to my chest like it's my inmate number. My quiche went forgotten in some corner.

I feel like the opposite of camera-ready. My features are too small *and* too big. Monolids. Mu-legs. Extra pounds. Bad posture and worse clothes on top of it. This whole time, I was so focused on the cooking. But that won't cut it for TV.

I'm cursing myself for coming on this audition. For thinking I actually had a shot.

너 같은 애를 고르겠냐?

I am *such* a babo for thinking I actually had a shot at this audition. Halmoni was right.

"Speak up, Jacqueline Oh," Host Dennis says. "We can't hear you."

I can tell he's annoyed. He keeps glancing at the door, like Contestant 4894 is about to walk in any second and save him from the drudgery that is me.

Am I usually this mousy? Imposter syndrome's affecting my ability to deliver halfway intelligible answers. I keep thinking about the thousands of other more qualified contestants—Pacojet users and child actors with agents and coaches—standing on the other side of the door.

Also, I'm kind of mad. They made us wait for *four hours*. My elderly grandma was on her feet the whole time and standing out on the sidewalk in the hot concrete jungle that is New

York in late June. And I'm going to fail world history. Forget the Ivies—there go my safety schools.

Umma and Appa will never let me live this down.

Host Dennis gives the universal signal for *Wrap it up.* "Tell us about your signature dish, Jacqueline Oh!"

"Judges," I start, "today I've made for you a quiche Lorraine. I adapted the recipe from Judge Stone's cookbook, and . . ."

As I describe my quiche, I feel the confidence creeping back into my voice. Judge Kelly turns her quiche sideways and taps the bottom with her fork. *Tap-tap.* A nice crispy, hollow-y sound because I blind-baked the crust so it wouldn't get a soggy bottom. Judge Johnny digs in. But Judge Stone jiggles the plate, causing my quiche to quiver. He frowns.

"Why did you go with a diluted cream ratio?"

Of course he spotted the difference.

"I wanted the filling to taste more like egg," I say. "I didn't like how milky your original recipe was."

Halmoni, sitting in the corner, lets out a sharp *hsst!* of nun-chi. I realize my mistake: I've insulted the guy who literally wrote the recipe.

Judge Stone's frown deepens. "Unbalanced milk-to-egg ratio notwithstanding"—he crosses his hands, elbows high up on the table—"I don't see how this dish meets the brief. How is quiche Lorraine part of *your* narrative?"

I don't know if it's a rhetorical question, or what.

"It's not *terrible.*" Judge Kelly says it like it's supposed to be some kind of compliment. "But I don't see *you* in this dish. It feels like a failure of creativity."

"Where's the spice?" Judge Johnny says. "Give us some kimchi flavor!" And . . . now he's winking at Halmoni. "Amirite, Grandma?"

Halmoni bursts into giggles. I can't tell whether she's laughing because (a) she genuinely thinks Judge Johnny is funny, (b) she's thrilled to be singled out by a *Burn Off!* celebrity, (c) she's laughing out of embarrassment, (d) she's laughing out of obligation, or (e) all of the above.

Kimchi flavor? Would they have asked Brown Ponytail if he brought the fish 'n' chips flavor? Or the sauerkraut flavor, or wherever in Europe his people obviously hail from? If KT were auditioning, would they tell her to up the Sichuan flavor, even though her family's from the eastern mainland?

But nunchi tells me now is not the time to voice that question.

Nunchi—there's no direct translation for it in English—is like this unspoken code of conduct you're just Supposed to Know as a Korean Person, even if you're three generations removed from the Korean peninsula. Nunchi tells me what I should and should *not* do, because doing or not doing that would make me a Bad Person with Bad Family Values.

You know how in Victorian society, everyone just knew their place, and if you stepped out of line, you'd get cut down with a flutter of the eyelashes? People were shooting nunchi-daggers all over the place like it was a mafia takedown. Like how in Brontë's *Jane Eyre* (they made us read it last year; it was not bad), Jane just sat behind the curtains and never joined in all the rich-people parlor games because, well, nunchi!

Just like nunchi tells me now's not the time to list all the painstaking French techniques of the dish, so I stand there and take it as they hate all over my dish—which I'm coming to see was a huge kimchi-free mistake.

Judge Johnny goes, "You got a lot of talent, kid. But the whole point of this show is to cook *your* food."

The judges don't even tell me if the dish tastes good or not. And I don't bother to ask because even I have the nunchi to read a room.

AT THIS POINT, THE AUDITION is lost—like it's over before it even began. It doesn't matter that I rock the "technicals" portion of the interview, demonstrating my knife work and basic cooking skills, because it's so obvious I am not the contestant they're looking for. I had one chance to wow them, and I blew it.

As a matter of formality, Host Dennis asks me my last question: "Jacqueline, why do you want to be on *Burn Off!*?"

Have you ever heard of the "oh, hell" moment? It's when you know you're done for. When you know your ship is already sinking. When you dance like no one's watching because you're going to get the hook pulling you offstage anyway?

So I just Truth it.

"I know exactly what you thought of me when I walked in that door," I start. "You think I'm some nerdy Asian girl robot who has zero personality and flavor. Well, what you don't know is I'm actually a badass in the kitchen. And I can serve up *all* the flavors. I can chop and fry better than any of those 'child actors' out there. Put any four ingredients in front of me, and I'll give you sixteen different dishes you've never tasted in your life."

The judges look like I've just punched them in the face.

Halmoni flaps frantically at me, signaling me to *shut it down*.

But I'm just getting started.

"Plus, I suck at school! Do you know I'm skipping my final exam in world history right now to be here? Which means I'm getting a zero and failing the class. Which means my parents are going to kill me because I'll never get into Harvard. At this rate, I won't even get into Queens Community. I don't even want to go to Harvard, anyway! Why? So they can dress me up in sweater sets and pearls and marry me off to some future JFK? Yeah, no thanks.

"All I know is, I don't want to be the chump sitting around for the rest of my life, wondering what if."

Judge Stone's eyes flicker.

"But . . . whatever," I go on. "I guess we'll never know how good I could've been on your show."

I catch my breath. "Also, by the way, I made the quiche with a three-to-one egg-to-dairy ratio because your way gives me indigestion."

Judge Kelly's mouth drops. Host Dennis bites his lip. Judge Johnny stifles a laugh. Halmoni shoots me a furious look. And Judge Stone . . . he goes red in the face.

"Where was this passion earlier?" he asks. "If you're not going to bring it, don't bother wasting our time. I think we've seen enough."

Judge Stone stands up, signaling we're done. Halmoni and I rush to grab our stuff and scurry straight for the door.

She doesn't get her selfie with Host Dennis after all.

BUSTED

We leave the Marriott in defeat.

"Let's go K-town, eat pat-bingsu," Halmoni suggests. "Cheering up."

I've failed the final. I've bombed my audition. I could use all the cheering-up bingsu I can get.

We debate whether to walk the thirteen blocks south and two avenues over, or take the subway one stop. "Walking good for us," Halmoni decides. "So you don't get too fat, Jackie-ya."

That's Halmoni. Offering to buy me shaved ice dessert and insulting my weight at the same time.

A figure down the street is rushing toward us. Power-suited and power-walking. Unswerving. Carrying something—a box. I blink, focusing my eyes.

It's Umma.

Oh bleep. Her tracker must have found me.

Umma's face is a weird combination of fury, confusion, relief.

"I don't even know where to *start* with you!" Umma hisses. "Tell me you didn't miss your history final!"

". . ." I'm caught too flat-footed to come up with a lie.

Halmoni looks at me with wide eyes. "You have test today, Jackie-ya?"

"And you!" Umma turns her cold glare to Halmoni. "You go behind my back and pull *my daughter* out of school? You're supposed to be the adult here!"

"Josie-ya, I explain," Halmoni says in her *let's be reasonable* voice. "Today Jackie have once-in-life opportunity. *Burn Off!* TV audition. But if I know Jackie have test today—"

"A *what* audition?" Umma demands.

I explain. Sheepishly.

Umma sets down the cardboard box she's been carrying.

"What's up with the box?" I ask her.

"Don't try to change the subject," Umma says, putting a hand to her forehead. I am one more headache on her long to-do list.

"Josie-ya," Halmoni adds. "It not matter anyway. They not like Jackie. Zero percent chance she get on TV."

"Halmoni!"

"I don't know what's worse. That you"—Umma points at Halmoni, who flinches—"thought *in any way, shape, or form* that this was a good idea? Or that you"—she aims her finger at me—"lied to us, went behind our backs, to follow this rash, delusional impulse . . ."

I know what I did was wrong. But this isn't a *rash, delusional impulse.*

This is my dream.

"Do you have any idea how worried sick I was? Of course you don't; you only think about yourself. Don't you *dare* shut off your phone like that again. I couldn't find you, Jackie! I thought—you'd been . . ."

Halmoni turns sharply to me. "야! 이나쁜 계집애!" *Hey! You bad little she-rascal! Hurry up and tell your mother sorry!*

I do as I'm told. "I'm sorry, Umma."

"그거 갔고 돼?" *You think that's going to cut it?*

I try again, casting my eyes to the ground. I'm trembling as I offer up my apology—a deep, heartfelt, sincere apology—to Umma.

I'm terrified. Not of my mother—but of *Halmoni*.

I have *never* seen this side of Halmoni before. Not even with the worst of customers. And I have never, ever heard Halmoni call me, or anyone else, 이 나쁜 계집애—which I know sounds cute in the translation—*oh, you bad wittle wascal!*—but in actuality is anything but.

Then I turn to Halmoni and bow.

"할머니, 죄송해요. 저 잘 못 했어요. 다시 안 그럴 게요." *Halmoni, I sincerely apologize. I messed up. I never do like this again.*

I bow deeper.

"용서 해 주세요." *I beg forgiveness.*

I make a note to *never* get on Halmoni's bad side again.

To my surprise—as if the day could contain any more surprises—Umma says sharply, "엄마! Jackie 한태 leave alone 해!" *Umma! Leave Jackie alone!*

Pause: Umma's Korean is as bad as—maybe even worse

than—mine. I once asked Umma why. I was surprised when she answered me straight-up. "When I was a kid, it wasn't cool to be Korean. We didn't have K-pop and K-dramas like you do. We got teased and picked on for being Korean. I wasn't incentivized to learn the language. In fact, I was ashamed."

Unpause: "뭐라고?" Halmoni demands. *What did you just say to me?*

"내 딸한태 그렇게 말 하지마! 엄마가 my whole life 그렇게 감" [she means, "고함"] "질렀지만 *my daughter* 한태 절대로 no way!" *Don't say like that to my daughter! My whole life you shream* ["scream"] *like that to me, but to my daughter, never ever no way!*

Halmoni blinks, stunned. It takes her a moment to respond.

"그래. 엄마가 너 한태 잘 못했다. 엄마 미안 하다," she starts. "근데, 너도 마찬가지로 네딸한태 . . ." *You're right. I was bad to you. I'm sorry. But if you do the same to your daughter . . .*

Halmoni trails off.

"됐어." *Never mind.* She waves us on—"간다," *I'm off*—and heads toward the subway.

Umma grabs her arm. "혼자 subway take 하지마!" *No take subway alone!*

"낮 인데 . . . , 뭐." *It's daytime, no biggie.*

"그래도 taxi take 해." *Still, take taxi.*

"아이고야, 돈이 아까워." *Aigo, it's a waste of money.*

"내가 pay 할게!" *I pay!* Umma pulls out her phone to call up a cab.

Now Halmoni grabs her hand to get her to stop. "돈이나

애껴, Josie야. 그래 가지고 뼈 빠지게 일해야 되잖아!" *Save your money, Josie-ya. That's why you have to work those backbreaking hours!*

They're doing this thing—I don't know if it's a Korean thing or just-my-family thing—where they're holding each other's wrists and shaking heads, one refusing, the other insisting. I've seen Appa do this, too, with other relatives when they're fighting over the check.

Umma wins out.

When the taxi pulls up, Umma hoists up her cardboard box. "Why you carry heavy box, Josie-ya?" Halmoni starts. "No good for woman, *ung*?"

"I'm *fine,* Umma," Umma says.

"Maybe this why you lose second baby." Halmoni tuts, and disappears into the taxi.

. . . Which I can't even *begin* to process.

UMMA DOESN'T GO BACK TO the office. She and I head home. Down on the 7 train platform, she says, "You and I are not finished here. We're going to have a long talk with your father when we get home. This . . . *food* obsession of yours needs to stop."

Then she reaches for her phone; work calls. It never *not* calls.

"Don't worry about it," I retort before I lose her to the quicksand of emails. "Like Halmoni said: I don't stand a chance."

RESTAURANT VALUATION

The next morning, the whole family is hungover with too much fighting. It went on all night. Umma and Appa yelling about how *my failure* will now *jeopardize my chances for college, career, success!* They blamed it on my *laziness* and *lack of motivation.* I'm getting some serious déjà vu to the old fights they used to have with Oppa.

And, like Oppa, they inform me *my future is doomed.*

I know I messed up, big-time. But isn't there more to life than memorizing pointless history facts and drilling PSAT prep questions ad nauseam? Like Umma and Appa said: I should be looking to my *future.* Not someone else's past.

Dejected, I asked, "Then what do you want me to do with my life?"

Umma: "Get your MBA."

Appa: "Get your law degree."

Then they gave each other a look because they'd recommended the other's profession.

"Why?" I muttered. "So I can end up miserable like you guys?"

That didn't go over well.

I should have stopped there. Sometimes, you have to know when to call it.

But I couldn't stop. I kept going. I pulled the pin and launched another word grenade at them:

"I mean, what's the point? Having a perfect GPA and perfect SAT score that will get you into the perfect college . . . for what? It didn't change the fact that you have a son in jail and a daughter that's flunking out of school!"

Umma's face went red. Appa shouted, "That's *enough*, Jackie!"

"I don't *want* your life." It came out like a whisper. "I want to become a chef. It's . . . the only thing that makes me happy."

If only I could just skip high school altogether and leapfrog straight into adulthood. I'd live in a cheap basement studio in the last ungentrified part of Queens and quietly do my own thing, working my way up from line cook at Le Bernardin or Per Se.

The real highlight of my day would be preparing "family meal," which is the meal for all the staffers using up the bits and bobs from service. I'd shed the shackles of stuffy haute cuisine and cut loose: deconstructing mushroom tartlets into taco innards, repurposing the crust into a fruit crumble, that sort of blasphemous thing.

Then I'd go back to my crummy studio and watch reruns of *Burn Off!,* heckle the contestants, pass out on the couch, and start the day all over again.

But when I shared this with Umma and Appa, they couldn't hear the part about my passion and dreams. All they could hear was "drop out of high school and do something stupid with my life."

Furious didn't even begin to describe my parents. There was a weird tingling in the air, like lightning was about to strike everywhere. And not in a good, *jackpot!* kind of way.

I mean, like, total destruction.

UMMA AND APPA ARE THREATENING to pull me out of Bronx Science. They want to send me away from the city altogether. Umma is scheduling a call with a headmaster at a boarding school in the middle of Nowheresville. Somewhere plain and vanilla, with a culinary scene to match. Where there'll be no other Asians to compete against.

So that I might now have a shot at somewhere like Boston U.

They'll send me far away—just like they tried to do with Oppa.

If I'm out of sight, then I can't make them feel whatever the opposite of "proud" is.

OVER A GROGGY BREAKFAST OF bagels fresh from the freezer, Appa tries a new tactic. He wants me to "buy in" to their way of thinking. So he performs "backward induction" on the next fifty years of my life.

"What, exactly, is your end goal, Jackie? To own your own restaurant?"

I don't say anything, even though it's obviously "yes."

"Let me guess: an intimate 'small plates' table with, what,

twelve covers?" Appa squints at me. Nailed it. "Maybe in the West Village, tucked away on Carmine or Grove Street? Or let's say Brooklyn. Bedford Avenue or somewhere you young people go, with lots of foot traffic."

Appa slurps his black coffee. He has forever-bags under his eyes, even though he has a full head of black hair. Umma rustles her newspapers. It is five-thirty a.m.

"We actually did a valuation for one of our clients, a restaurant group." Of course he did. "Let's run the numbers, shall we? Okay, so you're looking at one hundred fifty to two hundred dollars per square foot a year in rent. You'd need a bare minimum of twelve hundred square feet. Ideally *five* thousand. So that's—"

Appa looks at me expectantly. He always turns every family meal into a mathalon.

"A hundred eighty grand to one million dollars," I say robotically.

"A hundred eighty grand to *one million dollars* a year in rent, Jackie," Appa repeats back, unfazed by my tone. "And commercial leases are usually fifteen years, so even if your restaurant shutters, you'd still be 'on the hook'"—Appa trying to sound hip—"for the duration of the lease term, even with a 'good guy' clause. More than half of all restaurants fail in their first year. And nine out of ten fail within their first *five* years, Jackie, which is something they never talk about in those 'Tables for Two' write-ups in *The New Yorker*. So unless you're a celebrity chef on TV, you're destined to fail before you even get out of the gate."

I chew on my freezer-burned bagel. The crust is tough, with no air pockets, like the dough was overworked. It tastes like how I feel: chewed-up and deflated.

Appa, oblivious, goes on: "Equipment costs—for argument's sake, let's say you pick them up used at auction—are going to run you fifty K. Twenty-five, if you're on a shoestring budget. And PR. Those PR ladies, you wouldn't believe what they charge for a launch campaign. And we haven't even gotten into overhead costs.

"And, Jackie, don't forget the *years* you have to pay your dues. Do you have any idea how much the average line cook makes?" I know, but it's not like I'm going to admit it to him. Appa answers for me: "It's below poverty level, I'll tell you that."

Appa meticulously calculates every line item of our hypothetical restaurant, charting its opening and failure in the span of a minute. By the time we're done, we are millions of doughnuts in the red.

"This isn't a wise career choice," Appa says in conclusion. "There's no ROI to speak of. Do you want to be poor and in debt for the rest of your life?"

That's the way my dad is. He thinks if he throws enough numbers at me, he can "logic" me out of my dream. It's pretty condescending.

Then again, he's a corporate Ivy League MBA.

"I know you think it's all just celebrity chefs and bestselling cookbooks," Umma says. "On TV, they make fourteen-hour days on your feet in a hot, cramped kitchen look glamorous. It's literal backbreaking work. Halmoni has arthritis and varicose veins. No one chooses restaurant work because they *want* to. Do you know what kinds of people show up at Melty's looking for a job? Two kinds: immigrants, or lowlifes. People who have *no other choice.*"

Umma pushes her plate away. She doesn't do bagels because carbs are the devil.

"You know how hard Melty's was hit during Covid. Halmoni and Haraboji are barely scraping by as it is. The food service industry is *extremely* risky."

"But, if I get on *Burn Off!,* it will prove—"

Appa lets out a sarcastic laugh. Umma leans back in her chair, arms crossed.

"You've got to be kidding me!" she says. "Even *if* you get on that show—big if—there is no way we're letting you go on. Not after that stunt you just pulled. This isn't some get-out-of-jail-free card. Ahem."

Appa's face pinches. Umma realizes her slipup too late.

My phone rings. It's a 310 number I don't recognize. Since my phone privileges have now been taken away, all I can do is look longingly at it on the table.

We all stare and stare until it stops ringing.

Then *Umma's* phone rings. Same 310 number.

Umma answers it. "This is Josephine Oh . . . no, no, not too early, that's all right . . . yes, this is her mother . . . sorry, where? Chop Chop?"

I look up expectantly. Umma shakes her head. Then she gets up from the table and takes the call in the other room, slamming the door behind her.

Part II

Part II

WEEK 1

KITCHEN CLASSROOM

Episode 1:
Welcome to *Burn Off!* High

Meet the twelve talented teen chefs who will compete on the first-ever series premiere of *Burn Off! High School Edition*. We've scoured the country far and wide to find the best teen cooks, ages fourteen to seventeen, who will fight in Kitchen Classroom for the title of Valedictorian!

When I was nine, I had my first—and last—piano recital. Teacher Cho arranged for all his pupils to perform at Queens College. I was so nervous because my parents had taken off work to watch me perform. They *never* took off work. We didn't even go on vacations as a family or anything, unless you count renting a house for a week in the Catskills so everyone could sit in front of their laptops and do more work.

I (practiced)[3] until I was perfect.

It was right after Oppa was arrested, and I felt this need to be "extra." To be the perfect daughter, to make up for the fact that my big brother had Messed Up. I don't know if it was pressure my parents were putting on me or pressure I was putting on myself. Probably both.

Umma and Appa didn't talk about what happened to Oppa. At home, they'd shut down my questions. Even H&H avoided the topic. I was scared, with no one to talk to. So I confided in my best friend, Chloe Han.

Big mistake. Right after I spilled, she ghosted me.

When Umma called her mom to follow up on yet another no-show playdate, Mrs. Han said, loudly enough that I could hear her even though the phone wasn't on speaker, "Jackie's got *so* much on her plate right now, and we just think the best thing is for Chloe to step back and give her some space? It's really what's best for *both* girls? What with the SHSATs coming up and all . . ."

The science high schools test wasn't until eighth grade, and we were only in fourth grade, but—whatever. I could read between Mrs. Han's lines: She didn't want her daughter to be friends with the girl whose brother was in jail. Because jail was something you could catch, like Covid.

"I understand, Yoojin," Umma said, using the same calm tone

she uses even with clients who call screaming at all hours. "Call me if you and Rob revisit."

When they hung up, Umma threw her phone across the room.

My mother did not hold and comfort me as I sobbed. I'd lost a brother and now my best friend. Instead, Umma said to me in her steeliest voice, "This is why we don't discuss family matters outside the home."

I never made that mistake again.

And not that Umma was the touchy-feeliest of moms before Oppa's arrest. But after, I felt the wall going up. Every tiny slipup I made was met with the apocalypse. I could do no right. Some days, it felt like perfect wasn't good enough for Umma. And Appa . . . I guess you could say he was easier on me, but it's because he just disappeared into his own work. According to those self-help magazines Umma has lying around, Appa "outsources the childcare and discipline" to Umma—if he's around to help out at all.

SO, THE RECITAL AT QUEENS College. Backstage, the other pupils and I stood awkwardly and attempted small talk. This one girl, Jenna Kim, was like, "I can't believe Cho is making me play Beethoven, it's so basic" and rolled her eyes. Nancy Jeong said, "At least it's not *Brahms*!" and pretended to barf, which made all the other kids laugh.

I was playing Brahms. But I wasn't about to volunteer that.

When it was my turn to perform, the notes I had meticulously memorized went poof—evaporating from my brain. Teacher Cho, standing in the wings, waved frantically for me to start. But I sat there frozen on stage. I couldn't think; I couldn't move.

My parents were sitting expectantly in the front row. I knew I was supposed to make them proud. But when their eyes met mine, they just shook their heads. Forget disappointment. The shame on their faces was unmistakable.

SO . . . YEAH. THAT PIANO RECITAL is nothing compared to what I'm feeling now in the *Burn Off!* studio, blinking under a thousand spotlights. I'm standing with eleven other contestants in *V*-formation, hands on hips, following the producers' instructions to "look badass!" The same nervous energy swirls in Kitchen Classroom. It's so thick, you can smell it. I feel dap-dap-hae—constricted, claustrophobic, uncomfortable—in the bulky white chef's jackets they've dressed us up in, and the pancake makeup they've powdered us down with sits heavy on my face.

The handlers kept trying to make me go down a size with my jacket—"for a snugger fit!"—but I feel self-conscious enough already wearing tight things, so I insisted on the bigger size. Not that it's a fashion contest, but I don't even want to think about what I must look like on TV.

Instead of Kitchen Coliseum, with its Grecian columns and grape leaves and naked marble statues, the studio is tricked out like a discombobulated cross between a kindergarten classroom, a science lab, and Hogwarts. A chalkboard, alphabet posters, and multicolored paper cut-out people are strung up on the walls; there are also beakers, a skeleton, and a periodic table that, for whatever reason, is missing all the noble gases, and these dark wood floor-to-ceiling bookcases. Green library lamps are placed at each workstation, hogging up precious counter space.

Host Dennis strides onto the stage. Gone is his usual Grecian toga getup. He's wearing black-framed glasses and a tweed blazer with elbow patches. He twirls a pointer stick. This must be Hollywood's idea of the brainy professor.

He's still orange as ever.

"Ladies, gentlemen, countrymen! Lend me your ears!" he says, starting his usual intro.

The studio audience is instructed to whoop. The studio audience is just our parents, like a sad Little League game. Umma looks up from her paper and pen—they don't allow phones or computers on the set, so she's probably answering work emails the analog way. She lets out a half whoop, a beat too late.

Things have been chilly between us ever since the *Burn Off!* phone call. Umma still hasn't forgiven me for lying about the audition, failing history class, threatening to drop out of high school, the whole shebang. She'd meant it when she said she wasn't going to let me come on the show, even if I made it on, because it would be "rewarding" me for my bad behavior.

It was Appa, of all people, who intervened on my behalf. "There's no erasing that F on Jackie's transcript," he said. "But maybe we can spin this. How many other kids will be putting 'starred in a nationally syndicated television show' on their college apps?" Appa was probably already envisioning my

"How I Spent My Summer in Hollywood" college essay. Plus, *Burn Off! High School Edition* was taping over the summer, so I'd be missing hagwon but not regular school.

But I had to promise I'd quit it with the "dropping out of high school" nonsense. Which I did. Appa volunteered Umma to be the one to chaperone me because his office is in-person five days a week. I thought Umma's was, too, so I don't know how this will jibe with her "being up for promotion."

Not like I was going to nose around and ask questions. I know better than to rock the boat.

HOST DENNIS CONTINUES, "WELCOME TO this very special season premiere of *Burn Off! High School Edition!* But this ain't just any old episode of your favorite cooking competition in the primetime slot. Tonight, we have twelve talented teen cooks *battling* in Kitchen Coliseum—I mean, *Kitchen Classroom!*"

He lets out a deliberate laugh, to let us know the gaffe was for real.

This is usually when the gladiator guy blows his Viking horn. But today they've dressed him in a scientist's lab coat. He holds up a school bell and lets it *rinnnnng.*

"These teens will chop. They'll fry. They'll roast! Each night, they'll be serving up sizzling sides, mouthwatering mains, divine desserts . . . and all before they can legally drive!"

Cue the laughter.

Host Dennis rattles off the winning prizes, and we all whoop again. I'd give anything for just *one* of those prizes. But to stage with Judge Stone? It'd take my cooking to the next level. It'd open doors for me in the culinary world I couldn't even *dream* of.

So . . . yeah. I kind of better win this thing.

If only to prove my parents wrong.

"Which one of these twelve talented teens"—the cameras zoom around us, then spin back to Host Dennis—"will win the title of *Burn Off!* teen champion? And which will be sent home? So as we say in Kitchen Classroom: Cook off, or—"

The studio audience finishes his tagline: *"Burn Off!"*

EACH EPISODE CONTAINS THREE ROUNDS: Homework, Quiz, and Detention. In Homework, we complete different techniques, and the winner gets Immunity for the rest of the episode. Then we get "Quizzed" on any challenge the judges cook up, and the winner is named "Teacher's Pet." If you're safe, you get "dismissed" to Recess. The lowest-ranking students get sent to Detention, where they'll have to duke it out among themselves and the loser gets Expelled. The season will end in a Final Exam, and the winner gets named Valedictorian of *Burn Off!* High.

Cute, right? Except I stopped having recess in like the eighth grade, and Bronx Science doesn't even do detention. It's a little cringe.

But I get it—it's TV. Lowest Common Denominator. They have to speak to the masses.

* * *

THE CAMERAS SWOOP AROUND US, like aggrieved geese. I blink and blink under the hot lights, dots dancing behind my eyes, trying to shut out the Greek chorus of voices in my head.

Umma: *Remember, this is <u>national television</u>.* Translation: *Don't humiliate yourself—or us—in public.*

Appa: *This will go on your permanent record.* Translation: *If you fail, you'll never get into a good college.*

Haraboji: *Jackie-ya, show America Korean food number one!*

Halmoni, interrupting Haraboji: *No. They think Italian food number one.*

Haraboji, revising: *Okay, Korea number-two food!*

Halmoni, no nonsense: *Number two is American food. They addicted to McDonald hamburger. Number three is Mexican, Taco Bell.*

Haraboji, resolved: *Fine. Number four.*

Halmoni, correcting: *Number four unlucky number. Give it to Chinese food.*

Oppa wrote me right before we left for LA, congratulating me for making it on *Burn Off!* But he also warned: Never take help . . . dont owe NOBODY . . .

KT didn't offer any advice. Because she and I haven't spoken since the day we walked away from each other at the Lions. When I texted to tell her I made it on the show, she just thumbs-upped to acknowledge my text but didn't write me back at all.

Host Dennis moves on to introducing the contestants. "First up . . . from Pasadena, California, is seventeen-year-old Betsy Fernández!"

A tall, thin girl takes center stage. She has glossy dark hair and long, tanned legs. Her plump lips are either bee- or Botox-stung.

I remember this girl from the hotel. We were all staring at her; it was impossible not to. I thought she was a model or an actor. I had no idea she'd be my *competition*.

"Hi to all my fans!" Betsy Fernández says. "Y'all know me as Baja Fresca. My thing is fresh, feel-good, healthy Cali food!"

We're all wearing the same white chef's jackets, but Baja has managed to make hers look like a chic blazer. She's wearing it over a miniskirt and strappy high-heeled sandals. Open-toed shoes are a safety hazard that would never pass a Department of Health inspection.

Then something weird happens. The cameraman aims his lens down low, at Baja's legs, then swoops up. It feels . . . gross? No, gross, period—no question mark. But if Baja notices, she doesn't let on. Her face is a perfectly made-up mask.

Suddenly one of the contestants pulls out of formation and runs up to Baja, red pigtails flying behind her. The girl—red pigtails, freckles—looks familiar, but I can't place her at first. Maybe she was on TV? Or maybe she just looks like all the other perky, freckly, red-pigtailed girls on television.

"Omg, Baja!" Perky Freckles cries. "I am *such* a fangirl! Can I have your autograph??"

I shake my head. This can't be for real. But Host Dennis laughs.

"Well, here comes our next contestant! You may remember Perky Freckles from *Jump! Rope! Jungle!* where she won hearts all over America. But can she win over our *stomachs,* too? Folks, please give a warm welcome to fourteen-year-old Annie Perkins, from Oklahoma!"

This girl's fourteen? She looks like she's pushing ten, tops.

"Gosh! I'm pleased as punch to be cooking for y'all! Yee-haw!" Perky Freckles curtsies, which makes the crowd go wild.

A skinny, bleach-blond woman—her mom?—is actually *mouthing along the words* with her daughter.

I'm starting to feel sick to my stomach.

River Waters, a lanky, brown-ponytailed seventeen-year-old from Portland, Oregon, tells Host Dennis he audited classes at the CIA.

Host Dennis laughs. "Aren't you too young to be a secret spy?"

River gives Host Dennis a withering look, which I totally respect. There are two kinds of people in this world: those who know what CIA is, and those who think it's the other thing.

I recognize Brown Ponytail; I think he was the guy on line in front of me during the auditions, talking up the Pacojet (which I've since learned is a food pulverizer thingy). But I now have a new sinking feeling. Something in my gut tells me this kid from Portland is the one to beat.

From the *other* Portland, Maine, is Sara Bass—a blond fifteen-year-old who does seafood. She looks incredibly serious, arms folded tightly across her chest during her whole intro.

The next contestants fly by. Constantine works in his family's diner in Chicago. Jo from LA does Mexican. Jill from Atlanta "lovessss" Southern cooking. Sharif from Michigan does "Middle Eastern fusion." Staten Island Calvin makes "Italian family-style"; and the other Asian, Mei from San Francisco, does "upscale Chinese." It all feels a little matchy-matchy.

None of the other contestants do classical French cooking, like me.

Host Dennis pries Mei's whole origin story: born in China, adopted to the States as a baby. She looks relieved when it's over and she returns to the lineup.

And of all the luck, or maybe it wasn't luck at all but a deliberate machination from the producers—I'm next to be introduced. Which means America will forever link the two of us Asian girls, back to back.

I hate how I have to worry about stuff like this.

"Our next contestant is from Queens, New York, . . . fifteen-year-old Jacqueline Oh!" Host Dennis booms. His bobblehead is really going at it. He makes some dumb crack about the First Lady, which he laughs at, but I don't.

"Now tell our viewers at home about yourself! What's your story?"

". . ."

My mind goes blank. I'm back on that piano stage. Frozen. You can memorize Brahms to perfection, but still the notes evaporate from your mind.

Host Dennis, sensing dead air, scrambles to fill in the silence. "I bet you make a mean bibimbap!"

"It's not as good as my coq au vin," I blurt.

I mean, I *do* make a mean bibimbap, but Host Dennis's question rubs me all wrong.

Host Dennis tries again: "Then what *is* your specialty?"

I don't see you *in this dish.*

Where's the spice?

Speak up. We can't hear you!

". . . I guess I'm here to figure that out, Dennis."

"Well, Jacqueline! We're here for it!"

He moves on to the next contestant. I'm hoping against hope I don't come off sounding and looking like a total idiot on national TV, but I'm 98.7 percent sure I did.

INT. BURN OFF! SET—OTF ROOM

Dark recording room with a green screen back-
ground. A camera is aimed at a single stool
in the middle of the room.

A PRODUCER (30s, white woman [interchange-
able], headsetted and clipboarded) directs ME
(15yo Asian girl, anxious, studious-seeming)
to the stool.

> **PRODUCER (V.O.):**
> The way these interviews work,
> Jacqueline, is we'll ask you some
> questions, and you'll give us your
> honest, OTF—that's Off the Fly—
> answers. They're *super* casual,
> so don't be nervous! We just want
> the folks back home to get to
> know you.

> **ME:**
> (looking nervously at PRODUCER)
> Uh, okay?

> **PRODUCER:**
> And don't forget to look into the
> camera when you talk!

> **ME:**
> (facing camera)
> Uh, okay.

> **PRODUCER:**
> (clears her throat)
> Jacqueline, you and eleven other
> contestants beat out *thousands* of

American teens to earn a spot on
the first-ever season of *Burn Off!*
High. Congratulations! How does it
feel to be competing on the show?

ME:

Fine?

PRODUCER:

Please try to refer to the
question in your answer.
      (beat)
Our questions won't air, but your
answers will.
      (beat)
Let's try again?

ME:

Sorry. I'm new to this. I feel
like the kid who showed up at
school and forgot there was a
test, ha ha.
      (nervous laughter)
I think I'm the only one here who
doesn't have an acting coach or a
celebrity stylist!

PRODUCER:

Let's roll with that. What do you
think about the other contestants?

ME:

I mean, not all of us can star
on *Jump! Rope! Jungle!* Or have a
half a million followers online.
Some of us are just regular old
nobodies over here.
      (pausing)

I mean . . . I've only just met
the other contestants. It's too
soon for trash-talking.
(laughs uncertainly)
Let's wait 'til we actually get in
the kitchen?

PRODUCER:
(hiding/not hiding exasperation)
Let's move along. How do your
friends and family back home feel
about you competing for a chance
to become the first-ever teen
champion? What was their reaction?

ME:
(shrugging)
My parents are just . . . kind of
blah about me making it on *Burn
Off!*? They think TV is dumb.
(hand to mouth)
Sorry, no offense! Anyway, they
weren't even going to let me on.

PRODUCER:
Your parents must put *a lot* of
pressure on you, huh?
(gives a knowing, *amirite?* look)

ME:
I was born here, and so were my
parents. So . . . I'm not sure
what you're implying?
(stares intently at PRODUCER)

PRODUCER:
Right, right.
(recovering)

Tell us about your first food
memory.

ME:
In the basement of Melty's . . .
sorry.
      (starts again)
My first food memory was in the
basement of Halmoni and Haraboji's
deli, Melty's, in Midtown
Manhattan.

PRODUCER:
Harmony and . . . ?

ME:
Sorry, that's my grandparents.
Halmoni and Haraboji. We watch
Burn Off! together every week.
Halmoni's a superfan of Host
Dennis, b-t-dubs. They've taught
me everything I know about
cooking. And there was the food we
cooked for the customers upstairs,
but then there was the food *we'd*
eat from the leftovers.
Anyway, Haraboji would make this
jjigae—that's like a stew and
casserole Voltroned together—where
he'd dump in the day's leftovers,
so that nothing would go to waste,
and cook it up into a spicy broth
with a packet of instant ramyun
noodles. It's called budae jjigae,
which I have no idea what that
means in English.
      (dreamy smile spreading
        across ME's face)

PRODUCER:
All right, Jackie, cameraman's
signaling it's his union break.
We'll wrap this up, but more to
come! Good luck out there!

END OF OTF.

HOLY TRINITY

Being on TV isn't as glamorous as it seems. We basically just stand around while they set up the camera positions, and stylists pat our faces to get rid of the shine, and as soon as they roll tape, someone on the crew goes on their union break, and then we contestants go on *our* scheduled breaks (because child labor laws), and Host Dennis keeps repeating his lines until he gets them right, and then we're all waiting around until we can start over again.

If TV cooking was anything like real cooking, where customers needed their food yesterday, restaurants would go out of business.

It's a lot of hurry up and wait.

Which is strangely more exhausting than just *doing*.

When we finish taping our intros, we get back to the hotel that evening and I promptly pass out. The hotel messed up and gave us one large queen bed instead of two doubles, so I have to share with Umma. I haven't shared a bed with my mom since, like, ever. But I'm too tired to complain. I just roll away from her and hit the zzz's.

Episode 2:
Back-to-School Basics

Homework Challenge:
"Holy Trinity"

Rules: Contestants must chop a mirepoix, aka "holy trinity," of ten cups of onions, five cups of celery, and five cups of carrots in a uniform dice. First to complete the challenge wins Immunity for the next round!

The next morning, we're back in the studio for our first-ever Homework challenge. Judge Stone has a whole chapter on the mirepoix in his book, *Foundations of Good Cookery,* so I know what's up. But from the confused looks on some of my competitors' faces, it's pretty obvious who knows what a mirepoix is and who doesn't.

Never mind the baskets of onions, carrots, and celery on display as a dead giveaway.

It's only when Host Dennis announces the rules that my competitors quickly recover, fronting like they knew all along.

He starts the countdown: "On your marks, get set, go!"

The twelve of us start clawing for the mirepoix veggies, all elbows and shoulder checks like it's a madhouse. Which is kind of ironic because French cooking is all about being refined.

I grab what I need and get out of there.

Everyone else starts with the onions first, but my order of operations is celery, carrots, onions. Easiest → hardest. I make quick work of the celery, breaking down ten ribs into five cups. I've guesstimated the quantity correctly, which means I just saved myself precious time by not having to run back to the celery basket again.

Next up are carrots. They're trickier to cut because their sizing's all over the place. After peeling them, you have to cross-section them, run your knife down the unwieldy stacks length-wise, then dice them down. If celery's $1+1$, then carrots feel like $x+y= z$, where you have to plug and play different values for each knife stroke. But soon I get eight carrots down to five cups. I had nine in my basket, so I'm all good.

Everyone around me is crying. Calvin, the spiky-haired Staten Islander, is furiously wiping his eyes with his onion-juice hands, which will only make the sting worse. And then they'll all have to chop their way through the "easier" veggies with bleary eyes.

Which is why I saved the onions for last. It's called common sense.

Onions are like the long division of the holy trinity. You'll get there eventually, but it's going to be messy.

I chop off the ends, cut them in half, and make careful cross-slivers, just like Haraboji taught me. As soon as the onion juices are airborne, I feel the milky burn in my eyes. I ignore it and keep working.

As I chop, I start to fantasize about Donghae Steel knives, which I just read a feature about in *Bon Appétit*. They're these custom steel-forged knives made by a hipster guy in Brooklyn whose Korean *grandfather* was a steel forger conscripted to work in a Japanese factory. He passed down his "trade secrets" to his son, who passed it down to the grandson. They're super lightweight, but sturdy and precise. My knives are okay—I saved up my allowance to get a decent chef's knife, and my others are a mishmash of Melty's leftovers. As soon as I make real money, I'm going to buy myself a set of Donghae blades.

Someone shouts, "Done!" breaking my concentration. It's Calvin, slamming down his knife. He was still crying not even a minute ago. How did he beat me?

Judge Kelly is the first judge to make it to Calvin's station. She peers into his Cambro container. "Why are there onion skins in here?"

"It's the everything-but-the-kitchen-sink approach, Kelly!" Host Dennis quips.

Host Kelly ignores him, reaching for a handful of onion slices, which are only semi-detached. The cuts did not go all the way through—like those paper people cutouts that are still attached by hand. Except not intentional.

"It will take all day to separate the good pieces from the bad, which will waste time and food, and make service late." Then Judge Kelly asks him point-blank: "Do you think this is acceptable work, Calvin?"

Calvin doesn't answer. But the scowl on his face is unmistakable.

Then she dumps all his onions out of the Cambro and tells him to start over.

Calvin mutters the B-word when Judge Kelly is out of earshot. So not cool. The cameras don't seem to pick it up.

I get back to my work. I'm *just* shy of the ten-cup mark. I could fluff up my onion slices so they'll hit the mark—but that feels like cheating. So I dice up another half onion. I'm tossing my slices into the Cambro when I hear a "Done!"

It's Constantine. During the intros, he said his family runs a diner in Chicago. Judge Johnny heads over to inspect.

"So, Constantine," Judge Johnny says. "Where'd a kid like you get a name like that?"

It sounds kind of . . . wrong?

Constantine blushes. "I go by Gus."

Judge Johnny inspects his work. I realize Gus was the only one of us not to gawk; he just kept his head down and worked. And now he'll come in first and get Immunity in the Quiz Challenge. I could curse myself for rubbernecking. Calvin's train wreck cost me vital seconds.

I slam down my knife and shout, "Done!"

Judge Stone heads to my station. I find myself getting nervous—sweaty palms and everything. I want to tell him he's my idol. That I've read every one of his cookbooks. That I want that internship at Icebox Plums *so* badly.

But I don't, because it's kind of a bit *much*.

Judge Stone unceremoniously dumps my onions, carrots, and celery all over my workstation. He sifts through the piles, holding each piece to the light. All around me, I hear my competitors shout, "Done!" and "Done!" At Gus's station, Judge Johnny cries, "We have a winner!" It feels a little unfair, how meticulous Judge Stone is being with me. My anxiety is *up to here*. One misshapen carrot dice is all it'll take to send me back to the end of the line.

Finally, after what seems like forever—

Judge Stone is done.

"Uniform cuts. Precise. Excellent knifework. You're quite the workhorse, Jacqueline Oh."

Quite the workhorse! Was this Judge Stone's first compliment to me? Relief, pride, all the things flood through me.

I'M IN SECOND PLACE, AFTER Gus. Not bad. But I didn't come on *Burn Off!* just so I could be "not bad."

I'm Jackie Oh.

I'm here to clean house.

SCHOOL LUNCH

Episode 2:
Back-to-School Basics

Quiz Challenge: "Sandwich-Off!"

Rules: Contestants will have twenty minutes to prepare their best School Lunch sandwiches. You must make four identical signature sandwiches: three for the judges, and one for "Beauty" shots. The chef of the winning sandwich will be named Teacher's Pet! The six chefs with the worst sandwiches will be sent to Detention, where they will face Expulsion.

We barely have a second to catch our breaths when it's on to the next challenge.

"Sandwiches!" Host Dennis announces. "You will have twenty minutes to make *your* signature sandwich. On your mark, get set—go!"

I'm all about the sandwiches. I make hundreds a day at Melty's. My favorite is the Madison Avenue, which is like the quintessential New York sandwich: pastrami and melted Muenster on toasted rye. But the best thing about the Madison is our house-made horseradish mayo.

But. As everyone flies for the pantry, I'm stuck in my own head. I wish this were a five-minute sandwich challenge instead; I'd switch into autopilot and I'd bang out an awesome-for-the-time-allotted sandwich without overthinking it. But twenty minutes is both too much and too little time to make a sandwich. It's not like I can go slow roast a six-hour pastrami or anything.

That's the trap.

I spot yellow plantains in the pantry, perfectly mottled and ripe. When you fry them up, each slice gets a hint of caramelly crunch, which is the best thing. Whenever Ratón brings maduros from home to share, we all fight for the last piece. But I'd level them up with some lime zest, to cut through the sweet and starchy monotony.

Then, in the fridge—a beautiful skirt steak. Skirt cooks quick; I'd throw it on the grill and whiz up a citrusy chimichurri. Add a shitake mushroom "pâté" schmeared on toasted baguette. Mandolin a green apple and cabbage slaw to add brightness, tartness, and crunch. Some chunks of mango mixed into the slaw, and a dash of chili powder, like the fruit cart lady

125

outside Bedford Park Boulevard station who sells spicy mango slices on a stick.

I can see my dish forming—

But—no. It's too basic, mishmash, and *unrefined*.

I move on.

Suddenly it hits me: the perfect sandwich that will show off my classical techniques and inspire the judges. I grab Gruyère, Parma ham, a loaf of sourdough, milk, butter, eggs. I grab mâche, shallots, lemon, honey. I'll make a croque madame with a microgreens salad. It's like a ham, egg, and cheese but *way* fancier. You can't get a croque at a corner bodega or anything. They only sell them at fancy brunch bistros. Croques are fried *and* broiled, with a bechamel sauce that needs to be babysat on the stove. I'll be lucky if I can pull this off in twenty minutes. The judges will be impressed.

I whisk flour into melted butter in a pan, making a roux that's the foundation for the béchamel. Then I add in hot milk and whisk vigorously. I could also add grated Parmesan to make it a Mornay sauce instead. To cheese or not to cheese is a big debate in the croque world. But there's already so much cheese *in* the sandwich, as well as sprinkled on top. I nix the Mornay; more cheese will be overkill. I hope the judges won't ding me for it.

I survey my competitors:

Baja is picking flowers, I kid you not.

Mei is doing something with a pork chop. Risky, since raw pork can kill you.

Calvin, with his "unacceptable" mirepoix, unscrews a jar of
marinara sauce. Basic.

Sara, the Mainer who placed third in the mirepoix, is dropping lobsters into a boiling pot. It'll take forever just to
pick the meat from the shell. Good luck.

River, the brown ponytail who came in fourth for the
mirepoix, has a large metal canister at his workstation.
Is that . . . *liquid nitrogen*?

I'm supposed to compete with *liquid nitrogen*?

I need to level up my sandwich. Instead of babysitting my
béchamel, I run to the pantry, searching for . . . le mot juste,
the *just-right thing* to add to my dish. I'm scouring the shelves,
but nothing inspires. I race over to the fridge—

When I collide with Gus, who's carrying a giant bag of flour.

Which means we're both sprawled on the floor, covered in
all-purpose dust.

I can just picture the slow-mo reel for the viewers at home.
My cheeks burn.

"Hey, *watch* it," I say, at the same time Gus says, "You okay?"

"I'm fine," I say, at the same time he says, "*You* watch it."

I pick myself up and get out of there before I lose more
time. But nothing in the fridge or pantry catches my eye. I race
back to my station empty-handed. Gus is already back at his,
kneading dough. That guy is *fast*. But he thinks he's making
bread in under twenty minutes? Yeah, right. Good thing he has
Immunity.

I check myself. Am I always this competitive?

At the stove, my béchamel has gone from white to brown. It's ruined.

Fifteen minutes left on the clock.

And I haven't even started my sandwich yet.

I scrape the burnt sauce into the trash and start again.

The minutes tick down. I assemble the sandwiches and fry them in a cast-iron skillet. Arrange them on a sheet pan and pour the finished sauce over them. Grate Gruyère on top, then pop the whole shebang in the broiler. While they broil, I whiz up a shallot vinaigrette for the mâche salad. Should I also do a side of frites? But there's a line for the deep fryer. Forget the fries.

The kitchen is chaos, but I'm starting to find my rhythm. KT used to describe her best debate tournaments as "getting in the zone." She's prepped inside and out, so when it's Show Time, muscle memory just takes over.

I wonder how she did at nationals. I hope she kicked ass; knowing KT, I'm sure she did. Even though I'm still mad at her, and I know she's mad at me, I miss her.

I wish things weren't so weird between us.

FIVE MINUTES LEFT ON THE clock. It's time to fry up eggs for the croques. I guess the sunny-side ups resemble ladies' hats, so that's why they're called croque madames vs. croque monsieurs that are sans eggs? I don't know; I didn't make up these names. As the eggs cook—I have a minute before the runny yolks turn into golf balls—I pull my croques from the oven. They are perfectly golden brown. Nice! I'm about to plate them up—

When a camera and mic are shoved in my face.

"Chef Jacqueline!" It's Host Dennis, sneak-attacking me. Because that's the way this show operates: quiet sabotage. "Tell the folks at home about your signature sandwich!"

"Croque madame."

My head is down, I'm focused on shimmying sunny-side ups out of the frying pan and onto the sandwiches. The last thing I need is a punctured yolk spilling everywhere, ruining my dish.

"Can you explain to the viewers at home what the *croak* is a croque madame?" Host Dennis laughs at himself.

"Google it."

Great. Millions of Americans watching at home will think, *What's up with that rude Asian girl?* I'll hear the guilt trip from H&H later: *You make ALL Korean people look bad, Jackie-ya!*

Add that to my 1,001 other worries as I rush to plate up. I grab the sheet pan with my bare hand and can practically hear my skin sizzle.

"Ouch! That's got to hurt!" Host Dennis waves for the medic. They have a floating medic because apparently contestants are constantly injuring themselves and the show does not want to get sued.

"I'm fine, I'm fine!" I say, but they insist on examining me all over. I *so* don't have time for this.

Host Dennis moves on to pestering someone else. But not before I hear him mutter to the cameraman, "Zero charm."

It stings, worse than the ointment they're smearing on my screaming fingers.

The medic finally finishes bandaging me up and lets me go.

With one minute left.

I finish throwing food down on my plate.

Then I remember, *Where's the kimchi flavor?* Judge Johnny's "feedback" during the auditions. Great. Are they going to ding me for not bringing "kimchi flavor" to my croque madame? The contestants who get *burnt* are the ones that "fail to incorporate feedback." I race to the fridge, where earlier I spotted a jar of kimchi. I throw some on my plate; it'll have to do.

Seven seconds left. Wiping down my plates. Did I forget any elements of my dish? Checking to see—

"Time!" Host Dennis cries. "Hands up, baby, hands up!"

The clock flashes 00:00.

JUDGES' TABLE

I survey my four expertly croqued madames and an ever so delicately dressed mâche salad. I could legit charge twenty-five dollars for this plate of food—well, except for the kimchi part. But that part's just fulfilling the brief. I'm feeling really confident about my sandwich—which is saying a lot because I'm not exactly the most confident person in the world.

One by one we're called up to Judges' Table. The first few sandwiches are a lobster roll with huge shards of shell just hanging out, a "deconstructed" meatball hero that's basically ground meat scattered across a hot dog bun and slathered in cold jarred marinara, and a char siu bao, with undercooked pork.

I know it's wrong or whatever to take pleasure in other people's miseries. But each not-good sandwich brings me closer to the win. I'm sorry, but I'm not one of those "you do you!" types who can afford not to care what everyone else around them is doing.

My whole life, I've always been compared to someone else.

First it was my cousin Sophia, who was prettier, skinnier, and did not suffer from ugly radish leg syndrome. At Science, teachers like Mr. D compare you to all the *other* overachieving Asian kids. At church, back in the days when we used to go to church, we were compared to the "better" families, i.e., the ones with kids who *didn't* break the law. At hagwon, popularity was ranked by practice test scores.

If you couldn't keep up, there was something wrong with you.

I've heard the horror stories about how all us Asian kids are competing for a handful of slots. Not just the Asian kids at Science, but all the schools in the city, tri-state area, and the country. Everyone's forced to one-up each other with orchestra this and varsity that, 4.0 GPAs and 1600 SATs, and still that isn't enough.

Last year, this (non-Asian) girl from homeroom was like, "Why are you guys, like, *so* competitive?"

I just stood there, dumbfounded. I was shocked by the question, both because it was so offensive and also the answer was so obvious.

There's not enough room for all of us.

It's almost like the system was designed that way.

GUS IS UP NEXT, AND his sandwich—flatbread with charred fennel, pine nuts, goat cheese, and pesto—demolishes whatever shreds of confidence I thought I had left.

"You made your own bread? In twenty minutes?" Judge Johnny says in disbelief. "This is the *bomb*!"

But Gus is screwing up his face, like his dish personally irks him. "It was no big deal," he mumbles. "I used yogurt instead of yeast, then grilled it on the flat top. If I'd had another minute to let the dough rest . . ."

He trails off.

Well, this explains the flour collision earlier. I'm a babo for thinking *he* was the babo for making his own dough. Note to self: Underestimate NO ONE.

"There are nice earthy elements here, with the pignoli and pesto," Judge Kelly says, "but the char on your fennel is not uniform."

Because she can't ever *not* find fault with a dish. It's kind of her thing.

"Uniform does not a char make," Judge Stone interrupts. "Therein lies the enigmatic beauty of the char. Of which, good sir"—he nods at Gus—"this dish contains multitudes."

Judge Johnny drops his voice deep. "Bring it in, m'man!"

He reaches across Judges' Table and gives Gus a half hug and dap.

I don't know if it's cool or cringey to be singled out like that.

From the uncomfortable look on Gus's face, maybe he thinks so, too.

BAJA FRESCA PRESENTS A DISH of greens and flowers, but no *actual* sandwich. "Show me the bread!" Judge Johnny demands, searching his plate comically for the missing element.

"Well, Johnny, and Stone, and Kelly!" Baja says, dropping the "Judge" like they're already besties. "Today I've cooked for you a deconstructed sandwich of luscious kale lacinato, silky roasted candy-cane beets, and sexy edible flowers to finish the palate. I think we've evolved beyond the literal walls of carbs."

"What about a burrito? Or taco?" Judge Johnny says.

Baja shoots him a withering look. "No."

"It's great you're thinking outside the box!" Host Dennis butts in encouragingly. Usually he lets the judges do their thing.

"What's the flavor component?" Judge Stone asks.

"Nutritional yeast for texture and umami. And a champagne vinaigrette with grapeseed oil for the omega-threes! Because I'm all about fresh, feel-good, Cali—"

"Your flowers are unwashed," Judge Kelly interrupts, holding up a tiny stone from her plate.

Baja looks flustered. "I'm sorry, I was rushing and—"

Judge Kelly turns on her heel, and the other judges follow.

PERKY FRECKLES'S SANDWICH IS, NO joke, an open-faced PB&J. It has a squirted jelly smiley face, butterscotch chip freckles, and the crusts cut off. She presents her dish all doink-doink, like she's expecting a biscuit or something.

Judge Stone does this thing where he rests his chin on his elbow, and you just know she's about to get "Stoned": "This explains what you did for the first two minutes of the challenge. What, pray tell, Ms. Perkins, occupied the remaining eighteen?"

Perky's face falls. Her eyes bunch up, like she's going to cry.

Judge Johnny goes, "Aw, phooey," waving a dismissive hand

at Stone. "For what it's worth, this PB&J tastes awesome! High-five on the butterscotch thingamabob!"

They slap hands.

I'm wondering which way Judge Kelly will go. She lifts up the sandwich and actually studies it all over. Her verdict: "The peanut butter is unevenly distributed, as well as the jelly. The cuts on the crust are not uniform. And most egregious is that the bread has become soggy. Chef Annie, you would have been better off toasting the bread, to support the structural weight of the fillings."

Perky Freckles looks anything but. Her face falls. Her mother, in the audience, stands up and starts booing. Like, *actually* booing, two thumbs down and all. Two production assistants rush over and have to calm her down before filming can continue.

A FEW MORE HO-HUMMERS RESTORE my confidence, kind of. But then River is next. His dish is a precisely round piece of meat stacked on a precisely round piece of bread, placed on the corner of the rectangular plate. Down the middle of the stark white plate is a paintbrushed streak of brown sauce.

It's not food—it's art.

"Judges, today I have for you a beautiful grass-fed Oregon Valley elk steak, reverse seared with foraged mushroom and pink peppercorn dust, on a country baguette, with offal jus, and a salted Rocky Mountain goat milk cream foam."

River pulls out a metal canister, shakes it up, and pours frothing white foam onto his plate.

I have *never* seen anything like it before.

You can hear our collective jaws drop in Kitchen Classroom.

"Hot diggity! That sandwich come with an instruction manual?" Judge Johnny says. But when he bites into the sandwich, he holds up both hands to signal a perfect ten.

"A goat milk cream foam?" Judge Kelly says, raising an eyebrow.

River nods, smiling. "I'm showcasing Pacific Northwest products at their most elevated."

Judge Kelly says, "I can't argue with your technique. But this foam has no place with the rest of the dish." And she *wipes* off the foam from the sandwich with the back of her fork.

Which wipes the grin right off River's face.

Judge Stone lifts the top off his sandwich. "Mushroom powder?" he says.

River, still a little shaky, says, "Yes, a blend of slippery jacks, matsutakes, and king boletes. To amp up the umami flavor."

Judge Stone takes a tentative bite. "An enlightened move, sir," he says. If you get a "sir," you're pretty golden for the round.

Unless the "sir" is sarcastic, which means he's burning you off.

Therein lies the enigma of Stone McMann.

I HATE THAT I HAVE to follow River's dish. My hands shake the whole mile-long walk up to Judges' Table.

But it's over before it can even begin.

Judge Kelly: "Serviceable."

Judge Stone: "It's rather . . . safe?"

Judge Johnny: "Not bad." Then: "What's up with this kim-chi? Doesn't go with the flow, know what I'm saying?"

But I did what they *told* me to do. I literally brought them "the kimchi flavor."

I delivered a technically difficult and flawlessly executed croque madame in *twenty minutes.* Just like I came in second during the Mirepoix-Off. I cooked my butt off today.

But all that work, all those extra steps of layering flavor—it's like they can't even see it.

LIBRARY

While the judges deliberate, we're sent to the Library, aka the greenroom, which isn't a green room at all but yet another studio where they're filming our every word. "Beauties" of our sandwiches flash on the TV screen in a continuous loop.

The twelve of us stare awkwardly at each other. We know what's up: This is where you're supposed to trash-talk each other. The greenroom is where alliances and factions are formed.

But I'm not playing this game. I grab some water and slump into a chair in the corner so I can go feel sorry for myself. *Safe? Serviceable?* They offered more feedback to a PB&J.

It's only now, after the adrenaline fades, that I realize how exhausted I am. I'm used to long shifts at Melty's, but they feel like nothing compared to cooking onstage. My feet, shod in Crocs and the support stockings Halmoni makes me wear—*Do you want varicose veins like me?*—are sore and achy.

I down my glass of water. It tastes . . . funny. I know California has a drought and all, but this water tastes plasticky, which does nothing to quench my thirst. It's like New York City tap is delicious by comparison.

Weird.

River comes up to me. "Nice croque," he says. "It's the béchamel that trips up most people."

He puts out his fist, so I bump it. But inside I'm cringing. Did River see me mess up my first sauce?

"Uh, thanks."

"You know what would have next-leveled your béch?" he adds. "If you caramelized the roux. White sauce is a little last millennium, feel?"

I wasn't even alive in the last millennium, and neither was he. Is this praise or a neg? Both?

"It's super easy," he continues. "All you have to do is let the butter brown, and . . ."

Either way, it's working. I can feel River worming into my head, psyching me out.

I'm shutting this down.

"Nope," I interrupt.

River is confused. "What do you mean, 'nope'?"

"Meaning, it'll make the roux brown, so it won't be a béchamel anymore, and you only use brown roux for gumbo or jambalaya, so, yeah. Nope."

They should invent a word for that satisfied feeling of putting a show-off in his place by dropping some serious knowledge. I bet the Germans have one. Except—

Wait. Why's River giving me a *Oh, you poor thing, you* look?

"That *was* the received wisdom, but like I said, last millennium.

All the molecular gastro chefs today are deconstructing the mother sauces. You do know the work of Snijders and Klausgård, right?"

They should also have a word for that panicked feeling when said show-off challenges *your* knowledge by dropping *his* knowledge, then looks at you expectantly for an answer, and now you're forced to either own up to the fact that you have absolutely no idea what he's talking about, or front like you do?

Yeah, that.

I choose to front. "Yup."

"Then you know Snijders' fjord de Noël uses the broken béch mushroom anglaise in a savory application, featured in this month's *Tidsskrift Gastronomique Molecular*?"

I literally have no idea what River's talking about.

"Uh, yup."

River goes on about liquid nitrogen, freezing points and dissolutions, and this Snyder person, who I guess is some gastrophysicist dude? I hardly follow, even though I did above mediocre in chemistry (93.4%).

You'd think because I go to Bronx Science, I'd be into the whole molecular gastronomy scene. But I'm actually not. I cook to de-stress. If cooking suddenly became all about following strict formulas and measuring down to the last milligram, it'd feel like homework.

I'll probably never be a baker, which is all science. I'm okay with that.

"So what'd you think of his reverse Swiss roll technique?"

"Uh . . ." Darn. I can't now *un*commit. "I would have stayed . . . classic."

"Classic, right." River nods, so at least I didn't give the *wrong* answer. "I've had it both ways. Réne made it for my dad and me in his lab at Poäng. You do know Poäng, right?"

"Who doesn't?"

"And you'd think reverse would be the way to go, but nope. Classic all the way."

"Classic all the way," I say, finding a foothold. "You know, Judge Stone talks all about preserving classical techniques. I read it in his—"

River groans. "*Don't* tell me you're reading McMann's *French*."

"Yeah, and?"

"I got galleys of it last year. Even back then it was dated."

What's a galley? I don't ask.

Around the room, the other contestants cluster in groups. Baja Fresca is working the room like it's a party. She flits from one group to the next, laughing all the way. How does she get her skin so dewy yet not at all sweaty-looking? I don't even *want* to look at myself in the mirror right now.

In fact, *all* the other girl contestants are TV-genic, and I can't help but compare myself to them. Perky, with her doink-doink adorability. Mei—"upscale Chinese"—is rail-thin. Maine Sara: ultimate girl next door. And Jill, with her blond bouffant, looks like a Southern pageant queen.

If we're just a "type," where do I fit in?

Maybe she saw me making eye contact, or maybe it was our turn, because Baja saunters our way, saving me from molecular torture. River perks up and runs his fingers through his hair.

He's so predictable.

"What are you guys talking about?" Baja asks.

"Molecular gastro," River says to Baja. "You know, like the work of Snijders and Klausgärd."

He gives her that same expectant look. Unlike me, Baja goes for option number one: to confirm.

"Yeah, I don't know what that is," she says in a dismissive and *I don't care* tone.

I'm in awe—and envy—of her confidence. I wish I was so cool I didn't care if I looked foolish in front of others.

"It's all like a little too freaky gen-mod, you know?" she goes on. "I think we should mess with food as little as possible. I'm all about the au naturel."

"I don't agree with you," River says, getting heated. "At Poäng, Réne pioneered the reverse Swiss roll fjord du—"

"Hey, can you go, like, grab us some drinks?" Baja flits her manicured fingers toward the beverage table.

River is thrown. He obviously wants to keep showing off to Baja about "molecular gastro," but he says, "Uh—sure."

"Take your time!" Baja calls out after him.

If Baja weren't my competition, she'd kind of be my new hero. Seriously, she should teach seminars on that—the art of making smug boys do your bidding.

Baja perches herself, uninvited, on the arm of my chair. "Wow. *That* guy. Am I right?"

Since we're now apparently girl-bonding/trash-talking, I go, "Yeah, uh. He basically read the whole Ikea catalogue aloud to me."

She laughs. "Wow. Jacqueline, right?"

I nod.

"So you really went for it with that ham and cheese. I *love* that for you."

Girl-bonding is now officially over.

"It's called a *croque madame.*" I say it like, duh. But the insult goes right over Baja's head.

"I'm not really into French food. It's so heavy, you know?"

I can feel her sizing me up. You know how when Stephen Min looks at me, I feel like eye-broccoli? Well, Baja's the type who's probably really into broccoli. Instead, she's staring down at me like I'm a greasy Big Mac wrapper.

Oh no. She doesn't get to do this to me. Not after the day I had with the judges. Not after River tried to make me feel like a fool. Not after the fights I've had with Umma and Appa, and the crummy nights of sleep I've been having, and jet lag on top of it.

I'm barely holding it together as it is.

So I say to Baja, "Most people are intimidated by French cooking. But that's because they lack technique."

Which wipes the smug smile right off Baja's face. She gets up from my armrest perch, looking all scandalized. As if she had no part in this. She goes to the table, taking a seat next to Perky Freckles. In a matter of seconds, they're giggling about I don't know what. But then they keep glancing back at me, like we're still in the fifth grade.

I go back to sulking in my chair.

Only two others are loning it: Seafood Sara, who sits in the corner with her arms crossed. Her face says, *Don't talk to me.* And Chicago Gus looks deep in his own thoughts, like he's troubleshooting his performance.

Smart. I should have followed their lead. They're not here to make friends—and neither should I.

GOOD ENOUGH IS NOT GOOD ENOUGH

The judges announce the winner: River. It was a close call with Gus, but River's sandwich was "next level." When we walk off the set, River's dad gives him a fierce high five. "*That's* what I'm talking about! Go get what's *yours.*"

The other parents hug and kiss their kids and offer up praise: "Great job!" "You were fantastic!"

The look on Umma's face tells me everything I don't want to know.

In silence we shuttle back to the hotel, then elevator up to our room. The second Umma waves the key in the lock, she barrages me with all the things I could have/should not have done, starting with the Mirepoix-Off, then on to sandwiches:

> wasting time with an aimless trip to the pantry
> burning my béchamel the first time around
> failure to "transform" the mâché

lack of acidity in the croque; lack of brightness in the dish
overall

failure to integrate the kimchi seamlessly into my dish, e.g.,
in the form of a kimchi chutney or spreadable paste

failure to anticipate Host Dennis's questions and prepare
coherent answers, thereby leading to

failure to engage with the audience back home

losing concentration and burning my hand

an overall mismanagement in time

lack of focus

too much rubbernecking

It turns out Umma wasn't answering work emails in her note-pad; she was scribbling notes on my performance. For someone who knows zilch about food—I've never seen Umma cook in my life—she lays down my every move with perturbingly pin-point accuracy.

I flop onto the bed. Our *shared* bed. Which feels like one more thing on top of everything else.

"Umma, can you chill with the performance review?"

Umma's sitting at the vanity, wiping off her makeup. She dabs cold crème on her face with a mini wand. One tiny jar is like five hundred dollars a pop. The awkward English on the label says, *Be 100% beauty!*

"You're the one who insisted on coming on this show." Umma's speaking to me through the mirror. "Jackie, do you think you did your best?"

I stare (okay, glare) back at her reflection. "Obviously *you* don't."

What burns me, so to speak, is how no one recognizes all the ways I went the extra mile—not the judges, not my own mother. I could have just dumped mayo on bread and called it a day, instead of executing a complicated sauce. Instead of cast-iron searing, then broiling the sandwiches, I could have served them up cold. All my efforts made absolutely no difference— I was still lumped into the same "safe" category as Baja's salad, Calvin's jarred marinara mess, and all the other forgettable, low skill, "mediocre" dishes.

I think of the other parents backstage, high-fiving their kids and telling them they did great. Even Mei's mom folded her into a big hug and murmured, "I'm so proud of you."

Proud of what? That her daughter's getting sent to Detention for raw pork?

"Wow, Umma," I say. "Would it kill you to say, 'Good job, Jackie!'?"

Umma sits next to me on the bed. All her makeup is gone. I don't often see my mother without her face on. She's already made up by the time I get out of bed in the morning and still on work calls all around the world by the time I go to sleep. *What's wrong with your face? So old and tired-looking!* I'm not trying to body-shame, but Halmoni's kind of right. Umma looks so enervated—despite her overpriced crème and its "100%!" promises.

"Because good enough is *not* good enough, Jackie."

Her tone softens a fraction. She reaches for my hand; I let her. "People like us don't get second chances. We have to be perfect the first time around."

Every day, I walk around feeling like I'm carrying an invisible backpack full of stress bricks. On top of my *actual* backpack loaded with textbooks, notebooks, and my laptop. I just feel all this pressure weighing down on me, all the time.

I beat myself up enough as it is.

I just survived my first two days in Hollywood. I didn't win, but I also didn't get burnt. Shouldn't that count for something?

Umma gives my hand a squeeze. I pull it away.

"You know what Oppa once told me? He said you have to be 'perfect' to be a member of our family." The words spill hot and angry from my mouth. "No wonder he ran away!"

Even if I wanted to, it's too late to take them back.

I stare up straight at the ceiling, blinking back tears big-time.

I hear the tightening of Umma's voice. "Good night, Jackie."

She turns down the covers on her side of the bed and climbs in. Then she rolls away from me and puts out the light.

I DRIFT IN AND OUT of sleep, my dreams disjointed. Umma, reaching for my hand. Appa, kicking Oppa out. Judge Stone, issuing my verdict: *Safe! Serviceable!* The banging of a gavel. Oppa in an orange jumpsuit, crumpled in the corner of a lonely jail cell.

People like us don't get second chances. We have to be perfect the first time around.

***

I NEED FRESH AIR. UMMA'S still passed out. I climb out of bed and creep from the room.

I sit in the hotel lobby, staring down at my phone. It's eight p.m. here, eleven p.m. New York time. It's too late to call anyone back home.

Outside by the pool, I hear laughter—no, giggling. It's Baja Fresca and Perky Freckles in their bathing suits. They're hanging out on the lounge chairs, trying on makeup.

"Pucker up!" Baja Fresca says, and spreads lipstick across Perky's mouth.

Perky studies herself in a handheld mirror. "I *love* it, Baja!"

They giggle again.

Perky's mom is sitting at the tiki bar. "Hey!" she shouts to the bartender, waving her empty glass. A cocktail umbrella tips dangerously close to the side of the glass. "I said, *hey*!"

In that instant, Perky Freckles freezes, winces. Baja's too busy with the lipstick that she doesn't notice. But I do. Suddenly Perky looks a hundred years old.

It lasts a split second. Then Perky breaks into a huge, freckly smile. "Omg, Baja! Have you ever, like . . ."

They giggle again.

The moment, whatever it was, is gone.

TOUGH LIKE STEAK

The awesome thing about dodging Detention is that I get to do PSAT practice tests instead. That was another condition of being allowed on the show: keeping up with hagwon studies in my downtime. I'm sitting with my Chwaego Hagwon prep book and my tomato timer, which Umma actually made me pack. Through my room's window, I see Baja, River, and a few others lounging by the pool.

H&H video-call me after the Melty's lunch rush. I'm technically supposed to have my phone off while I'm studying, but Umma's not here to panopticon me. It's so good to hear from H&H. We left New York only a few days ago, but it feels like it's been forever.

"You winning, Jackie-ya?" is the first thing Halmoni wants to know.

"Not yet, Halmoni," I say. I don't go into details, because NDA. For all I know, Chop Chop's tapping our phones.

"Maybe you not try hard enough," she tuts, and I laugh it off.

"Did Oppa send a letter?" I ask.

"Not yet," they say, even though I already know that's the answer. Halmoni says she'll text a picture of his next letter to me when it comes.

H&H catch me up on Melty's news—same old, nothing new—but I can read between the lines that business is still slow. Then they ask me to put Umma on.

"She's not here," I say flatly. "She's in the business center, working."

"Why she working when she—" Halmoni stops herself.

"When she what?"

"Nothing, nothing," she says quickly.

"She's *always* working," I say.

"Jackie-ya, you fight with your umma?" Haraboji asks. He must have picked up something in my tone.

"Not *fighting*," I say. "It's just . . ."

And suddenly I'm rehashing our argument, careful not to reveal too much about the show, and how Umma ragged on every little piece of my performance.

Halmoni isn't having it. "Why you complain?" she demands. "Daughter should be grateful when Umma tells her what to fix! Because she wants you to be chwaego, the best—"

"Well, maybe I'll never be chwaego!" I interrupt. "Then what's she going to do?"

Haraboji says, "Your umma tough, like steak."

"Wha . . . ?"

"When we immigrate this country, we just trying to survive. No time for 'mental health,' 'self-care,' what-you-call," Halmoni says. "We just throw your umma on grill, no marinade, no tinfoil, no protection, nothing! She all by herself outside world, of course she get burnt! That's why she so tough lady now."

". . . What's that have to do with me?" I ask.

"야, 이 바보야!" Halmoni says. *Hey, you fool!* "Your umma not wanting you get burnt by outside world, too! 그것도 모르냐?" *Don't you even know that?*

Halmoni throws in another 바보야! for good measure.

I guess *tough like steak* runs in the family.

"Jackie-ya," Haraboji says, "even though your umma tough outside, inside, she still tender. Don't you forget."

He goes on. "That's why we always so sweet with you, Jackie-ya. Because when you put sweet pear or kiwi in marinade, makes steak soft and juicy, not tough. But we never have time to marinade your umma. We made big mistake."

Halmoni being Halmoni, she adds, "Why you think we never yell at you, even when you do stupid thing, Jackie-ya? So many stupid thing! But always we keep our mouth shut. Is why you come out sweeter than your poor umma."

Halmoni strikes her chest. "Because back then, we 바보, too."

I GET BACK TO WORK. But the reading comp passage in my workbook is all gibberish.

Maybe you not try hard enough.

Jackie, do you think you did your best?

I laughed it off when Halmoni said it.

But how's what Umma said to me any different?

I SKIP TO THE ALGEBRA questions, thinking maybe cold hard math will get me out of my own head.

Tough like steak.

So old and tired-looking!

*You have to be **extra**ordinary for them to consider you ordinary.*

But inside, still tender.

The tomato timer goes off.

TEST KITCHEN

As soon as I finish my study quota for the day, I head down to the practice kitchen on premises. It's kind of cool they've given us our own workspace. On the way down, I glimpse the non-Detention-serving other contestants, still hanging out by the pool. But it feels fake to go over to them and make nice.

Plus, I have like zero confidence in myself in a bathing suit.

The hallway leading to the kitchen smells like bread baking. Just before I get to the kitchen, I pass one of the PAs, Erica.

"Hi, Mei!" she says.

"I'm *Jacqueline*," I remind her.

"Oh! Sorry!"

Erica looks a *little* embarrassed as she walks away, but not like, *full on* embarrassed. It's Mr. Doumann all over again.

Mei and I don't even *look* alike.

"I hate when they do that."

It's Gus, standing in the kitchen doorway.

"Oh . . . you caught that?" I say, feeling embarrassed, even though—why should *I* be the one to feel embarrassed?

"It's like we're all the same to them," Gus says. "You know in my last OTF, they kept asking me if Marcus Samuelsson is an influence? The guy's Swedish Ethiopian. I'm from *Chicago.*"

"I hear that," I say, nodding.

What Gus says strikes deep. When I first met Erica the PA, she also asked me to list my influences. I started with Escoffier, obviously. Then all the French-trained greats: Julia Child, Jacques Pépin, Eric Ripert, Anthony Bourdain, and Stone McMann, of course. But Erica was like, "What about David Chang? Is he one of your culinary idols?"

Like I'm going to idolize a guy whose idea of a good pizza is *Domino's*? Please.

I want to tell Gus how much I hate how the other judges act around him: from doing double takes at his name to *M'man! Bring it in!* and forcing him to give them daps.

But . . . I don't know if it's my place to say any of that. It might make him feel more self-conscious that I noticed than if I *hadn't.*

Also, it's not like we're friends.

So I just say, "Well, I'll let you get back to it . . ." and leave Gus to his cooking while I go to the pantry.

I'm not really cooking with purpose. I dice up potatoes and turnips here, grill vegetables there. I'm just kind of riffing. We cook in tandem, in silence. When Gus pulls loaves of bread out of the oven, I'm distracted by the smells: malty, toasty, with just a hint of sourness.

He sees me sniffing around. "Want to try?" he offers.

"Okay," I say. But I make it sound all casual and not too eager.

"I'm experimenting with different glazes," Gus explains, pointing to each loaf, which he's labeled with index cards. "This one, I sprayed with water and baking soda. This one has an egg yolk-and-water wash. This one's egg white only. And this one, I brushed with milk . . ."

He goes down the line, slicing pieces off each loaf and explaining why some have a lighter or darker sheen. And how the baking soda, for example, gives the bread a shiny, shellacked crust. Gus is methodical, like a scientist in the lab, changing one variable at a time. It's impressive.

I point to the one with a shiny crust. "You think this could work on bagels?" I ask.

Because bagels are one of my favorite food groups. (Everything is *everything*.) But each time I've tried to make them, they come out dull and flat.

"It probably could," Gus says, "but the thing about bagels is—"

"The water," we say in unison. Then we both kind of grin at each other, nodding.

"I didn't know you were such a bread guy," I say.

"I'm not," Gus admits. "Baking's actually the weakest part of my game. So that's why I'm drilling it."

KT does—did?—the same thing with debate team; she'd drill the weakest part of her game, like word efficiency exercises and "what if's."

"Promise you won't laugh?" Gus says.

"I don't make promises I can't keep," I say.

"Fair enough," Gus says, and holds up a tattered book called *There's No Business Like* Dough *Business!*

The cover is a corny cartoon drawing of a talking ball of dough wiggling its jazz hands.

It's physically impossible not to crack up.

"I know, I know," Gus says. "It'll never win a James Beard. But so many cookbooks talk down to the reader, you know? And even if you follow their recipes to a tee, you still feel like you messed up somewhere. But this book's super practical and helpful. And it *works.*"

I think back on Judge Stone's quiche recipe, and how I had to keep adjusting the custard ratio so it wasn't so liquidy.

"Anyway, you're welcome to borrow this book anytime," he offers.

"Yeah, maybe. Thanks." I nod. "I might *just dough it!*"

"Ha ha."

Gus asks about my practice dishes—potato pancakes, vegetable casserole. Now I'm kind of self-conscious because I'm not cooking today with any methodology, like how he is.

We sample each other's food, offering feedback. Gus takes notes as I compare his different bread textures. And he makes good suggestions for me, like subbing Yukons for the red blisses for a creamier texture.

But I also don't get it. Gus is openly transparent about his cooking: the baking soda tip, Greek yogurt in the pita dough, offering to lend me his cookbook. What game is he playing at, giving away all his trade secrets? Why's he being so helpful?

"Hey, Gus," I say. "Shouldn't you keep it tighter? This is a competition."

I'm joking/not joking.

Gus looks thoughtful. "Well . . . if I'm going to beat you, I'll beat you fair and square."

He smiles to let me know he's also joking/not joking.

"Ha!" I start cracking my knuckles, which is this nervous fidget-thing I do. It catches Gus's attention.

"You've cooked before," he says. "I can tell by your hands."

There's a blister bubble on my right thumb. A slice on my left index finger from the first time I wielded the cleaver at Melty's. Various scars and burn marks across my knuckles, from years of handling boiling cauldrons of water and pulling hot pans from the Blodgett, and my croque madame mishap.

Basically, my hands are a mess.

Self-conscious, I jam them in my apron pockets.

"No, I didn't mean . . . I mean, me too." Gus spreads his hands wide, turning them front and back for me to examine.

Gus's hands have cuts and calluses and welts everywhere. Burn marks slash the insides of his forearms, like minus signs. They look like, well, Haraboji's: big, red knuckles and lashes all over. With Gus, the wounds still look mostly fresh. With Haraboji's, the scars are smooth and shiny with age.

Gus points to each scar like he's palm reading not his future, but his past: "This one's from the time I grabbed the cast iron but didn't know the back burner was on. And this one involves lamb shank, garlic, and a dull cleaver."

"Ouch," I say. Been there, done that, if not exactly those combinations.

"You and me, we know work. Which is more than I can say for everyone else around here." Gus clears his throat. "If you ever want to practice again together and give each other feedback . . ."

Suddenly, the alarms go off; my defenses go up. What *is* this? I'm not like Baja. Guys don't just ask me to do *anything* together.

I see exactly where this is headed. Gus just wants to plus and minus my strengths and weaknesses. He wants to pit them against me. Just like how River was trying to play mind games with me.

Never take help . . . dont owe NOBODY . . .

"Yeah, uh, maybe . . ."

But Gus can read the *no thanks* all over my face.

"Forget I asked," he says, matching my tightness.

This competition is so confusing. How am I supposed to make friends with my competitors? I can't trust anybody here. Oppa trusted his friends—and look where that got him.

Better to keep the wall up. Better to be always on guard.

Since I was the one who made it awkward, I leave the kitchen first.

Burn Off! is what Appa would call a zero-sum game: Everyone here wants you gone so they can stay alive.

ELEVATOR BANK

I'm waiting for the elevator in the lobby when I hear voices approaching: Perky Freckles and her mom. Detention must be over.

"You didn't try hard enough, Anna! You should have been out there, making every single one of those damn judges fall in love with *Jump! Rope! Jungle!* Perky!"

They're rounding the corner toward me.

Suddenly Mrs. Freckles trips—over nothing—and pitches forward, but Perky catches her from falling and steadies her.

Mrs. Freckles keeps talking like nothing happened, like she didn't just trip over air and almost fall splat on her face: "What's left for us now, Anna? Every casting agent in town says you've aged out of everything. This show was our last shot. *Our last shot!*"

For a millisecond, I see a look of *relief* flooding over Perky's face. It's so jarring with her normal cutesy-wootsy act that I think I'm imagining it.

I'm not imagining it.

Then the look is gone.

"I'm sorry, Mommy," she says, her voice small. "I'll try much harder next time."

But Mrs. Freckles goes, "There won't *be* a next time! Because you didn't give it your all!"

Now it's awkward because Perky and Mrs. Freckles are brushing right by me. I pancake myself against the wall to let them pass. Mrs. Freckles doesn't notice me—she stumbles past, her Gucci purse swinging and hitting me straight in the gut. But Perky does. She breaks into a sudden perktastic smile.

"Hey, Jacqueline! *So* sorry about my mom. She's had food poisoning, she's kind of out of it!"

Then she rushes her mom down the hall.

Not at *all* what I was expecting.

But . . . dang. That was some primo acting. Brava, Anna Perkins, brava.

Yo, Jackie Oh.

> Who is this

Stephen

Min

> How did you get my #

From my cuz ji who got it from some girl named ambrosia who got it from this guy kris

So random

Who names their kid after the worst dessert in Greek history

Anyways my dads putting in the produce order how many bell peppers u need tom

idk lemme check

Doesnt your dad have my harabojis #

Guess your h's not picking up

Texts with Haraboji:

Haraboji 내일 Min Produce order bell pepper 몇 상자?

5 green 2 red

Jackie, Highting!

ㅌㅋH!

Texts with Stephen:

5 green

2 red

And my Harabo totally picked up

Maybe ur dad needs to
check his phone

yeah maybe lol

U gonna be at Meltys tom

Hook me up w ur bacon egg n cheese

Thats the bomb

No

No u wont be @Meltys or no to a BEC

Havent seen u in a min

Jackie?

WEEKS 2–3

TEAM WORK, DREAM WORK, YADDA YADDA

With the elimination of Perky Freckles, *Burn Off! High School Edition* snaps into focus. Even Host Dennis (mostly) drops the cutesy act. The fluff gone, the competition gets leaner, tenser with each challenge.

But I'm still just "middle-pack." In the "Truth or Dairy" challenge, I make fondue three ways, and it's not enough to wow the judges. In "One Hot Wonder," my candied bacon pommes dauphinoise "gets the job done." In "Bake Sale," my French vanilla crème brûlée with berries macerated in Framboise (fancy Belgian raspberry beer) literally don't sell.

"Now if you'd made me a matcha brûlée . . . !" Judge Johnny says, and starts dancing around Judges' Table singing, I kid you not, *Fiddler on the Roof: "Matcha-maker, matcha-maker, make me a matcha!"* Which is (a) cringe, (b) offensive, (c) probably violates fair use IP laws . . . and (d) would still make H&H crack up at home.

Nothing I do seems to catch the eyes *or* palates of the judges—my dishes are technically precise, but utterly forgettable.

Michigander Sharif, Wisconsin Jesse, and Southern fried Jill are expelled—for a cherry pasty "explosion," "too dry" tater-tot cheese curd hot dish, and "oily" peach beignets, resp. And River and Gus basically keep rotating who comes out on top.

IN THE LIBRARY, RIVER DOESN'T really come up and talk to me anymore. Which I should be relieved about—conversations with him are *so* exhausting—but actually makes me more worried because he no longer sees me as a threat. I'm "basic." He's moved on to chatting up Gus instead.

We're eight, down from twelve. I'm still alive, so there's that.

But what's the point of surviving each round when you just feel invisible?

UMMA AND I MOSTLY AVOID each other. When we're not in Kitchen Classroom together, she's either holed up in the business center or at the gym, and I'm studying or going to the test kitchen. Beyond "hello" and "good night," we barely talk.

I *especially* try to avoid her eye when she's standing in the studio audience, arms crossed over her chest. Thinking, if not saying, that I've failed to do "my best."

Episode 6:
Dream Team!

Host Dennis is dressed in a coach's jersey, sneakers, and a whistle around his neck. "Team work makes the dream work!" he says. "Now draw straws and pair off for your first 'Blind Date' challenge!"

I'm dreading this challenge so hard. Group work is basically a time-suck of people tossing out stupid ideas, and in the end one person does all the work while the other person coasts.

We draw straws, and I'm paired with Staten Island Calvin—he of Jarred Tomato Sauce fame.

Calvin's been inconsistent with each challenge. There was the holy mess he made, and that sorry excuse of a meatball hero; he was even sent to Detention in "Truth or Dairy" for his limp lasagna. (Seriously. Who messes up *lasagna*?) Just when I thought Calvin couldn't boil water to save his life—he comes out of nowhere with the "Bake Sale," winning the challenge with a beautiful caramel green-apple cake shaped like a giant candied Granny Smith. Upsetting the apple cart, so to speak, of Gus/River's consecutive winning streaks.

On camera, Calvin and I fake smile and high five, but we're both fronting it. The way he keeps staring at River and Gus, who get paired together, I bet Calvin wishes he was teamed up with one of the "bros." Neither of us are happy about this pairing. All I know is, Calvin better not take me down with him.

For the blind taste test, I get nine out of my ten right, mistak-
ing oregano for marjoram. But Calvin gets the most basic things
wrong: chicken for turkey, quinoa for oatmeal, lavender for cilan-
tro. He only gets two of ten right, but he nails them with surpris-
ingly specific accuracy—demerara sugar and Tahitian vanilla bean.

Humiliatingly, they flash our scores on a big screen:

Baja/Mei: 20
Sara/Jo: 18
Gus/River: 14
Calvin/Jacqueline: 11

HOST DENNIS REMINDS US THAT Baja and Mei have won Immunity, then announces a twist: "For the rest of you, this up-
coming Quiz is a *double-elimination*! Only one other team will
be 'safe' and join Baja and Mei in Recess! You're only as good
as your teammate, so make the dream work!"

Which means the rest of us will be sent to Detention. The fear of that sinks in for all of us. We have a 33 percent chance of being the other team that makes it through to Recess.

Except, not. The odds are even worse.

Gus and River have consistently been the strongest competitors. So the odds tip in their favor. But Maine Sara and LA Jo are also no joke. Sara's got amazing technique—though the judges ding her creativity—and Jo's bold with flavors, but they don't always execute with finesse. Sara-Jo will make the perfect pair.

The statistical likelihood of me making it out alive rounds down to 0 percent.

I glance over at the deadweight that is Calvin. Unless the Quiz ends up being another cake challenge, which it won't because they never repeat challenges on *Burn Off!*, I know I'm going to have to be the one to carry our team.

Quiz Challenge: "Copy That!"

Rules: Teams will have seventy minutes to replicate three classic dishes demonstrated by Judges Johnny, Kelly, and Stone of increasing difficulty: meatloaf, spaghetti Bolognese, and the soufflé.

The two lowest-ranked teams will be sent to Detention. There, the judges will decide which two chefs will get burned.

This challenge is a double-elimination.

"In school, it's *bad* to be a copycat," Host Dennis says for the next challenge. "But in Kitchen Classroom, it's a *good* thing to 'Copy That!' At least, it will be on your next Quiz! Judges, any advice for our teen chefs in this challenge?"

Judge Stone says, "This is not about showing off your own food, hashtag I'm a unique snowflake. Save the flair for another day."

Groans fill the studio.

"In a commercial kitchen, you'll be making other people's food," Judge Kelly says, interrupting the groans. "Set your egos aside and watch each step carefully."

"But don't forget to have fun out there!" Judge Johnny says. "Do you copy?"

And we're instructed to answer, "Copy that!"

Bah-dum, ching. These jokes practically write themselves.

The PAs pass around marbled composition notebooks and number-two pencils so we can take notes during the judges' demonstration. I notice four things:

1. Baja and I are the only ones actually taking notes.
2. Judge Kelly warns us to add ice-cold water to the pasta dough one spoonful at a time. "This sounds gross, but your hands will add moisture as well as heat to the dough."
3. While separating eggs for the soufflé, Judge Stone drops a little yolk into the bowl of whites. He keeps going like nothing happened.

4. Calvin only pays attention to Judge Johnny and Judge Stone. *Not* to Judge Kelly.

Thanks to TV magic, each judge brandishes a miraculously finished dish mere seconds after their demos—including a perfectly risen soufflé. No one else seems to notice Judge Stone's secret mistake.

WE'RE GIVEN TWO MINUTES FOR a team huddle. "Listen up," Calvin says. "I'll take the spaghetti, and you do the soufflé. Whoever finishes first starts the meatloaf."

"Who died and made you team leader?" I say. "Nice try, sticking me with the hardest dish."

"Spaghetti's hard, too!" Calvin argues back.

I open my notebook. "Look. I've timed out the steps. Meatloaf's technically easiest, but it takes the longest. So we should start with that—"

"Like I said, whoever finishes first will just pop it in the oven, easy," Calvin interrupts. "I'll probably be finished before you anyways."

Ten seconds left in our huddle. We don't have time to argue.

"Fine," I say. "But it has pork."

Meaning, *Get that thing in the oven pronto so we don't serve raw meat.*

"Duh," Calvin says, just as the bell rings. I hope he's picked up what I'm putting down.

SOUFFLÉS ARE THE PRIMA DONNAS of French cookery. Which is saying a lot because all French food is pretty fussy. (Sorry if that's racist.) Honestly, even though I acted put out for getting stuck with the soufflé, I'm actually relieved to be in charge of the dish instead of Calvin.

Remember when Judge Stone spilled some egg yolk in his bowl of egg whites? Yeah, no. If he'd cooked his original batter from start to finish, he would've baked up a flat crêpe. The fat from the yolk schmutz in the bowl would have prevented the whites from whipping up. A textbook rookie mistake; Judge Stone should have known better.

The first time I ever tried making a soufflé, KT was at my house. We were working on our Honors Bio lab, and I offered to make us a study break snack. Back then, I was all about JC— Julia Child—and I insisted on baking up a cheese soufflé. It took too many Goldilocksian tries—from soupy to grainy to cratered—to get it "just right."

The thing I learned about soufflés is this: You have to do all the upfront work to get it in the oven, but once it's there— don't touch it! If you keep helicopter-parenting it, opening and closing the oven door to "check in," you'll ruin the souf-flé. You have to leave it alone and trust it'll do its own thing. Even though you're watching every second tick down like an anxious gargoyle.

I get my batter going, but Calvin's still struggling with his pasta. The dough looks dry, like crusty bits of Play-Doh stuck to the rim of the lid. That rock-hard lump's supposed to be our future spaghetti.

"Hey, Calvin!" I call out. "Judge Kelly said to add ice water—"

"Don't tell me what to do."

"But your dough looks kinda dry—"

"I *know* how to make pasta," he interrupts. "I don't go barging into your kitchen and telling *you* how to make kimchi."

"What the—"

But I stop myself. As weird as this sounds, maybe Calvin has a point.

If he'd tried to Koreansplain to me how to make kimchi, hells yeah I would have shut him down. And maybe there's some Korean Korean girl in Seoul who's like, *Who the hell's this Korean American girl, trying to make our people's national food?* And maybe there's a granny in Busan who's thinking, *Who the hell's this city slicker youngster, trying to make my kimchi?* And maybe there's some marauding Mongolian who's like, *You damn Koreans, fronting like you invented kimchi!*

. . . Where does it end?

So, I leave Calvin to his spaghetti. If I keep backseat-driving him, his mistakes are going to distract me from *my* dish.

THAT TIME I MADE SOUFFLÉ for KT—she didn't ask for it. She probably thought I'd grab chips 'n' dip from the pantry, something quick. If I'm being honest-honest, I was just looking for an excuse to stop studying and get in the kitchen.

. . . Leaving KT to finish off our lab report. She basically had to carry our team.

I'm struck with an awful analogy.

Was I: KT, what Calvin is to me?

GREATER GOOD

I did something I'm not exactly proud of: I made the best soufflé of my life. And this makes me a bad person, which is why,
once again, I hate group work.

I'll explain.

I was taught to put your individual needs aside for the
greater good—especially when the greater good's in a tight
jam. Right? So at Melty's, if I'm on the right side of the
grill, and Ratón's on the left side of the grill, and suddenly
he's slammed with a bunch of omelet orders—I'm going to
jump in and help him out, even though I'm still on meats and
potatoes. And yeah, my next few orders of bacon and home
fries won't be my finest work, because suddenly my attention
will be split trying to push these plates out. But that's the way
it is. Time is money, people needed their food yesterday, and
group work means we're all working together for the greater
good.

At least, that's how it is in real kitchens.

But it's precisely the stuff that gets you burnt on *Burn Off!*

I can't tell you how many times I've seen a contestant in the group challenge volunteer to help out her struggling teammates, which means she (it's almost always a she) now has less time to focus on the bain-marie for her cheesecake or whatever. And I know what she's thinking: What good is the perfect dessert if the main course comes out scorched? Her contributions helped make the *overall menu* better, but of course it comes at the expense of her individual dish.

On *Burn Off!*, those shes are the ones who always get sent home.

In competition, you never get rewarded for putting your group's needs before your own. In fact, you get punished. And I don't know if this is a reality TV show thing, a society in general kind of a thing, or is just selfish *me, first!* human nature?

A lot of *Burn Off!* chefs use group work to show off their individual awesomeness, to hell with the group.

So for the Group-Off, I ignored the part of my brain that said, *Team work makes the dream work!* I let Calvin churn out the sorriest excuse for spaghetti Bolognese, resisting the urge to take over and make it better myself. I focused my energies on baking up the best soufflé imaginable. Calvin, of course, overshot his deliverables—he was still feeding dry-as-a-cracker dough through the pasta machine—so it was on me to get started on the meatloaf.

But by the time I popped the loaf into the oven—thank God we have split ovens, so at least my soufflé could bake undisturbed—there wasn't enough time for the meat to cook all the way through.

I called an audible. I yanked the meatloaf out of the oven, sliced it up, and fried the pieces in a pan because $>$ surface area $\rightarrow$ faster cooking time $\therefore$ $<$ likelihood judges will die of dysentery.

If I served the judges raw pork, I'd never live it down.

Neither would they.

The risk I take is almost worth it.

Judge Stone says my soufflé's "the best bite he's had all day."

Judge Johnny says my soufflé "beats Stone's by a country mile."

Not even Judge Kelly has any of her usual criticisms, which is—progress! They've heaped more praise on me in the past thirty seconds than they have in the last two-plus weeks combined. I start thinking, hoping that, based on the strength of my soufflé, our team just might push through. Especially when only Jo/Sara did "so-so" with their soufflés, and all the other teams served pancakes.

But. Our spaghetti "is an insult to Italians everywhere." And Judge Johnny looks down at his plate of "meatloaf" and says, "The Hamburglar called, he wants his patties back." But it's Judge Kelly's response that kills me most.

She says: "If you know the ship is sinking, are you just going to let yourself go down with it? It should be on you to right it. No excuses."

Then her face gets scarier than Umma's worst *You have failed me* looks.

And my soufflé wasn't enough to make us "safe," let alone to win the group challenge.

And I hate, more than anything, how this show has made me do things I'm not proud of.

Because I was tired of being overlooked.

And I wanted to win.

SURPRISE, SURPRISE: JO AND SARA win "Copy That," and Calvin and I are sent to Detention.

I'm furious with him. Calvin's seriously the opposite of what Umma keeps nagging me about—he's *ordinary,* acting like he's *extraordinary.* If only I had the confidence of a mediocre boy! As we walk off set, I let him have it: "You literally know nothing about cooking! Seriously, how'd you even get on this show? And now you're going to get me sent home!"

I fully expect Calvin to go into attack mode: *Me? What about you?* I expect a whole diatribe in his thick Staten Island accent about how it's all my fault, how I'm not even really *from* here, and *us people* should all just go back *from whence we came.* Because that's the kind of stuff his people usually say to my people.

Because I've only seen it my entire life.

So I'm wincing, bracing myself for this barrage. But all Calvin does is turtle his shoulders. He says, in the smallest, most terrified little boy voice, *"Dad is going to kill me."*

INT.—*BURN OFF!* SET—OTF ROOM

> **PRODUCER:**
> Jacqueline, how does it feel to
> get sent to Detention?

> **ME:**
> Are you for serious?
>   (seeing PA's deadpan expression
>   and walking it backward)
>   . . . Oh. You're absolutely being
> serious. Okay. Sorry.
>   (straightens face)
> It feels "not great" to get
> sent to Detention. It actually
> feels . . . terrible. This is
> really doing a number on my "self-
> esteem," which TBH wasn't all that
> great to begin with.
>   (Beat)
> I'm not great at school. I'm not
> pretty, popular, whatever. But
> cooking is—was—my thing. It was
> like the only thing that made me
> feel confident because I knew I was
> good at it.
> And being on *Burn Off!* . . . it's
> really shaken me up, you know?
> Like every week, I'm busting my
> butt for the judges, and it's like
> they don't even *see* me.
> I know the "right" answer is I
> have a lot of fight left in me.
> But . . . I'm not sure I do.
>   (shaky voice)
> Maybe I deserve to go home.

PRODUCER:
How do you feel about your
chances, heading into Detention?

ME:
I feel nervous about my chances,
obviously. It's me, Calvin, Gus,
and River in Detention. See?
There's an example of getting
thrown under the bus when
you're trying to help your team.
Gus tried to pitch in and save
River when his whole agar-agar
soufflé experiment blew up in his
face. Which meant Gus took his
eyes off his meatloaf, and it got
overcooked and dried out, and here
they are.
So yeah. Chances. They don't look
so good. If this was a normal
Detention, my chances would be one
in four, right? But this one's a
double-elimination. Even though
they're saying Detention will be
individual challenges, I'd say my
actual chances of getting expelled
are more like a hundred percent.
So . . . yeah. And to add insult
to injury, Calvin and I will
probably end up on the same flight
back to JFK.

PRODUCER:
Why didn't you jump in to help
your teammate, like Judge Kelly
asked?

ME:
(sighing)

Stuff like COOPERATION! HELPING!
SHARING! is what gets you burned
off. That's the ethics your
show is peddling, right? You
get punished for helping your
teammate. I wasn't going to be
that chump.
I feel like I'm damned if I do
or don't. If I'd jumped in to
help Calvin, then my soufflé would
have fallen flat and we'd get sent
to Detention, anyway. And *then*
America would remember me as the
girl with the bad soufflé. Like I'd
be defined by the worst mistake in
my life . . .
   (shakes head, as if overcome by a
        sad sense of déjà vu)

PRODUCER:
Is there anything about your
family you'd like to share?

ME:
Not really.

PRODUCER:
What about your brother, Justin?

ME:
How . . . do you know about Oppa?

PRODUCER:
Did he have a big influence on your
cooking? Did you used to cook
together? He is currently serving
a prison sentence, right?

                    ME:
                  (trembling)
I repeat, *How do you know about my
brother?*

                  PRODUCER:
How does he feel about your being
on the show? Do you write to him?
Do you visit him regularly? How do
you feel about his crime? Is he
your motivation for winning the
show?

                    ME:
I can't . . . I just . . .
        (shaking, convulsing)
Are you *allowed* to ask that?
Where is my mother?

                  PRODUCER:
That's all, Jacqueline. We'll
resume another time.

END OF OTF

FEEDBACK SANDWICH

"I don't want to hear it," I say to Umma back in the hotel room. She's sitting there with her lips pursed, and I'm just waiting for the barrage of should-have-dones that will come pouring out of her: *You should have tried your best! Good is not good enough!*

But . . . Umma doesn't say any of that. She says, "Anyone could see you were carrying the team, Jackie. I'm speaking objectively, not out of motherly bias. It's why I hate group work."

I can't compute the words coming out of her mouth.

"Wait, *what?*"

"One person gets stuck doing everything, and the rest of the team free rides off their hard work."

"Right?" I say with disbelief. I'm still not processing a universe where Umma and I agree on anything.

"Actually," Umma continues, "I thought it was pretty *baller,* as you kids say"—it's not, but I let it go—"when you refused to get sucked into Calvin's incompetent vortex. You looked after your own with that soufflé."

"But don't you think I should have . . . tried to take on everything? Meatloaf *and* spaghetti? To save my team?"

If you know the ship is sinking . . . it should be on you to right it.

"That's what I tried to do," Umma says. "At Leviathan, I worked as hard as I could to keep the whole ship afloat. I thought, *rising tide floats all boats,* etc. But it's a culture that only rewards the big, grand gestures—not the million invisible things you do to keep the engine running. Who cared if you were going to need a new motor in the next quarter, when your polish job on the yacht *this* quarter was looking ace? I probably should have done what you did."

Umma's not speaking in the usual voice she puts on the phone with clients or in her perpetual lectures to me. She sounds . . . personal. Like she's actually confiding in me.

"But Umma, I'm not sure that's the way I want to live," I admit.

And because Umma's opened up to me, I find myself opening up to her. I tell my mother about my dread of being paired with Calvin, his arrogant posturing, my debating over the greater good.

"I had a Calvin," Umma says, nodding, understanding. "Maybe if I'd done the same at Leviathan—"

Umma stops abruptly.

I narrow my eyes. "What *about* Leviathan?"

Umma doesn't answer at first. It's been weird, how she even had the time to fly out to LA with me. And she heads down to the business center later and later in the morning when we're not at the studio.

"Umma," I ask. "What about your promotion?"

"They . . . went with the other candidate."

"What!" I'm stunned. "Umma, why didn't you tell me?"

"The board feels Kayla's more 'likeable.' More 'a good fit for our culture here,'" Umma says. "I could stick around and watch my former junior report now boss me around. But it's best if I leave the company. That's pretty much what was implied. So . . . I quit. I've had it with them! I'm *done.*"

Don't worry about it. Umma's cardboard box. Halmoni's back-tracking. So that's also how Umma was able to take the time off work to come babysit me for *Burn Off!*

"*Wait,* so have you just been getting up every morning and *pretending* to go to work?" I ask, incredulous. "Like those Japanese businessmen that get laid off, and every morning they still put on their suits and pretend to go to work and they just sit on the train all day and their families, like, never know about it?"

"They do that here, too," Umma says. "And for your information, I've *been* keeping busy. Meeting with headhunters, planning my next move, etc., etc."

And now Umma starts blinking like crazy. "Kayla's always calling out at work. One kid gets the sniffles, she stays home. Then the next, she stays home again. Then after all that, she needs a 'self-care day.' When you and your brother"—Umma's throat catches—"when you two were little, I never missed a single day of work! I checked my personal dramas at the door when I showed up at the office. I *never* wasted the firm's time. I was *reliable.* I had *accountability.*

"And this is how they reward me. Do you know how many group projects we've worked on together, where Kayla skips off and I'm left holding the bag? Yet because she talks a good game, she swoops in and gets all the credit. I—"

Umma gulps air, struggling to contain herself. She's barely holding it all in. I don't know if I should reach out and hug her. I'm afraid it'll only make things worse.

Suddenly, she's shaking her head. The storm passes. "I'm sorry, Jackie. But watching you today in that group challenge . . . it was triggering, I'm not going to lie. I'm sorry. This isn't about me. It's about you."

Your umma tough like steak.

Umma has *never* opened up to me. We've never really had a heart-to-heart before. This whole time, she's been dealing with her own stuff. But I was too obsessed with my own dramas to check in about hers.

I'm a pretty terrible daughter.

"Why didn't you tell me sooner?" I ask again.

"I was . . ." Umma's groping for the word. "I was ashamed. And humiliated."

"I'm so sorry, Umma." I really mean it, even though it feels too little, too late.

Umma's regained her composure. "But that's the way the real world works, Jackie. So maybe this is good practice for you. Also, there are definitely things you can do to improve . . ." She trails off. I'd already chewed her out about her constant criticizing of me.

"You know what Halmoni and Haraboji said to me? They said I should be nicer to you. That I should understand where you're coming from when you're always breathing down my neck."

Umma laughs. "They called me up to say the same thing about you," she says. "Proving you're never too old to get lectured by your mother."

Now I laugh.

"Feedback is supposed to be delivered like a sandwich, that's what they say in our managerial training sessions," Umma says. "Positive bread, negative meat."

"Um . . . ?"

"I guess with you, Jackie," Umma goes on, "I've taken the 'bread' for granted. You were the daughter that never gave us any trouble." There's another hitch in her throat. "From a young age, you were *so* good at anything you put your mind to. First, schoolwork. And now cooking. Albeit at the *expense* of your schoolwork, and when all this *Burn Off!* business is done, we're going to sit down and have a *serious* conversation about your future—"

"*Umma*—"

"—and, so, with you, Jackie, I never led with the praise, the bread, the filler. Because everything you did well, well—it was so *obvious.*"

"Umma," I say slowly, "it *wasn't* obvious. Not to me, at least."

"I should have made that clearer." Umma nods slowly. "When you and your brother were growing up, I had to be mindful. If I went too heavy on the praise with you, I was afraid it would hurt Justin's feelings. Things came . . . later for your brother. He learned to read later, speak full sentences later, potty training, even. And you remember what his grades were like."

"You could have encouraged us *both*," I say. "You still could have given us each the 'positive bread.'"

She stares down at her hands. "There's a lot I regret, as a mother."

"Umma," I say. "They asked about Oppa. In my OTF today."

"They did what?" Umma is furious. She demands details.

"I mean, I'm sure it wasn't hard to research," I say.

"I will have a word with that producer, Erica."

"I was upset, when they brought it up out of nowhere," I say. "But it got me thinking. Like . . . why do we never talk about him?"

"Jackie." Umma looks so *tired and old-looking*. "You're asking the impossible of me."

"It's just—this is the most I've ever heard you talk about Oppa, ever since he"—I swallow down the words—"since he went to prison."

"Jackie. We all have our ways of coping. This is not the time nor the place to have this kind of conversation. Not tonight."

"Then, when?"

Umma doesn't answer.

"I miss him, Umma." My chest heaves. "I miss him so much."

"So do I, Jackie-ya." Umma's holding me now, and I can't stop the sobs bursting from my chest.

I'm crying for Oppa, for me, for Umma. I'm crying for all of us.

She smooths my hair back and whispers, "More than you could ever know."

KITCHEN DRILLS

After the tears, and a totally hits-the-spot order of room service cheeseburgers and fries that Umma spares me the agita about, we talk about cooking.

"You know, Jackie," Umma starts, "there are still things you could do to tighten up your game."

"Oh boy." I crumple up my greasy napkin. "Here comes the 'negative meat.'"

With near photographic precision, Umma proceeds to list each dish I made, the techniques I used, and where each of my dishes' weaknesses lay.

"The béchamel," she continues. "If you're thinking in UX terms, the sauce was too runny and hard to handle. The user experience was also your downfall with the brûlée. Who wants to spoon custard in the middle of a bake sale? You should've gone with something more portable."

My first instinct is to get defensive. Umma holds up a hand as I start to protest.

"I know that's traditionally how it's done, but isn't the whole point to improve on a classic, versus a direct interpretation of it? Like, I don't know, a gochujang béchamel on the side."

"That's actually not a bad idea," I say, considering her suggestion. "Umma, since when do you know so much about food?"

She looks at me point-blank: "Jackie, who do you think invented the Madison Avenue sandwich?"

I'm all disbelief. "That was *you*?"

Umma buffs her fingernails against her shoulder and blows them in response. "There's more to people than you think."

I've learned more about my mom in the last ten minutes than I feel like I have my whole life.

"Umma," I say, my voice going small. "I feel so . . . humiliated. I don't think I can face going back in that kitchen again. I'm already second-guessing everything I know about cooking. I just *know* I'm getting Expelled."

Usually Detention is the day after the Homework and Quiz challenges. But due to a change in the production schedule, Detention's not until next week Tuesday.

I have a long weekend to prepare for my Inevitable Doom.

"I understand that instinct, Jackie," Umma says. "It's natural to want to hide out in a corner and lick your wounds. I did that the first time I lost a trial. I kind of want to do that now that I've lost my job. But then, how will you ever learn from your mistakes? I'd get up and keep drilling over my mistakes until I got it right," Umma says.

I think of the practice kitchen in our hotel room.

"That sounds like torture," I say. "Let's do it."

***

SO THE NEXT MORNING, UMMA and I head to the kitchen. We start with croque madames with different sauces. They grow lighter in mouthfeel and texture; I experiment with citrus and spices to add brightness and depth. I practice on all the different breads, the different cuts of meat, which I grill/sauté/roast.

Just when I think I know croques *cold,* Umma starts calling out drills: "Make a croque . . . with one hand tied behind your back!"

"Make a croque . . . using only a butter knife, a dinner plate, and bamboo steamer!"

"Make a vegan croque!"

By the time we're done, I don't *ever* want to look at another sandwich again.

We repeat this for each dish I've made during the competition.

Next Umma starts to invent challenges, and they get increasingly wackier: "Make a pizza . . . in the microwave!"

"Make dumplings . . . using only five ingredients and the deep fryer!"

"Make a stir-fry . . . using only an oven set to three hundred seventy-five!"

"Make a stew . . . using only ingredients that begin with the letter *X*!"

"Okay, Umma, that one's just *ridiculous.*"

"Jackie, I am trying to teach you to think on your feet!"

Back in our hotel room, she makes me write index cards,

memorizing different flavor profiles and ratios. I study for *Burn Off!* harder than I've ever studied for anything else in my life.

It never feels like homework—even though it totally is.

I READ SOMEWHERE THAT FAMOUS athletes practice every type of shot, over and over again, so they're ready for anything come game time. Chess players apparently do this, too. Through my kitchen drills with Umma, what I'm realizing is this: When you're passionate about something, you do everything you can to go the extra mile, even if you're putting in all this effort and only *slightly* getting better at it. Appa would call it "diminishing marginal returns." There's little ROI on your added efforts.

When you truly love what you love, and you want to be the best at it, then "good enough" will never good enough.

IN THE HOTEL LOBBY, I overhear a cameraman and the new PA (Erica quit and/or was fired) complaining our shooting schedule's been pushed back because Judge Johnny's off promoting his new spice line.

"Like the world needs another Cajun spice rub," the cameraman grumbles. "This mean I'm not getting my time and a half?"

The new PA attempts to reassure him. "Maybe, like, consider it a mental health day!"

The cameraman's not having it.

So this must be why we're doing a double-elimination. And

even though the statistical likelihood is high that I'll be sent home—I'm so ready to burn.

I SPOT GUS JUST ONCE over the long weekend. He's leaving the practice kitchen just as I'm arriving.

"Hey," I say, trying to figure out how to address the awkwardness between us. "I'm sorry about, you know . . ."

And now I've officially made it More Awkward.

"About us both getting Detention?" Gus finishes for me. "Yeah, sucks. But it is what it is."

I say, "If I had to lose to anyone, I wouldn't mind if it was you."

Believe it or not, I meant it as a compliment. But Gus lets out a sarcastic laugh.

"You *wouldn't mind* if it was me?" he repeats back. "Gee, thanks."

"No, I mean—" I square my shoulders. "It's a competition. *Obviously* I want to beat you. But, you know." I shrug, unsure of how to say it without sounding so corny. "I respect you as a chef. You're really good. So, like, yeah. I *wouldn't* mind."

Gus considers this. "I wouldn't mind, either."

We're just standing there in the doorway like that. I want to tell Gus I'm sorry I blew him off before. How in a different world, I would have really liked to practice cooking with him. I remember the way he showed me the scars all over his hands. The way he'd looked at mine.

"I wish it didn't have to be like this," I start. "We shouldn't have to compete against—"

My phone buzzes. Gus clears his throat.

"I should go." He pushes out the door. "Good luck, Jackie."

"Good luck to you too—"

But Gus is already gone.

HALMONI TEXTS WITH AN UPDATE on Melty's: Madison Avenue's still the number-one sandwich of the week, followed by the Downtown. Stephen Min's been filling in for his dad all week, what a good son he is; I don't know why she thinks I care?

Though now I'm thinking of Stephen's idea for a breakfast juk bar, toppings and all.

And since I'm plum out of ideas for practice, I start making the rice porridge—toppings and all.

It's actually a not-bad idea.

ON MONDAY, WHILE UMMA TAKES some "work calls," I head down to the test kitchen again without her. Baja, of all people, is there, stirring something at the stove. I peek at her through the windows of the door. She's standing over a pot of food. She leans in and takes a deep whiff.

Just when I think she's going to plate up and eat her own food, she dumps everything into the trash. Weird. She doesn't even taste what she's cooked. Then she makes for the door.

Where she bumps into me.

"Oh, Jacqueline!" She looks wide-eyed and suspicious. I've

clearly caught her in a private moment. "I was just . . . anyway, see ya later!"

She busts out of there *so* fast.

The night of our Big Talk, Umma told me to watch out for Baja. "That girl knows her way around the kitchen." I'd waved her off and said, "Baja can't cook to save her life." Even though Umma gave me a *We'll see about that* look.

But the kitchen now smells delicious: spices and herbs and roast meat and slow-cooked beans and rice. Did Baja really cook all this?

This is going to sound super gross. But after Baja leaves, I go to the garbage can and take a bite of Baja's food. I mean, in my defense, I go for the food sitting on a heap on top; it's not like my spoon goes digging around to the bottom of the pile and touching all the other trash.

Baja's food isn't just okay; it's *delicious.*

INT.—*BURN OFF!* **SET—OTF ROOM**

> **PRODUCER:**
> Hi, Jacqueline! Can you walk us
> through what was going on in your
> mind during Detention?

> **ME:**
> I guess . . .
> > (looks thoughtful)
> You know that expression, dance
> like no one's watching? I guess
> that's what was running through my
> head that day. Cook like no one's
> watching. It's like I stopped
> caring about impressing anyone.
> Instinct just kind of like . . .
> took over. I cooked what I'd
> want to eat, based on the flavors
> I know. I didn't care anymore
> whether it pleased anyone else.
> Maybe because I already felt like
> I was going to get sent home, you
> know?

> **PRODUCER:**
> Tell the viewers at home about
> your dish.

> **ME:**
> The Detention challenge was to
> make pasta carbonara, with our
> spin. I got nervous at first,
> because they were continuing the
> Italian theme. And I was competing
> against Calvin—

PRODUCER:
Did you feel intimidated by
Calvin? Especially knowing he's
very "at home" with Italian
flavors?

ME:
I guess I should, right? But I'm
not trying to cook "pure" Italian
food. The second it left Italy
and touched U.S. soil, it became
American. Just look at our pizza
versus theirs.
Also, Calvin needs to finesse his
technique. His problem is that he
isn't open to learning. He didn't
once crack open his notebook while
the judges—hello, the experts in
their field—were demoing their
dishes during "Copy That." How are
you supposed to get better when
you think you know it all? If he
keeps that up, he'll be stuck at
"mediocre" forever.
So anyway. I was starting to make
the carbonara, you know, noodles,
eggs, cream, Parmesan, beige on
beige on beige. It's so gloopy and
one-note, you know? It's a super
heavy dish. And I felt it needed
something earthy, but without the
fat.

PRODUCER:
So you reached for the fermented
bean paste.

ME:

So I reached for the dwengjang. It was like, instinctively I knew it would amp up the "umami" funk or whatever. I needed to cut through all that richness, you know?

PRODUCER:

Why umami in air quotes?

ME:

Because my grandparents would say that's the language of our Japanese oppressors. I try not to use the word "umami" if I can help it.

(Shudders)

PRODUCER:

How did you come up with the cucumber slaw?

ME:

One of my favorite dishes is jjajangmyun. That's these noodles in black bean sauce, it's technically a Korean Chinese dish. It's like what chop suey is to America, jjajangmyun is to Korea. So anyway, jjajangmyun comes served with cucumber matchsticks on top. And it's kind of my favorite part of the dish. You mix it in, and everything gets smothered in the jjajang sauce, but every now and again you get this surprise crunch of fresh cucumber. It's the best thing. I

wanted to replicate that in my
carbonara.
Plus, Haraboji always tells me a
dish needs some kimchi element to
be a complete meal. So it was also
paying homage to that, you know?

PRODUCER:
Judge Stone said your dish was
"awesomeness personified on a
plate." He said it was a "winning
dish."

ME:
I just told my truth on a plate.
Take it or leave it.
Also, I've read every one of Judge
Stone's cookbooks. He is my food
hero. His comment meant everything
to me.

PRODUCER:
How do you feel about Calvin
getting sent home for raw pasta
and unfinished sauce?

ME:
I should probably be happy, right?
Calvin's the reason I got sent to
Detention in the first place. Not
only did he have raw pasta, he
didn't even have time to get the
sauce on the plate. But . . .
(Eyes clouding over
with sympathy)
I kind of feel bad for the guy.
Especially when . . .

PRODUCER:

Especially when?

ME:

I mean, did you see the way his
dad basically yanked him off the
stage? He called him "a goddamn
disgrace." Sorry.
      (holds up hands)
Don't kill the messenger over
here.

PRODUCER:

And how do you feel about the
other contestant who got Expelled?

ME:

Honestly, I never saw it coming.
Gus? He never should have been
burnt. He couldn't help it that
his pasta water wasn't on! Or
maybe
    (looking angry, sad, confused,
        all the things)
it got shut off. Gus never
should've been sent to Detention,
let alone expelled. If you ask me,
he was *robbed*.
     (Continues glaring angrily
       at the camera.)

END OF OTF.

WEEKS 4–5

TEACHER'S PET

I start killing it. In "Who's Got Beef?," I win with my take on a shepherd's pie: kiwi and soy-marinated braised short-rib, topped with scalloped goguma and mu. ("Craic-Kor Jack"? "For Craic's Sake!" "Unite, Fellow Sufferers of Centuries-Long Oppression from Small Island Imperialists!" Yeah, still working on that title.) I win again in "That's a Wrap!" with gochujang-smothered chicken with blistered scallions and green chili oil in perilla leaf and Parmesan tuile "taco" shells ("Ssam Like It Hot!"). And again in "Hog-Wild!" with braised and reverse-seared jok-bal—pig's trotters—with apple-dwenjang schmear, served over steamed rice infused with sesame oil and a whisper of apple cider vinegar, topped with seaweed flakes, toasted sesame, and, yes, a jammy soft-boiled egg (darn you, Stephen Min, for inspiring "Some Pig"!).

Pig's trotters—aka feet—probably sounds gross. But I've been reading a book on unpopular and discarded animal parts, and how some chefs are really embracing these "leftovers." It's also more sustainable. I found the book in the Library, buried under all the celebrity gossip magazines.

The judges are beside themselves with each win. Judge Johnny does a comic double-take, like he's seeing me for the first time. Judge Kelly finds nothing negative to say—which is praise in my book. But it's Judge Stone's words that make me start to tear up: "Wow. Just, wow. You've rendered me speechless, Jacqueline Oh. Where did you come from? You've been our little dark horse this whole time."

I look out into the audience, at Umma. She's not looking down at her notepad, thinking about work. She's tearing up at Judge Stone's hard-earned praise, too.

"SOME PIG" GETS ME THROUGH to the semifinals. Three of us will compete in the semis, and two of us will face off in the finals! My odds of winning are one in three—maybe even higher?

Do I dare to let myself hope? That I . . . might be the winner of *Burn Off! High*? How ironic that I, Jackie Oh, might be named a Valedictorian of anything.

MEI GETS EXPELLED IN EPISODE Seven, and LA Jo in Episode Eight. In this episode's Quiz challenge, "Hog-Wild," River comes in dead last: his "Mother Earth" suckling pig-drinking-from-a-bottle-of-sow's-milk experiment literally blows up in his face. He's sent to Detention with Baja, who's made pineapple-barbecue pulled "pork" jackfruit on homemade tapioca flour bun sliders. Judge Stone tells Baja, "Your veggie act was only going to get you so far."

For once, watching someone get Stoned doesn't feel so satisfying anymore. Because, for one, it feels cheap, like he's punching down; and for two, Baja's "veggie act" really *is* good. I kept getting distracted by the delicious aromas wafting from her station to mine.

Umma was right: The girl knew her way around the kitchen.

It only took me a full month into the competition to realize it.

BACK AT THE HOTEL, BAJA Fresca is waiting in the lobby with her million suitcases. Which means she's been Expelled. I don't know why, but I'm overcome with sadness for her. Watching her cook made me learn a lot. It also made me question my own cooking practices. Why *don't* we cook more veggie-forward? Why *don't* we eat more sustainably?

Maybe it would've been cool to cook with her in the semis.

I go up to Baja to say goodbye. She's wearing sweatpants, glasses, no makeup. Her hair's tied up in a greasy bun. I have never seen her looking anything but camera-ready.

"I'm sorry, Baja. You're actually a really good cook. Like, your 'beef'-steak tomato cups—"

"Actually?" She lets out a sarcastic laugh. "You don't have to act so surprised, Jacqueline Oh. I'm tired of you people acting like I don't deserve to be here. Like I'm not a serious chef or whatever."

So much for trying to compliment someone.

"You made a salad in the first challenge, Baja."

"So?"

"And you totally threw shade on my 'ham and cheese.' For being too *fatty*."

Baja colors. "That's not what I meant! It's—" Baja stops. "I just don't cook with animal fat."

"Good for you."

"No, it's just—heart disease runs in my family." She's blinking, big-time. "I lost my—" She chokes up. "Sorry, I can't."

I don't know what to do—should I pat her arm? Hug her? Or will that make it weirder since we're technically frenemies?

I settle on a sincere "I'm so sorry, Baja."

"Don't be. You didn't know my mom." Baja wipes back the tears and straightens herself. "You know, Jacqueline, Baja Fresca isn't just some act I put on for likes. Contrary to what you people believe."

And maybe it's because Baja's leaving, and we'll probably never see each other again, but I just Truth it. "It's not fair, Baja. I only have one thing: cooking. But you have, like, both."

"Both what?"

I stare back at her like, *C'mon!* Either Baja's playing dumb, or she really *is* dumb.

Something in Baja's face loosens.

"I don't know what you're so insecure about, Jackie," she says. "You're fine. In fact, you'd be really pretty if—"

"If only I lost a few pounds," I interrupt. "Yeah, thanks. I've only heard that my whole life."

Baja shakes her head. "I was going to say, if only you didn't look so pissed off all the time. You might want to work on that, Jacqueline Oh."

Baja's ride pulls up. She grabs her bags and strides away.

RIVER'S BACK TO HIS MIND-GAME antics, chatting me up in the Library with his unsolicited feedback: "Gochujang and Parmesan, huh?" "Jok-bal instead of pork belly? Hm."

"You know what?" I finally say. "Just, don't."

"Don't what?" He's confused.

"This whole—thing." I wave my hand dismissively at his whole situation. "You think I don't see what you're doing? Snyder-this and fjord-that?"

"It's Snijders," he corrects, "with a 'j.'"

"Exactly my point!"

This whole competition, River's been getting in my head, making me feel foolish that I don't know what's "au courant" in the foodie world. Finally, I confided in Umma.

"The boy's insecure," Umma pointed out to me, "Only insecure people namedrop like that. The obscurer the reference, the better. This means he considers you as a serious threat. See it for what it is and move on. Let your work do the talking."

What's the point? Just let your work do the talking.

KT said that once after a debate meet freshman year. Back then, on a free Saturday I'd watch KT in action. The other team was the worst. Backstage they were making fun of KT's accent, exaggerating it for comic and racist effect. I was *fuming*. I started marching toward those jerks, armed with my best insults—ready to launch them grenade-style to defend my friend.

But that's when KT stopped me and said what she said. I couldn't believe how chill she was about the whole thing, like those guys weren't worth her energy.

Then KT went into the next round and "won a bid," which is debate-speak for "kicked some serious ass."

And those guys didn't.

She'd let her work do the talking.

YEAH, YEAH, I'LL LET MY work do the talking. But Umma is Umma, KT is KT, and since I'm also me, I add: "River, please. You're as obvious as a bouillon cube." Sara and I have gotten close—or as close as anyone can get in a competitive TV show. Maybe because she grew up in Maine, and her mom's was a lobsterwoman ("The work's seasonal," she says, shrugging, not elaborating), but I've never seen anyone scale and fillet a fish or shuck an oyster faster than she can. Sara also works at a lobster shack in her summers off. Her dad is a groundsperson at a college called Whyder. Actually, I can't do any of those things at all—seafood's my weak point—so when I saw her go at it during a "Go Fish!" Homework challenge, I was in awe.

But I feel bad the judges are always negging Sara about her food being "boring." They're always telling Sara to "add more spice" and "expand her culinary horizons beyond your fishy waters" (Judge Stone, if you couldn't tell).

"Like, I *like* other foods, but that's not my food tradition, you know?" Sara confided in me in the Library, after she'd gotten Stoned.

I didn't know what to say to make her feel better. Because the judges were basically telling me the same thing.

SPAM DREAMS

Dear Jackie

Yo its crazy to think ur up in Hollywood being famous on TV. Congrats on being the 1st famous person I know lol!

I had a weird dream. I dreamed I was eating Harabojis budae jjigae. That part wasnt the weird part. Ill get to the weird part in a minute.

You know how much I crave the budae. It haunts me like every day not just nighttime. By the time I get out of here I bet its not even gonna be as tastey like I remember. I mean itll taste aight but not as good as my dreams.

Memorys mad funny like that.

Anywayz. Back in the day I asked Haraboji whats up with budae jjigae. Its so random. I said it in Korean

214

and u know my Korean sucks so I dont know if he understands me. Haraboji says thats the point. Not this or that is the hole point. Budae tastes like being poor feels. And I go jigga wha? And he goes budae jjigaes the food that made me want to immigrate to the US of A. Bc if this is what Americans call trash then can you imagine how good their actual food tastes like? He says BJ means Army Stew and it got invented bc the GIs in the Korean war were like here villagers take our leftovers from the commisery & the starving Koreans were like ok well take ur random blue meat cans but we gots to make it OUR food. so they put it in a soup with mad gochujang and gochugaru and their like damn thats not bad actually its pretty tastey & THATS how budae jjigae was born.

Yo when u think about it budae jjigaes the OG stone soup.

All of this happened for reals right? I havent gotten to the dream part yet.

Anywayz back to my dream.

I dreamed Haraboji and I had the exact same convo we had in real life way back which was kinda freaky. In the dream, theres this big pot of jjigae on the table and were all STARVIN MARVINS so Haraboji starts pouring it into bowls for us when SUDDENLY this one piece of spam turns into a snake! it jumps up out of the pot and bites Haraboji in the face!

I woke up in sweats!

That dream was last week and I still cant shake it from my head. I know Halmonis into supersticion so when you get a sec ask her what it means. Does she still have that dream book with all the symbols and mumbojumbo. I thought she said meat in a dream is lucky or maybe she said chicken is lucky but pork is bad but I forget its only been <u>7 Yrs</u> in this joint.

Anywayz. Enough about me. Hope u kick some ass.

But even if u dont I m still mad proud of u lil 똥생.

DUMPSTER DIVING

And then, just like that—I make it to the semifinals. It's down to just me, River, and Sara. First we were twelve, and now we're three.

It's weird. Before, I kept wanting to thin the herd, but now, I miss the other contestants. I'm still mad/sad Gus got burnt. Sometimes I find myself wondering what his take would have been in the different challenges. Because I think his best was yet to come.

I don't want to compete against Sara. We speak the same language, dorking out about food in the Library, exchanging ideas and comparing and contrasting cooking techniques. It was so cool to see how we'd all take the same "assignment" and interpret it differently. Friendships like that don't come around all that often.

I wish we weren't all competing against each other. Because in a different world—

I could see us maybe all hanging out.

Or I wish we could go back to when we were all strangers and stuff. Because this makes it *so* hard.

Because if I try my best, if I give it my all—

I could be sending my new friend home.

IT FELT—FEELS—LONELY AT SCIENCE. I didn't speak the same language as my classmates. They were fluent in OMG GPA PSAT SAT ACT AP ED RD AUGH. To Common App or Not to Common App. Extra currics to pad out your college app and make you look "well-rounded."

I used to think KT and I were on the same page. Freshman year, believe it or not, we bonded over food. In our first-ever conversation, when I found out she was from Chinatown, I asked if she knew Dandong bakery on Bayard.

"Ohmigod, Dandong has the *best* pineapple buns!" KT said.

"Right?" I said. "Those buns haunt my dreams!"

Then we both giggled because there are some words you should never say aloud in public.

The next week in lab KT brought us a pineapple bun to share, and that's when I knew: This was friendship gold. I returned the favor by bringing her black-and-white cookies—we make them from scratch at Melty's. The secret to black-and-whites, I told her, is the lemon zest in the batter. Back then, KT actually listened when I talked on, and *on,* about food.

Then, something changed—I can't pinpoint when exactly. But it seemed like the more I talked about cooking, the less interested KT became in it. In fact, she just seemed annoyed whenever I brought food up. That day at the Lions, when she said I was *lucky*? It burned me up. KT didn't know the first thing about my life.

Then again, maybe I don't know the first thing about hers, either.

I cringe, thinking back on our soufflé study date. I was so focused on getting my soufflé right, I honestly didn't care if I failed our lab report. I wasn't going to stop until my food was perfect. KT must have recognized this and stepped in to save our sinking ship.

I need to tell KT I'm sorry—for the bio lab, for flaking on our last study session, for not being the best friend I could be to her. I said some pretty hurtful things the last time we saw each other.

But . . . she also said some hurtful things to me, too.

We need to talk. As soon as I get home from LA, I'll call her so we can meet up, face-to-face. Because I think this friendship is worth salvaging. I don't think it's, in *Burn Off!* parlance, *burnt*.

We're all gathered in Kitchen Classroom. They have us standing on these stumpy podiums, which look like the Kitchen Coliseum columns lopped off. They've tied bandanas around our heads like we're Rambo or maybe gladiators, ready to duke it out.

Host Dennis is there in his elbow-patched blazer. But there's something that looks . . . sad? in his eyes. Like he's about to deliver bad news.

"Ladies, gentlemen, country*people*! We've reached the semifinals of the first-ever season of *Burn Off! High School Edition*."

The audience cheers.

"These remaining three teen chefs have grilled-off, baked-off, and even"—Host Dennis winks—"served Detention for poor performance!"

The audience laughs, but my cheeks burn, remembering my near expulsion.

"Tonight's episode will be different." It's nine a.m. California time, but it doesn't matter. The show will air in a prime-time evening slot. "Tonight, these teens will compete for Sudden Death!"

We're instructed to gasp. We do as told.

"After this one Midterm challenge, only two of you will move on to the Final Exam. And one of you will be *burnt*.

Remember! For this 'Ode to Joy!' Challenge, absolutely nothing in the pantry is off-limits—not even the garbage! Ha ha. Are you ready? So cook off or—"

I can only join in half-heartedly: "Burn Off!"

Food memory. Joy. The words are stuck, like a puzzle. We almost never eat together as a family. Umma and Appa are always on different schedules, leaving the house before I'm even up in the mornings and coming home late, after I'm in bed. My only food memories are with H&H. But even at Melty's we have to eat in shifts because someone always needs to be on the floor to serve the customers.

Then, suddenly, I remember Oppa's letter. When we were little, we'd peer over the kitchen counter, watching Haraboji throw this and that into the pot.

You know how much I crave the budae.

This soup tastes like being poor feels.

U.S. Army leftovers.

Nothing's off-limits. Not even the garbage.

In the fridge, I go hunting for leftovers. I spot the chickens we butchered for our last Homework challenge, where Sara was fastest by a long shot. I grab the bones and bits, foraging for this and that.

Sara has veggie scraps at her station. I point to her refuse pile. "Hey, you gonna use those?"

"All yours, J."

"You're the best, S.!"

I scoop the scraps into my bin. She nods in the direction of her meat scraps. "You can take those, too."

Sara gets what I'm putting down.

On my way back to my station, I see River dumping food into his garbage can. Lamb bones with chunks of meat still clinging to them because they haven't been butchered efficiently.

"Hey, River, can I have those?"

"No."

"But you just threw the bones in the garbage."

"I might need them."

This is the way River wants to play the game? Fine.

"Thanks anyway."

Also, why's he searing his lamb chops a half hour before service?

Oh well. Not my problem.

At my station, I dump the chicken bones and meat and veg scraps into a pot of water. The judges are murmuring, wondering what I'm doing. Host Dennis is making his way over to me.

"Jacqueline!" Host Dennis says, shoving the mic under my face. "Tell the truth: Are you dumpster diving? There's plenty of food in the pantry!"

"My dish is going to be an ode to leftovers," I say.

"Is there method in the madness? Or only mayhem?"

"You'll just have to taste and see." I add, "And just call me Jackie."

He laughs. "Jackie Oh! It's got a nice ring to it."

"Tell me something I haven't heard my whole life."

As the cameras turn away, Host Dennis gives me a look like, *You might make it in this business yet.*

My chicken bone broth is simmering. I head to the pantry, looking for the key ingredients to my dish.

Gochujang paste, gochugaru flakes, dried kelp, scallions, carrots, onions, zucchini go into my basket. No instant ramyun noodles, though, so I grab flour. I spot an open bag of Doritos and grab that, too. My basket looks, well, like a basket case. But I trust my gut.

I knead flour, water, salt, and a splash of vegetable oil into a ball of dough, and set it aside. Next I shake the Doritos dust from the bottom of the chip bag into a mortar and pestle, and ground it up with gochugaru flakes and salt, to mimic the flavoring of the ramyun seasoning packet. Once I strain my broth and skim off the foam, I add the spice mixture in.

There's no Spam in the pantry. Spam is *the* central part of this dish.

But then I spot a package of hot dogs. Nathan's all-natural beef. That'll do.

Browning the meat has always been a point of contention between Haraboji and me. I think frying before adding it to the soup adds another layer of flavor, because I'm all about the Maillard reaction. But Haraboji says Korean people don't like burnt food because it'll give you cancer. Oppa was always Switzerland on the Maillard matter.

Because budae jjigae was always Haraboji's dish. As his sous-chef, I had to cook it his way.

Today, I get to do it my way.

I slice the hotdogs on a bias and sear them, the edges getting nice and caramelized, before adding them to the broth.

Forty-five minutes isn't enough time to make and ferment kimchi, so I'll make a quick pickle with napa cabbage, cucumbers, and mu, brined with white vinegar, rice wine vinegar, and sugar. Mul-kimchi, aka *water-kimchi,* is not spicy and will be a balanced banchan to the spicy jjigae.

I size up the ball of dough I made. What was I thinking? I can't reproduce ramyun noodles, *or* kalguksu—knife-cut noodles—because the thin strands will expand in the liquid and become bloated by service.

Unless I make sujaebi. It's like if the dumplings part of Southern chicken and dumplings met matzoh ball soup.

Here goes.

Five minutes before service, I rip off pieces of the ball of dough. Rustic, kite-like pieces float in the broth. I set out four bowls, set out smaller bowls of the mul-kimchi, and wait for the hand-torn dumplings to cook through.

***

WHEN THE DUMPLING-KITES FLOAT TO the top, they're done. It only takes a couple minutes. I spoon the whole stew into the four bowls, making sure each person gets enough of everything. Nothing worse than a soup that's all broth and no meat. Harboji says that's cheating the dinner. And just as I'm ladling the last bowl, and wiping down the sides, Host Dennis calls time.

JUDGES' VERDICT

River presents his "Ode to Joy!" first: "Lines Composed on Nord-Jan": sous vide lamb chops with a lingonberry gremolata and volcanic ash, inspired by a backpacking trip to Norway with his father, where they foraged for berries in a field dotted with sheep, then took part in a farm-to-table cooking collective. The lamb symbolizes birth, the ash death; his dish represents the whole life cycle.

Kitchen Classroom doesn't have access to volcanic ash, per se, so River recreated the effect by charring up some peppers and scraping off the burnt bits. Oh, and the lamb chop should be enjoyed by dipping it into the volcanic ash, cut side down.

Judge Stone picks up a pork chop. "I can't wrap my head around this," he says. "I don't know whether you represent food's future, or its demise."

River takes it like a compliment.

Judge Johnny nods. "I'm going to go with 'future.' River, man. You're the one to watch. You are *going* places."

Judge Kelly lifts her ramekin of "volcanic ash." "May I ask you a question, River?"

"Shoot."

"Do you respect your eater?"

"*Excuse* me?"

"You're so intent on these thought experiments, that sometimes it feels like you're talking *down* to your diner." Judge Kelly pushes the plate away. "I don't feel 'joy' eating your dish."

River doesn't seem angry, or embarrassed; he's . . . smug.

"That's just *your* opinion," he says.

Judge Kelly looks taken aback. And I know all the things she could say: I have twenty years in this business on you, kid. I've been cooking for longer than you've been alive.

But she doesn't say anything. Neither do Judges Stone or Johnny. They don't jump in to defend Kelly and put River in his place. They just let their fellow judge get disrespected on TV. They don't have her back. It's ugly.

Because no one says anything, River walks away thinking he got the upper hand.

I want to beat him *so* badly.

They're about to move on when Host Dennis asks, "Chef River, tell the judges how you utilized the lamb bones and scraps in your dish."

My mouth drops open. Host Dennis practically never interrupts during deliberation. I realize what he's doing—

"I . . ." River pauses, eyes shooting to the left, then right. Then he seems to recover. "I used them for the gremolata."

"You mean, the ones that are still in the garbage?" Host

Dennis gestures to an on-the-floor cameraman, who shoots his lens into River's garbage pail.

River neither confirms nor denies.

Off camera, Host Dennis winks at me. Now I get why he's Halmoni's fave. He has nunchi. He has heart.

I wink back.

SARA'S NEXT. I DON'T ACTUALLY know what she's made for the judges. At one point, I saw cod and cream at her station. At another point, tomato sauce, shrimp, and lobster tails?

She walks up bowls of murky soup? stew? to Judges' Table.

"Today, for you, I've made . . ." Sara can't even get the words out.

Then the judges fill in the blanks for her.

Judge Stone: "Is this a clam chowder?"

Judge Kelly: "The cream's split. It must be a soup."

Judge Johnny: "Shrimp and tomato. And I'm getting a whiff of Cajun spices. Is this étouffée?"

Sara's facing the judges, so I can't see her face. But I can only hear her voice, which comes out as a thin warble: "You told me, to expand my culinary horizons . . ."

Oh, no. I realize what she's done: She kept second-guessing herself, starting in one direction and pivoting halfway to another.

Instead of trusting her gut.

The judges are baffled by her Frankenstew. They don't see

228

all the invisible work behind it: the meticulous scaling and filleting, the expert knifework.

"You should have stayed true to your roots." Judge Stone
looks sternly at her. "I'd take a lobster roll and Whoopie pie
any day over this slop. Washed down with an ice-cold Moxie."

And just like that: Sara's been Stoned.

I'M UP NEXT.

"Judges, my 'Ode to Joy' is budae jjigae, Coney Island–style,"
I say, "with a Hershey's chocolate kiss on the side. I used to
make this 'army stew' with my haraboji out of leftovers, and it's
the ultimate Voltron: The sum becomes greater than its parts."

As I explain the origins of budae jjigae to the judges, how
it was the stew Korean civilians made from leftovers from the
U.S. base camps during the Korean War, to Haraboji's childhood joy over a can of Spam and a Hershey's bar that the GIs
would toss his way, I have one of those corny eureka! moments.
Budae jjigae is world history, in a bowl. It's war, it's peace; it's
occupation, colonialization, imperialism, treaties, and DMZs.
It's humble, stick-to-your-bones nourishment, infinitely adapt-
able to its environment.

Not this or that is the whole point.

I don't claim I invented budae jjigae. I'm not trying to pull
a Christopher Columbus and act like I discovered something
that was already there. And anyway, the judges already know
about budae jjigae, which makes them extra critical:

"What'd you use for the seasoning?" Judge Stone asks. "Instant ramyun noodles weren't available to you in the pantry?"

"I used Dorito dust, gochugaru, and Himalayan pink salt for the ramyun seasoning."

Judge Johnny practically loses it. "That is some crazy talk!" he says, shaking his head. "But it *totally* works."

Judge Kelly puts down her spoon. "We saw you going over to your contestants. Were you collecting *garbage* from them?"

"Yes," I say, owning it. "My dish features leftovers from Sara's station," I say, doffing my imaginary hat to her. "But no lamb." To underscore the fact that River is a nonsharer.

"You displayed the ingenuity of a restauranteur," Judge Kelly goes on. "Owning a restaurant is all about managing waste."

"How does this dish reflect you?" Judge Stone asks me, point-blank.

The same question he asked me during the auditions.

And I realize it as I say it.

"I'm Jackie Oh from Queens. And I make New York–style food." I pause, then add, "Even if that means I'm digging through other people's trash."

River snorts, Stone and Johnny laugh, and Judge Kelly nods. For the first time maybe ever in Kitchen Classroom, I feel completely seen.

OTF:

PRODUCER:
What made you forage through the
garbage?

ME:
Trash, treasure. What, I got to
spell it out for you?

As we head to the greenroom, I'm feeling pretty safe. Okay, more than safe. My dish was the only one of the three that the judges universally liked. I don't want to toot my own horn, but I can feel in my bones that I'm MAKING IT TO THE FINALS!!!

But here's the real question: Am I going to compete against Gastro-Molecular boy over here? Or my new friend?

It will all boil down to whose dish they hated more: River's future/demise of food or Sara's seafood stew that suffered from an identity crisis.

Deliberation is over, and the judges call us back to Kitchen Classroom. Host Dennis does his recap.

Then Sara's name is called. I'm gutted—for her. But a small part of me is . . . relieved? That I won't have to go head-to-head with my friend.

Before she walks off stage, I give her a hug.

"You're an amazing chef, Sara."

She whispers back, "Go beat him, J."

Host Dennis says, "Which means, River and Jacqueline, you are moving on to the Final Exam!"

The song "The Final Countdown" floods onto the studio. I'm happy but also sad. I can't believe I made it this far. And now I'll be moving on to the finals. Just me and River.

I hear two voices in the audience shout, "Jackie-ya! Fighting!"

The spotlights suddenly swing to the studio audience. It's H&H!

"Surprise! We've invited back the families of our contestants!" Host Dennis announces.

I don't care if it's proper protocol or not—I run right off the studio set and into their arms. The three of us are jumping up and down, laughing and cheering and crying. Standing just beside them is Umma. I feel a little pang of guilt for not running to her first. But Umma smiles, which lets me know it's okay.

The whole stage is cheers and hugs and cries and balloons and streamers suddenly raining down on us. The judges come over and congratulate us.

Halmoni grabs Judge Stone's shoulder and strong-arms him to take a picture of her and Host Dennis. He laughs—because this is probably the first time in his life someone did not give two bleeps about him. She hands Stone her phone, and he snaps a pic—but it's not good enough; she makes him take five more. Haraboji sneaks up behind them and photobombs the picture.

I look out at Umma, still standing behind all the commotion. She's not one for crowds. She lifts up a bicep and mouths, *Jackie-ya. Fighting.*

I lift a bicep back.

Part III

FAMILY MEAL

On the plane ride home, the Final Exam menu is all I can talk about. We're given one week at home to plan a four-course tasting menu that represents my food POV.

"I don't want to go *too* Korean," I say. I'm sandwiched between H&H in a three-seater. Umma sits alone across the aisle from us. "I can't cook 'pure' Korean as well as you guys, so I won't even try."

"So you want to cook pure American?" Halmoni asks.

"Like what? Steak? Side of potatoes and boiled veg?" I shrug. "That's so boring."

"Maybe boring to you," Haraboji says, warns, as we fly over the heartland. "But American people like boring food. Comfortable for them."

Haraboji has a point; he always does. But my main beef—no pun intended—with Western food is that it's only about one thing. That one thinginess gets the solo, and the rest of the plate is just the supporting cast. I've sat through so many

237

meals where the star protein was a dry lump, and the sides—interchangeable mounds of mash and veg—have nothing to do with the protein. They're like culinary benchwarmers, just there to round out the team, called up only when the main star twists an ankle.

In the brief time when I was Teacher Cho's piano pupil, we learned about counterpoint and polyphonic music. Bach would have the left hand sneak across the DMZ that is middle-C and grab the solo, while the right hand was sent to the cheer from the bleachers. I guess that's what was considered badass in the eighteenth century, like getting a motorcycle and a tattoo.

Could that apply to food? What if, instead of a meal being about just *one* thing, a bunch of things formed the meal itself like . . . okay, not the New York Philharmonic, but close?

The menu ideas are firing. I try to explain my thinking to H&H, flying somewhere over Kansas. But all they tell me is, "That sounds too 복잡해."

Crowded, chaotic, busy. Too many things at once.

Like New York City itself.

"So what?" I say. "I'm all about bokjaphae."

Halmoni says, "You want to confuse judges? You should do what *they* like, not just what *you* like! Why you trying to lose, Jackie-ya?"

Haraboji says, "You know, when I first come America . . ."

Usually, H&H's "when I first come America" spiels are designed to make us feel both guilty and grateful: guilty for all the suffering they faced as immigrants that we did not, and grateful

238

for modern privations—electricity! toilet paper! gochujang in squeeze bottle form!—that we have that they did not.

But today is different.

Haraboji says, "When if I first come America, they start building Twin Towers same time. I so lonely. But you know what Haraboji favorite thing is? Every day, after long hard day, I eat different food. Hot dog cart. Knish. Pretzel. Pizza slice. Twin Tower nothing but giant hole in the ground. And I think: I'm same like Twin Towers. Right now, I'm nothing. But one day, I building my American dream."

I blink, and blink. And even though it's probably maybe a little corny, it's also really touching. I blink until the tears drain back the other way.

"Haraboji lying!" Halmoni interrupts. "Every day he complain American food so boring, so 심심해! Needs kimchi to make food wake up."

"I forgot that!" Haraboji says. "No kimchi back then. No H-Mart. You know how I solve no-kimchi problem?"

"How, Haraboji?"

"Kosher dill pickle! Closest thing I can find." He laughs. "I eat *lot* of pickles."

We all laugh.

Which now explains why there's always a vat of Vlasic at the dinner table.

Haraboji puts a hand on Halmoni's arm. "Maybe Jackie right. We keep telling her, 'Do like this, like that.' But she the one cooking. Let her do her way."

Then Halmoni reaches for my hand, and we form a chain. We fly our way home.

WE TOUCH DOWN AT JFK. Appa's there to pick us up. He asks, "Jackie, what food do you miss the most? Any cravings?"

The answer's obvious: "Nino's, with a side of kimchi."

Most people would think Nino's on Springfield Boulevard is Nothing Special, but it's the only pizza I crave. It's not Patsy's or Grimaldi's or DiFara's or Lombardi's or Lucali's. Nino's isn't trying to be anything other than what it is: slice joint pizza, right down to the sticky red booths and the finger-trap napkin dispensers. And that's the beauty of Nino's Pizzeria—which, by the way, is owned not by Nino but a guy named Kevin.

I'm surprised when Umma, carbophobe that she is, agrees.

"Nino's all the way," she says. "You can't get a decent pizza in LA to save your life."

ON THE DRIVE TO H&H'S house, Appa says, "Jackie, I've been doing some research on colleges." It's the voice he uses when he's trying to sound casual but is actually about to come down hard on a talking point. He only uses it like all the time. "Did you know that Cornell has a program in restaurant management?"

The name "Cornell" does not escape me.

"Appa, let it go," I say. "I failed a class. I'm not Ivy League material."

"Hey, you never know what doors being a *Burn Off!* champ

might open for you," he says. "Let's leave it on the table. We could drive up to Ithaca this summer to visit."

"And let's not forget Johnson and Wales, in Providence," Umma adds. "They have a highly ranked culinary program. And maybe you could cross-register for classes at Brown."

Another Ivy. Because Umma and Appa are going to Umma and Appa.

WE HEAD TO BAYSIDE FOR a pie from Nino's, kimchi, kosher dill pickles, and other odds and sods from H&H's fridge and freezer. I'm looking around the table, and everyone looks so *happy*. Even Bingsu looks content because she's reunited with Haraboji. (Appa had to watch her while H&H came to see me in LA, and she suffers him as much as he suffers her.) I don't think I've seen my family in such a good mood in a long time.

We're just missing one thing.

It used to make me feel guilty to laugh or joke around. What right did I have to have a good time, when Oppa was *serving* time? I look again at all the smiling faces at the table. And I realize all of them are strained.

We're only halfway to happy.

UMMA AND APPA AND H&H have a surprise for me. They hand me a giant box that's practically the size of a kimchi fridge. Not that we could fit one in our apartment. But the box is way too light to be a fridge. I unbox it to find a smaller box inside, and so on, and so on. Appa is cracking up as I do it. That's his sense of humor for you: Matroyshkan.

Until, I finally—

"Oh my God!" I can't believe it as I unwrap the present. It's Donghae steel-cut knives.

The hilt of the chef's knife fits perfectly into my palm. It's lightweight, pivoting with every flick of my wrist, yet I can tell they're strong and powerful.

My brain is trying to compute the time it took to order the knives, let alone have them custom-made and delivered. The latest it could have possibly been was after that first episode. When Umma didn't even want me to be on the show. Plus, how'd they even know my hand size?

"A mother knows," Umma says, with deliberate and vague mystery.

Then I remember. When Umma tried to reach for my hand, during our Epic Fight in the hotel room.

I'd pulled away.

Sneaky Umma.

"Ya," Halmoni says, holding out her palm. "Pay up!"

"What?" I say, confused. "I thought these were a gift."

"Give us each a penny," Halmoni instructs.

"It's a superstition," Umma explains. "Weapons have to be 'bought,' so it's considered an even exchange."

"Or else somebody get hurt," Haraboji adds.

So, I pay up. I don't carry a wallet or anything, and the only cash I have is an emergency twenty tucked into my phone case, so H&H have to give me change, and it's a whole to-do.

"The knives were actually Justin's idea," Umma starts.

"What? I thought you never . . ."

"I write your brother every week."

As if on cue, Halmoni hands us each a letter from Justin. Turns out we've each used H&H's address in secret.

I'm hit with too many new things. All at once.

I sense Appa getting uncomfortable.

When Oppa was first incarcerated, we used to visit him more. Well, "more" isn't saying much: twice a year, around Christmas and his birthday. The last time, Oppa and Appa got into an argument, I don't remember about what, exactly, but it was a small thing that got made into a bigger thing. Oppa said, *Don't bother coming anymore.*

So we never did.

That night at the hotel, when Umma and I talked long into the night, she said, "Jackie, I know you think your father and I are some kind of monsters for not visiting your brother. But Justin put us on a Do Not Visit list. He's an adult, and we have to respect his wishes."

"Yeah, but he only *said* that," I said. "He didn't actually mean it."

"Jackie—" Umma stopped herself, midthought, then changed course to "I'll see what I can do."

And Umma and Appa reveal their next big surprise: Oppa approved our visitation request.

We're heading up to Placid Falls Correctional Facility later this week.

PATIENCE & FORTITUDE

The *Burn Off!* final echoes in my head like a college essay question: *Prepare a four-course tasting menu that represents you.* So I treat it like the assignment it is—and head to the Lions.

On Forty-Second Street, there's traffic everywhere: cabs/ cars/buses/scooters/cyclists honking, swerving, screeching, all of it. Smells everywhere: bitter coffee, street meat, car exhaust, cooking exhaust, stewing garbage—odors clinging to the humid air. People everywhere: coming in hot and fast and shouting a million different Englishes.

New York is $(chaos)^{8,500,000}$. It's a shock to my senses. Three weeks in California, and I've already grown soft. I have no idea how I'll make it across Forty-Second Street alive. It's all just too much.

But maybe that's the whole point? New York *is* too much. It's streams—stampedes—of people, sights, smells, sounds, tastes, all up in your face. It's madness and method, jammed up in the same tight space. Yet somehow, when you put all the mishmash this and thats together, New York forms its own smorgasbord.

Mild doesn't cut it here. You've got to be bold and assertive; you've got to get in there and take up space.

I jump in.

AT THE LIONS, A LIBRARIAN helps me with my research: history books, documentaries, cookbooks, food memoirs, news articles—anything and everything I can get my hands on. I come across a book on the history of immigration of New York City. Each chapter is devoted to a different immigrant group that shaped our city. And not just immigrant groups; one chapter is on the Great Migration, where African Americans from the South moved North.

And suddenly the ideas come, hot and furious. I make a mind map:

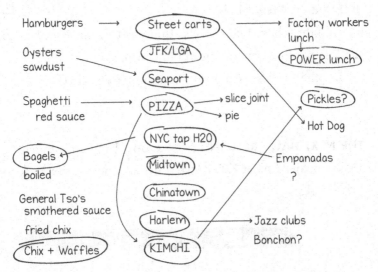

Crowded, chaotic, busy, bokjaphae. Too many things at once.
Not unlike New York City itself.

I RESEARCH LIKE I'VE NEVER researched anything in my life. I never studied this hard for school or hagwon. Certainly not for Mr. Doumann's class.

Who knew history was so useful?

And I'm discovering what each migrant group has in common: They came to New York to create a new and better life. The food cultures that each group brought with them kind of got lost in translation—due to lack of OG ingredients, tools, etc. You can get mad/sad about it. Or, you can embrace the Frankenfood as its own awesome, delicious, culturally confused thing.

And I'm actually excited for U.S. history next year—even though I didn't get into AP USH like KT obviously probably did. And . . . "regular" is okay.

And that's how I come up with my tasting menu: A Day in the Life of a Korean American New Yorker.

In other words—America, According to Jackie Oh.

THE NEXT DAY, I RETURN to the Lions. I put in a morning session before I meet KT. I texted her as soon as I got back to New York:

> Hey, I'm back from LA. Can we meet up to talk?

I don't want this friendship to end is what I wanted to add but didn't.

It took her a day to respond to me, the ". . ." appearing and disappearing. I didn't know if it was a good or bad sign.

Finally, the dots stopped.

yes.

Ten minutes before we're supposed to meet, I pack up my stuff and head down to the lobby. I'm not sure if we're meeting inside or outside. So just in case, I get through security and push my way through the revolving doors—

Just as KT's doing the same.

"Hey," I say.

"Hey," she says.

We're spinning around each other. So we step outside.

"How's . . . your summer going?" I ask.

"Fine. How's yours?"

"Fine."

Ugh, I hate this so much. We're being *so* awkward. You know how when you used to be close with someone, but then you fall out, and now when you run into them, you don't know if you should act the way you used to be, or the way you *used to* used to be?

So I just come out with it: "I hate how we left things when school ended."

"Same," KT says. "I kept writing and erasing texts to you. I had no idea what to say. I was still kind of mad at you. But then, I didn't know if I had the right to be mad, since I know I also made *you* mad."

Relief floods through me. Because I've been feeling exactly the same.

"I've been a bad friend to you, KT," I say. "I'm so sorry."

And KT goes, "I'm sorry, too. I haven't been the best friend, either."

And we both spill. I tell KT how sorry I am for all the ways I haven't been there for her—from the bio lab/soufflé incident up to our study date for the final, where I was just checked out.

"I appreciate your saying that," KT says. "Yeah, that lab report was kind of . . . annoying. And I should have said something. But I didn't. Though not gonna lie—that soufflé *was* pretty good."

We laugh. At least, I think it's okay to laugh?

KT goes on. "If I'm being honest . . ."

She looks at me, like she's asking my permission. I nod, *Go for it.*

"You're always talking about food, and it makes me uncomfortable. Like, I know my lunches are boring. But I don't eat the same rice and beans every day because my palate is 'basic.'" She scoffs at the word. "It's because . . . it's cheap."

"I . . ." My mouth falls open, but no words come out.

How did this never occur to me? *Food insecurity.* I now remember two PAs mentioning the term in passing. I could kick myself for how nunchiless I must have sounded all those times I teased KT.

"I'm so sorry, KT. I had no idea how much that hurt you. It was wrong of me."

"If I'm being *honest* honest," KT continues, "I felt resentful toward you. Your parents were born here. They went to Harvard." Only Umma, but I don't correct her. "It kind of felt like you were deliberately choosing to flunk out. I don't have that choice, Jackie. I know you think I'm weird for being grade-obsessed and whatever. But. It's on me to lift up my whole family."

A determined look floods KT's face. And something about the way her jaw is set reminds me of Umma.

"That's like a lot of pressure on you," I tell KT.

She nods. "It is."

Now she looks down, then starts slowly, "We're not like you guys, Jackie. My family . . . we're undocumented. We could get kicked out of this country at any moment."

I almost don't catch the word *undocumented*. KT says it cagey, like a whisper—like she's afraid the word will get snatched away. She's looking down, anxiously gripping the straps of her backpack.

It all hits me at once. How KT's had to keep this massive secret, how much it must have weighed on her. Home really *isn't* home for KT and her family—the way it is for my family and me.

Lucky you. Now I realize how wrong I had it.

Everything I've been able to take for granted, KT hasn't. "I'm so sorry, KT," I say. The words feel so horribly inadequate. "I had no idea you were going through all this. I . . . should have been more sensitive. I should have been a better friend to you."

"I'm not saying this to make you feel bad or anything," KT

says. "I was just, so insecure, you know? Plus, I was too busy judging you for not studying and everything. I shouldn't have done that. *I'm* sorry, Jackie."

KT is crying.

I fold my friend into a hug. But I can feel KT holding herself so tight, like she doesn't want to let anyone in.

She breaks away from me and wipes her face.

"You and I, we're just, different," she says. "You're obsessed with food and cooking. And I'm obsessed with studying. I don't have time for hobbies."

I pause. "I get that my family has more privilege, KT. My parents are American, they speak English, and they're higher earners"—I tumble out these words as fast as I can, so it doesn't seem like I'm gloating—"and it wouldn't be authentic to not acknowledge that. But I was a really bad friend for not seeing things from your point of view. How it must have felt like, I don't know, that I was complaining about stuff, when I've had it so much easier compared to you."

KT nods. "Thanks for saying that, Jackie."

"But—hear me out?—I think we're not actually *that* different," I continue. "We both geek out about the things we're passionate about. Cooking for me, and for you, debate team and public policy and . . . really, everything you're so good at; you're so frigging smart, KT, and you're so going to be our next future president!

"Presidents have to be U.S.-born," KT points out.

"Maybe they'll change the rules by the time we're thirty-five."

KT laughs, because I know she didn't expect me to whip out a U.S. History fun fact.

"So like . . . could our shared nerdery, and our obsession with process, be what connects us?"

"Nerdiness," KT corrects.

"Nerd-whatever-dom," I pile on. "I know we're different. But . . . you think . . ."—I'm getting *so* shy—"two big nerds could still hang out?"

"Depends," KT says. "What are the perks of being friends with a *Burn Off!* champion?"

I pull a Tupperware out of my bag.

"Would a black-and-white cookie sweeten the deal?"

"Are you trying to *bribe* me, Jacqueline Minhwa Oh?" KT looks scandalized.

"You wouldn't be the first future politician to accept one." I wave the giant cookie in her face.

"Yeah, well, two can play that game." KT reaches for her bag and pulls out a pineapple bun.

"O. Henry!" we cry. And even though it's not exactly "Gift of the Magi," which every New York City public school fifth grader was forced to read, it's close.

"This is pretty good." KT's mouth is already full of cookie. "But the design on this is pretty basic." She adds ruefully, "More basic than my rice and soy sauce!"

I turn red. "I promise to *never* make fun of your food again, KT. I'm so sorry." I point to my face. "Can you see? How cringy I am? It's even cringier on the inside!"

"I mean, I wouldn't mind a change-up," KT admits. "You know, zhuzh up my lunch."

"Rice and beans are so versatile," I say, the gears spinning. "You could cook it a hundred different ways, and it wouldn't have to cost you extra. I can show you how, if you're down . . ." I trail off. Am I going overboard again?

"I'm *so* down." KT smiles. "Jackie, you should like, start a lunch club at school."

"Let me win *Burn Off!* first."

KT looks at the black-and-white. "What if you changed up the design?"

I guffaw. "What, like an ombré effect?" I think of Baja's latest hair trend she just posted on her account. Perky—sorry, Anna Perkins—who follows her, posted a similar style.

"Or like, a yin and yang?" KT traces the up-down wave with her finger.

"That's—" I'm about to dismiss the idea, but then I see it forming, taking shape.

"That's not a bad idea, KT."

"I'm full of not-bad ideas, Jackie Oh."

We're sitting at our usual spot by our favorite lion, Fortitude, because there's less pigeon poop by him than by Patience. We eat our treats, we talk about our summers. KT works in an auntie's trinket shop on Canal Street by day and studies for the PSATs by night. I tell her what I can about *Burn Off!* that won't get me slapped with an NDA lawsuit breach. And I tell her about my food history project, which KT thinks is really cool.

"I know Mr. D is, well, a big A, but I'm glad you found a way to connect with history after all, Jackie."

"Right?" I say, nodding. "Who knew I'd care about world history only *after* flunking out."

We laugh.

I have something I need to get off my chest, too. Something I've been keeping secret for far too long.

"We're visiting my brother Upstate, later this week," I say.

KT frowns. "You have a brother? Why didn't I know that?"

"Yeah, uh. Because . . . he's in prison."

I wince, half expecting KT's eyes to go round with disgust, like Chloe Han's did back in the fourth grade. I'm afraid she'll judge me, and my family, just like how all the other Asians judge our family.

But she doesn't.

"You want to talk about it, Jackie Oh?" KT asks gently.

And I do.

FANTASY FUN TIME

After I meet with KT, I leave the Lions and head to Melty's. The lunch rush is over, so I can practice my new ideas without getting in anyone's way. I can't wait to try out my new recipe ideas with my Donghae knives, which I asked H&H to store for me since I can't exactly pack heat in a metal-detected public library.

Segundo and Ratón are impressed with the Donghaes. "¡Jackie la Samurái!" Segundo whistles.

"Samurai es japonés," I correct Segundo.

"Korean people *scholars,* not warriors," Haraboji inserts emphatically, on his way to the walk-in box with a pan of broth. "We too busy studying. Only Japanese people like fighting, because they Remove!"

I shrug at Segundo and Ratón as Haraboji goes to the walk-in. Does this make Haraboji a racist? *All Koreans are this. All Japanese are that.* But KT says it's okay because it's punching up and not down, and also Chinese people have beef with the Japanese from the war, too. I remember Umma's favorite novel, *Pachinko*, about Koreans being oppressed in Korea *and* Japan during the Occupation.

But . . . isn't Korea now on top, compared to Japan? *Now we're rich, because Samsung and K-pop.* Who even uses Sonys or Nintendos anymore? And most Hondas I see around are old and used. And Appa keeps talking about the plummeting yen (JPY).

I don't even know what to think anymore.

Speaking of cars, H&H have finally taken theirs to the shop. So now they ride the Q27 to the 7 to work while they wait for their car to be fixed.

Thunk-a-thunk-a-thud. I hear the familiar clunking down the stairs. It's—

Stephen Min, with his hand-truck. Except it's not loaded with boxes; it's empty. I don't know what he's doing here. It's too late in the day for deliveries.

Haraboji clamps him on the shoulder. "Stevie-ya, 왔구나! 밥 묵었나?" *Stevie, you're here! Did you eat yet?*

"안녕하세요, 사장님!" *Hello, Boss!* Stephen, ever the kiss-ass, bows deep at Haraboji, and bumps fists with Segundo and Ratón.

"Guapo," Segundo says. "You know La Jackie was on *Burn Off!*?"

"Seriously? You? On TV?" Stephen Min's eyes go wide, like, *never in a million years.*

So I counter with a cold, "What are you even doing here."

"I was in the area—" Stephen sees the knife in my hands. "Whoa, is that Donghae Steel?"

"You know Donghae?"

"*Bon Appétit* just did a feature on it." Stephen gives me a look. "And yes, Jacqueline Oh, I read *Bon Appétit*. I'm not a Neanderthal."

"Well, if you'll excuse me, I have to get back to—"

"So what's this about *Burn Off!*?" Stephen groans. "That show's so stupid."

Ratón and Segundo look scandalized.

"Watch it, Stephen Min," I retort.

Stephen waves his hand dismissively. "*Burn Off!* is to being a real chef what gladiator games were to being a real athlete. You're simply there to provide entertainment for the masses."

Segundo and Ratón go, *"Ohhhh,"* like we're in junior high and a fight's about to break out.

I say, "Please. You wouldn't last two minutes in the kitchen."

Segundo and Ratón go, *"Ohhhh"* again.

"Right here, right now," Stephen says. "You and me, battling in Kitchen Coliseum, *Burn Off!* style. Unless . . . you're afraid you'll get *burnt*?"

"Oh my God, you're one of those *closet* Burnees!"

Stephen tries, fails, to play it off. "Anyway, you chickening out or what?"

Are we seriously doing this? I'm waiting for Haraboji to just end it: *Now Business Time! No Fantasy Fun Time!*

But Haraboji says, "Jackie-ya. You got to put the money where is your mouth."

So I have no choice but to put my money where is my mouth.

SEGUNDO AND RATÓN ESTABLISH THE rules. All the leftovers on the counter are fair game. Pantry items are limited to oil, butter, salt and pepper, and Korean condiments from H&H's personal stash. Twenty minutes to make a signature main course.

Haraboji adds a twist: "Plus dessert!"

"*And* dessert?" Stephen Min says. "With this stuff?" He surveys the trays of mostly savory foods. "Impossible!"

"Now *you* chickening out?" I taunt him.

"No way. But let's up the ante." Stephen Min rubs his hands together like a supervillain. "Loser has to treat the winner to lunch."

Segundo and Ratón and Haraboji exchange a look I don't understand. Actually, I do. But it's not like that. Stephen Min is "guapo," so I don't even let myself think it's the thing they seem to think it is.

He's just looking for an excuse to make me look stupid in front of everyone.

Segundo sets up our prep stations so there's no cheating.

Ratón, in dead-perfect imitation of Host Dennis, says, "Ladies! Gentlemen! Countrymen! So cook off, or—"

And we all join in the chorus, Stephen too: *"Burn Off!"*

"Time now!" Segundo calls, and we're off.

My head is crowded with so many dishes; none of them

make sense. Sugar steak? Scallion brownies? You'd think, after all that time in Kitchen Classroom, cooking on the fly would be like muscle memory. But my mind goes blank. Meanwhile Stephen's already finished dicing onions and garlic and tossing them in a hot pan. He's scooping oatmeal in a bowl, cracking eggs into it, crumbling in bacon.

I'm stunned.

Stephen Min, son of Min Produce, moves around the kitchen like he's been doing this his whole life. Since when do boys like him cook? Stephen's mom probably packs him a dosirak of his favorite kimbap each morning. At school, I bet all the girls line up with homemade cookies and brownies or whatever.

Some people have it *so* lucky.

Meanwhile, Segundo and Raton are cheering/heckling from the sidelines: "¿Qué haces? ¡Vamos, vamos, Jackie! ¡Sí! ¡Tú puedes!"

Fifteen minutes left on the clock. I snap to. Start chopping peppers, sausage (not bacon, since Stephen's obviously using that), and whatever cooked veg and protein I can find. My new knives are *excellent;* they quickly respond to my every turn. This must be how Harry Potter felt when the wand chose him. I dump everything into a bowl with eggs and whisk in milk. I'll make a kitchen-sink frittata pie with a hash-brown crust in the cast iron. But—wait. Isn't that way too easy? Of course it's too easy. I need to level up. I'm a *Burn Off!* finalist, soon to be *Burn Off!* Valedictorian!

I stop, change course. I need to be practicing all the menu ideas I've been jotting down in the library instead.

I ditch the egg mixture and race around for another free bowl, when I hear Ratón say, "En el lado de Jackie, ¡mucha confusión!"

Segundo says, "Guapo, ¡adelante con el deep fry! Guapo le pasa la pelota a Guapo, otra vez Guapo a Guapo, y . . ."

"¡¡¡¡¡¡¡¡¡¡¡¡¡¡¡¡¡¡¡¡¡¡¡GOL!!!!!!!!!!!!!!!!!!!!!!!!!!!" Segundo and Ratón scream in unison.

And I hear the dunk and sizzle of the deep fryer.

What on earth is Stephen Min making?

"Hey, no peeking!" he calls out over his shoulder.

That's what first got me in trouble in the Mirepoix-Off! I stop busybodying and get back to work.

"빨리 빨리, ¡rápido, rápido, Jackie!" Segundo cheers/heckles from the sidelines.

But now a new idea takes shape, so I start over *again*. I mix up a quick pancake batter, add scallions and seltzer (which gives the pancakes all those nice air bubbles, so they're light and fluffy), and dump it into the waffle iron. Then I heat up pulled pork from today's tacos in a pan, and slice up some cabbage and red onions for a quick slaw.

By now, Halmoni's finished up work upstairs and is back in the basement with us. And—Et tu, Brute—she starts cheering for the enemy *instead of her own granddaughter*: "Highting, Stevie-ya!" she cries, punching her fist in the air.

Shoot, I haven't even started on dessert! No time. I take

yogurt and fruit, toss on brown sugar, brûlée it with the torch, and hope for the not-worst.

Stephen Min is done with two minutes to spare. He plates up and buffs his fingernails while I am racing to the finish.

"Show-off," I say, shoulder-checking him on purpose as I place my finished dishes on the pass, just in the nick of—

"Time!" Ratón cries. "¡Ya está! Hands up, baby, hands up!"

Stephen has made bacon-and-cheddar oatmeal "risotto balls" with a side salad. Which is the biggest cheat because all he did was take the leftovers from the salad bar and plop them on the plate. He didn't even make his own dressing! For dessert he serves strawberries dipped in chocolate. The ganache—or whatever attempt at one—hasn't hardened, so the berries are swimming in a puddle of gooey chocolate.

The totally biased panel of judges dig in.

"맛있다, Stevie-ya!" Halmoni goes.

"¡Muy bien, Stevie-ya!" Haraboji goes.

"¡Qué rico! Highting, Guapo!" Ratón goes.

"와! 대박, Guapo!" Segundo goes, thumbs-upping.

"I'm going to remember this tomorrow!" I warn them all.

As for my food, nobody's a fan of my barely warmed-over pulled pork and slaw over greasy scallion pancake waffle, and my last-minute yogurt parfait.

"El yogur sufre de una falta de transformación," Ratón says, trying to be helpful.

"You need something crocante," Segundo suggests. "Everything's same texture."

"But what about the waffle?" I argue. "And the slaw?"

"Not bad," Haraboji says, more out of charity than anything else. "But too much egg in the batter. And too greasy. Maybe because waffle maker not get hot enough? Too bad you rush, Jackie-ya. Then you put wet slaw on top, make waffle even more soggy. And slaw too sour. Make sweeter to balance." He ticks off my mistakes on his fingers. "But, not bad."

"And too much scallion," Halmoni adds, even though no one asked her.

"And the winner is . . . Guapo!" Ratón and Segundo grab Stephen's arms and raise them up, like he just KO'd me—which basically, yeah. "Jackie, you got *burnt*. Prepare to leave Kitchen Coliseum!"

"Jackie, success never tasted *so* sweet," Stephen gloats.

"This game was rigged!" I grumble.

"Jackie-ya," Haraboji warns. "Nobody likes sore loser."

"Listen to your haraboji, Jackie-ya," Stephen says, gloating some more.

"And nobody likes a sore *winner*."

Stephen and I swap plates so I can taste for myself what all this hoopla is about. And that's when Segundo, Ratón, and H&H suddenly make themselves scarce. They scatter to other parts of the basement to continue breakdown and cleanup.

I crunch down on one of the oatmeal risotto balls. "Not bad," I say. "Five out of ten points for creativity."

"Only five? Damn, Jackie. You're cold."

Stephen Min's dimples are going off all over the place, making it hard to concentrate. "Fine. They'd be elevated to 'enlightened' if they had some kind of dipping sauce."

"Hmm." Stephen looks thoughtful. "Maybe like a plum sauce? Something tart?"

I nod. It's actually a great idea. "Yeah, and sweet-salty, to play with the other flavors."

We move on to my dish. And as we dig into the pork-scallion pancake situation, it turns out all the critiques were spot-on. I pretty much fell flat on my face with this challenge. And the brûlée brought nothing to the party.

"You self-sabotaged, on purpose," Stephen says, trying to be nice. "You were throwing me a bone."

"I actually . . . wasn't," I admit.

"How exactly did you get yourself on that show again?" Stephen says, bumping my shoulder with his. Tingles everywhere. "Teasing. No, I've always thought you were pretty badass in the kitchen. It was an honor to cook with you, Jackie Oh."

I don't get it. "Stephen Min, why are you being so nice to me?"

Stephen acts like this is news. "When am I *not* nice to you? I'm always nice to you! Way nicer than you are to me, at least."

"Is it just because I'm, like, on TV now or whatever?"

I hate how imposter syndrome-y I sound. But I need to know the truth. Because guys like Stephen Min don't look at girls like Jackie Oh. He's in a completely different league. It's like Stephen plays for the Yankees, and I'm the equipment manager for the Brooklyn Cyclones.

"What?" Stephen cries. "Jackie, I didn't even *know* you were on TV until like, now."

"Yeah, exactly. So—"

"Yeah, exactly, so—what?" He puts down his fork. "I don't know. I like"—Stephen's whole face goes red. Is he angry? No; he's blushing—"*like* you."

"Shut *up*."

"I'm not joking, Jackie. And . . . it'd be kind of cool if you liked me back." His eyes dart nervously. "No pressure."

I don't know what to say. But I'm suddenly self-conscious. I look down at our plates.

Stephen's fork clinks mine. When I lift my eyes, he's smiling at me.

And . . . I smile back at him.

"많이 먹어, Jackie-ya," Stephen says. *Eat up, my Jackie.*

PLACID FALLS

Placid Falls Correctional Facility is so far north of the city it's practically Canada. It takes Umma, Appa, and me all day to drive up. We'll spend the night in a roadside motel before visiting hours tomorrow.

Stephen Min texts me on the way up.

> Hey how u doing
>
> Hope it goes ok today

As we ate our *Burn Off!* dishes in the basement of Melty's, I confided in Stephen about Oppa. He looked confused. "Is your brother in 'jail' awaiting trial, or is he in prison serving a sentence?"

That's funny, since I only use the word *jail* for the benefit of other people because most don't know the difference between *jail* and *prison*.

There was no judgment on Stephen's face, no omg-I-can't-associate-with-you-anymore look. And I'm starting to realize that it's okay to let people in—on my terms.

And Stephen shared his story with me. His mother passed away from cancer seven years ago, the same year Oppa was arrested. Every day he'd come home missing her food, so he taught himself to cook from videos online. He now cooks all the meals at home for his dad and older brother.

That's how he schooled me in Melty's kitchen.

So . . . no girls throwing baked goodies his way.

And no doting Umma sending him off to school with his favorite lunch. He said no matter how hard he tries, his food never tastes the same as hers used to. And maybe it never will.

I read Stephen Min all wrong. He's nothing like how I made him out to be in my mind.

I've been misreading a lot of people lately.

Yeah, I should stop doing that.

KT TEXTS ME ON THE drive up, too. Checking in, sending me virtual biceps. At the Lions, she listened—without her face erupting with judgment or vicarious shame. When I was done, she talked about the debate research she did on prison advocacy. She cited some staggering stats: "The data's a little old, but from 1990 to 2000 alone, incarcerated Asian Americans increased by two hundred fifty percent. That's *a lot,* Jackie. But our communities . . . we don't talk about it. Neither does the media. That's a big problem."

And it kind of feels like if you're not the perfect model minority, then your story gets forgotten.

KT taught me a new word: recidivism. It's when formerly incarcerated people return to prison. In America, recidivism rates are very high. "But studies show that recidivism rates are lower for those who have more support from families, friends, and social networks."

It makes me feel bad for how the last seven years went down. We could have been more "there" for Oppa—beyond my dinky once-a-week letters.

Also, I learned we don't use the word "inmate" anymore. It's better to say "incarcerated person." Because they're not just a number in a system, defined by the worst mistake they've made in their lives.

They're human, too.

YOU CAN'T JUST SHOW UP at a prison and say, *What's up? I'm here. Let me in to see my bro.* There's a whole formal process. Umma made all the arrangements from LA so we were able to come visit the week I was back.

I begged, *begged* Appa to come with us. Finally, he relented. Because when you're a finalist on a major nationally syndicated television show, you suddenly have leverage.

But when we pull up to visitor parking at Placid Falls and get out of the car, Appa doesn't follow us in.

"Aren't you coming?" I ask.

"I forgot, I have—work."

Appa drives off before I can call him out on his BS.

WE'RE HERE ALMOST TWO HOURS early for our appointed time. We're all waiting to get in. There's an old woman next to us who is suddenly staring big-time at Umma's boobs.

I'm about to say, *Excuse me!* when the granny whispers something discreetly to Umma.

Umma clamps her hand to her mouth, like she forgot. She shimmies off her bra under her shirt and throws it into a garbage can nearby.

"What was *that* all about?" I whisper to Umma.

"They won't let you in with an underwire bra."

I totally miscalled it. I smile a grateful smile to the granny. She smiles back.

IT'S A GOOD THING THE granny helped us out. Because a guy on line in front of us gets denied entry for wearing flip-flops. You should see the way his face falls as they turn him away. "I got regular shoes in my car! I'm just trying to see my dad!" he cries, but the guard tells him too bad, come back another day.

Maybe because the last time I came here I was kid, and they were nicer to me, but . . . *unpleasant* doesn't even begin to describe the screening process. Imagine if you combined the suspicion of TSA agents with the disgruntlement of DMV workers with the sterile, *I'm over it* look on the faces of DSNY workers as they heave-ho disgusting bags of garbage . . . and that kind of, sort of? approximates the way they pat you down and push and prod you through. At the end of processing, you feel like you've lost your human dignity.

If this is how they treat us on the outside—

I can't even imagine how Oppa gets treated every day on the inside.

IN THE WAITING ROOM, IT'S hard not to notice we're the only Asians here. There're two white families, and most of the other visitors are Black and brown. We all seem so different at first. But then I recognize the same strained keep-on-keeping-on expression—the one I always see on Umma's and Appa's faces— are shared by the other visitors as well. Like it's all they can do not to slump down with gravity.

We exchange polite nods and smiles with the other visitors. I know what we're all thinking: Our loved ones are *just* on the other side of that wall.

And there's absolutely nothing we can do about it.

FINALLY, THE GUARDS BRING OUT Oppa. I only recognize him because he's the only Asian guy in the room. I can't believe how much he's changed, how much older he seems now! Maybe he's thinking the same about me. He looks both more jacked and more haggard, if that makes any sense.

"What up, lil 똥생!" Oppa says. "What's a *Burn Off!* star like you doing in a place like this?"

We all hug. We keep the hugging brief because we don't want to get nunchi-daggers—or worse—from the correction officers.

"Damn, you got big, Jackie," Oppa says.

"I'm not *that* big," I say, blushing. Of course I'm shy. I haven't seen my brother since I started seventh grade, when our visits stopped.

"Justin, are you eating enough?" Umma asks, her voice coming out thin and wobbly. "Your face looks so thin."

She raises her hand, as if to touch his cheek—but Oppa flinches. Umma drops her hand.

"Thanks for coming," Oppa says. "You didn't have to go through all that trouble."

"Trouble? No trouble. Justin, stop talking like that." Umma tuts. "Are they treating you okay in here? Are you—"

"I'm fine," Oppa interrupts. "Where's Appa? Wasn't he supposed to come, too?"

"Your father . . . had a last-minute work emergency."

Oppa gives a *Yeah, right,* look. "Anyways, tell him thanks for the cash."

He sees my confused look.

"He posts money to my account at the commissary," Oppa explains. "Keeps me in peanut butter sandwiches." Then, turning to Umma: "Tell him I'll pay him back once I'm out. With interest."

"Justin, please—"

Oppa shrugs. "Isn't that all he cares about?"

The awkward silence is spreading, so I rush in with, "We got Nino's the other night."

This gets Oppa's attention. "Nino's is da bomb," he says. It's funny to hear Oppa talk, how same but different he sounds like in his letters. And he speaks in old-school slang no one really uses anymore. "And did you guys eat it with kimchi?"

"Of course."

"And pickles?"

I nod again.

"What is *up* with Haraboji and those pickles?" Oppa says.

"Believe me, he's been doing that since *my* childhood, too," Umma puts in.

"There's actually a funny story behind it," I say, and launch into what Haraboji told me on the plane—Twin Towers and all. It's the first time Umma and Oppa are hearing that story. It makes them both laugh, and even tear up a little. I can't tell if they're laughing-too-hard tears or the other kind.

Then Oppa tells us about working in the kitchen at Placid Falls. He was placed on chow duty when they learned he used to work in a family deli.

"Last night was beef stew," he says proudly. "First I dredged the beef chunks in flour, to give them a nice coating . . ." Oppa talks about each ingredient and what he would have substituted if he could—shallots for the yellow onions, filet mignon for the beef chuck. "But, whatever. It's all about improvising and making the most with what you've got."

I wish more than anything we could have brought Oppa a

homecooked meal. But they don't let you bring in food from the outside. All we have are the quarters we feed into the visiting room's vending machine.

"Anyways, the guys gave me props. Which is saying a lot, since it's still prison food."

Oppa trails off. His smile is 65 percent. Oppa's totally just putting up a brave front. He's smiling for us because he doesn't want us to worry about him.

We lapse into silence. It's like we've run out of the "safe" things to say, and we're afraid of venturing into "unsafe" territory.

I can't even say my true feelings: *I wish you were coming home with us, Oppa.* Because Oppa doesn't need any more reminders of him being on the inside while we're on the outside, and my saying it doesn't make the time tick down any faster. If anything, it will only make him feel worse.

I hope . . . Oppa knows how much he's loved.

"Oh, I forgot!" I say. "Thanks for the Donghaes!" I don't know if they let you say *knife* in prison, so I don't risk it. "Umma told me it was your idea. They're *so* awesome! You should have seen how fast I diced through an onion!"

"Right, 똥생?" Oppa says. "I saw them in *Bon Appétit* and knew they were perfect for you. Just had to convince the old moms to pony up." He nudges our mom. "Right, Umma?"

"Oh Justin," she says, batting him away.

Do you ever wish you could just hit pause and stay inside a moment forever? We're playing the perfect family—right here in the prison visitor's center—sitting at a table, eating a meal of Doritos, Oreos, and cans of Coke. Is this what our family might have been like if Oppa never got arrested? If he never did the thing that got him put away?

Or . . . maybe it'd be exactly the same as it was before he left.

Oppa and Appa, still fighting across the table.

Umma on my case about my grades, clothes, all of it.

Conversation strained, all of us texting on our phones, relieved when our family meal is over so we can stop spending forced time together.

Maybe we're *all* just putting on a brave front.

And Appa's not even here. Because he chickened out at the last minute.

I hit unpause.

"Hey 똥생," Oppa asks, interrupting my thoughts. "You got my letter, right?"

"Yeah."

"So what'd Halmoni say my budae jjigae dream meant?"

"Huh?" Then I realize what he's talking about. "I totally forgot! Sorry, Oppa. I'll ask later."

"Forget it. You were busy."

I'm sensing I need to make this up to him somehow. "But did I tell you? Your last letter? About the budae jjigae? It inspired me to—"

"Jackie, don't forget about the NDA," Umma warns.

"Right." I stop myself. "Sorry. Well, I guess you'll just have to wait and watch, Oppa."

"Guess so."

Oppa says he's been bragging to all the kitchen guys about

his little sister on the show. They promise to let him get a front-row seat when it airs.

He tells us about his correspondence classes and how, as long as the state doesn't pull funding, he'll be wrapping up his college degree soon. He already got his GED in prison. Now he's taking classes in economics and political science.

"Well, keep at it, Justin," Umma says when we're nearing the end. "I'm proud of you."

"Yeah, well." Oppa grunts. "That's a first."

"Your father is as well."

"That's BS and you know it."

"Justin—"

"Umma, enough. It's not Harvard or even Columbia. No point pretending like it is."

It's like the light in Oppa's eyes goes out.

OUTSIDE THE PRISON GATES, APPA'S there, waiting to pick us up.

"How was your work call," Umma says flatly.

"It was . . . fine."

"Well. I hope it was worth it."

We're barely on the highway when Appa suddenly pulls off on the shoulder. At first, honestly, I think he has to go to the bathroom and couldn't hold it. But Appa's hunched over the steering wheel. His shoulders heave up-down, up-down.

He starts to cry.

I have only seen my father cry once in my life. It was at

Chin-Halmoni's funeral, and he sobbed—a full-throated sob, just like he's doing now, like he's a little kid. I didn't even see him shed a single tear when his father passed away.

Appa looks into the rearview mirror—not at me, but the road behind us. His eyes are bright red. Tears fall in furious streams down his cheeks. His face is sadness, anger, despair.

Finally, he stops, shakes his head, composes himself.

"Gaja," Appa says. *Let's go.*

I don't know why he says it in Korean. I don't know why he says it at all; it's almost like he's ordering himself to move forward. Even when it's clear he doesn't want to—or can't. In the rearview mirror, his face is hard, jaw clenched.

Appa pulls onto the highway without looking back.

FINAL EXAM, PART I

Just like that, it's time to leave home again. We fly back to Holly-wood. The whole plane ride over, Umma and I talk nonstop about food. Funny how different this flight is from the first time around. Back then, we sat in chilly silence: Umma pissed that I sabotaged my grades to get myself on national TV; me resentful that she almost wouldn't let me cook.

"Now, Jackie, let's go over the timing again."

My prep list is broken down by each of the four courses, and broken down into further lists. My first course looks like:

Hors d'oeuvres

Bagels:

1. Roll dough into bagel shapes

2. Boil bagels

3. Make everything spice blend.

4. Brush with baking soda water slurry.

5. Dip bagels in everything spice blend.

6. Bake.

7. Slice bagels into coin-sized cross-sections. Bake cross-sectioned coins to dry them out.

8. Fry quail eggs.

9. Spread gochujang aioli schmear on chip.

10. Top bagel chip with egg, cheddar chunk, sprinkle with seasoning.

Pizza:

1. Roll out dough and cut out 2" rounds

2. Assemble pizzas

3. Feed wood in oven. Get to 800 F.

4. Bake pizzas.

5. Make basil chili oil. Drizzle on top.

Empanadas:

1. Cook ground beef and onions.

2. Hardboil eggs. Separate yolks, save for another use. Chop up egg whites. Add whites to filling.

3. Chop parsley and Spanish olives. Add to meat and egg mixture. Let filling cool.

4. See step 1. Pizza.

5. Heat frying oil.

6. Stuff empanadas. Crimp seams with fork.

7. Fry empanadas, turning over on each side when golden brown.

8. Set on paper towels to drain.

9. Make minari chimichurri sauce.

Pickles:

1. Slice Kirby cucumbers in quarters vertically, but leave hinged at one end

2. Boil white vinegar, sugar, salt, green peppercorns. Let cool, then add dill.

3. Submerge pickles in brining liquid.

I groan. "Umma, do we have to? I know it cold."

Umma lays off, but in typical Umma fashion, she still gives me a look like, *You sure you want to be doing that?*

I close my eyes, but sleep doesn't come. I snap them open again.

"Fine. Let's go over the drills again."

And we do.

Final Exam

Assignment: *Design a four-course tasting menu that represents you and your food POV.* The four courses will be

(1) Hors D'oeuvres

(2) Appetizer

(3) Entrée

(4) Dessert

Rules: On day one, you will have ninety minutes to prep. On day two, you will have two-and-a-half hours total to cook and serve your four courses. Each course will be served in staggered start times.

You are permitted to bring one un-transformed food item from home.

Judges will award for originality, taste, and presentation.

> The winner will be named Valedictorian of the series finale of *Burn Off! High!*

On day one of the Final Exam, I use my time strategically: get all my meats in their marinade, make my New York dough so it'll have time to proof, and make my tomato sauce as well as mozzarella from scratch. I soak black beans and prep some side dishes. I also need to make my Korean empanada filling tonight: I boil eggs and chop them, sauté ground beef, chopped onions, Spanish olives, japchae, and parsley, and assemble the filling so it's cooled down by tomorrow. You can't stuff an empanada wrapper when the filling's hot, or it'll get gummy.

There's not as much of a show on day one, but Host Dennis still makes his rounds. Over at River's station, I hear Host Dennis asking the same questions. River's "one ingredient from home" is handmade foie gras. Which is weird, because I thought foie gras was banned, but I guess you can smuggle it in across state lines? Also I thought we were limited to one ingredient, not one whole prepared product. But . . . whatever, I guess.

I try not to pay attention to my competitor. But occasionally, on running back and forth to the pantry, I spot River at work. He's filleting a fish, I think? But most of the fish carcass ends up in the garbage. Each time I run to and fro the pantry, more of his food piles up in the garbage. What a waste.

When Host Dennis asks me about my special ingredient from home—a jug of tap water—he looks at me like I've lost it. "You know we have water in California, Jackie Oh." He waves his hand in the air, like it's fifty-fifty. "Sort of."

"Nah, your water's no good." I pour the water into my flour well and start kneading the dough. "This is New York City's finest tap."

I explain I'm making New York dough and how you can't make anything New York is famous for without our soft water. I talk about mineral and sodium levels. I used to find Host Dennis's Obligatory Interruptions *so* annoying—hello, I'm trying to concentrate on my work!—but now I kind of look forward to them. And I get to show off a little, you know?

When I get into the ratio of grains per gallon of $CaCO_3$, Host Dennis stops me—with a full-out belly-filled laugh.

"I swear, you're a mad scientist, Jackie Oh."

"There's method in my madness, HD." I wink.

Which surprises both of us. Me, wink? Me, who has zero charisma for the camera? But there's just something about Host Dennis. He brings out this charm in you. It only took all summer.

"And what do you plan to do with your dough, Jackie?"

I give the dough a last punch in the gut. "New York dough," I correct. "I'm splitting it three ways to make everything bagels, mini-pizzas, and Korean empanadas—"

"Korean empanadas!" Host Dennis exclaims. "Now that's an oxymoron if there ever was one."

I give him a look like, *Really?* He looks chastened.

"And how do you feel about your chances in the Final Exam, Jackie Oh?"

I look straight into the camera. "Dennis, I feel ready to *burn*."

BACK IN THE HOTEL, STEPHEN Min texts me: Oh, Jackie, Fighting! and a string of virtual biceps. We've been texting ever since our Melty's Fantasy Fun Time. I apparently still owe him a victory lunch. He's picked out this pizza joint on Arthur Avenue up in the Bronx, which is right by this bakery with the best cannoli.

So . . . I guess it's a date?

It's unreal that Stephen Min and I are now kind of starting to hang out.

KT texts good luck, too. She sends me a link to breathing and meditation exercises she does before her debate tournaments. The article is confusing and more than I have the bandwidth for, but I appreciate it.

KT's gonna KT, and I'm gonna me.

I crash in bed with Umma. This time, the hotel did *not* mess up—they gave us two double beds—but for the finals, I'd prefer to sleep in the same bed as my mom, like I did during all of the taping. Which I know makes me sound like I'm five, but I don't care.

I'm so exhausted from the adrenaline, and the jet lag. I fall straight to sleep. Umma, too.

* * *

UNTIL WE'RE WOKEN IN THE middle of the night by the phone. Umma rushes to answer it. She lets out a sharp *"Huh!"* and goes to take the call in the bathroom.

I'm now up. So I knock on the bathroom door: "Is everything okay?" Even though I know, I sense, it's not.

I hear Umma cry out again. *"To Appa?!"* Then the fumbling of faucets and gushing of running water drowns out the sounds.

I knock again. "Umma?"

No one calls in the middle of the night with good news. Something happened to Haraboji. I just know it.

Sniffles. The fake regaining of composure. More sniffles.

"Jackie," Umma says. "Go . . . watch TV or something."

Umma never tells me to go watch TV. I do as I'm told. There's some home improvement show about tiny houses. I'm not even processing.

"What happened to Haraboji," I demand when Umma gets out of the bathroom.

"Oh, you know your grandfather. He had more last-minute pizza advice. But I said you need your beauty rest." Umma fake laughs.

I know what Umma's doing. She's trying to shield me from bad news because it's the night before the finals.

Then I remember: the car. How many times Haraboji had to turn the key before the ignition caught. Then it'd putt-putt down the LIE like it was on its last legs.

My hand flies to my mouth.

"Haraboji got into a car accident," I say, knowing it in my bones.

"No." Umma turns to face me. On the TV, the tiny house people are climbing the tiny ladder to their tiny lofted bed. "Listen, Jackie. It's the night before your finals. Get some rest—"

I interrupt her. "Just give it to me straight."

Umma sighs. There's a hitch in her voice.

"Haraboji did have an accident, but it wasn't in a car. He was . . . attacked on the subway, on his way to Melty's. He was alone: Halmoni had an appointment with Dr. Hong that morning. Her arthritis was acting up." (She means an herbal medicine—doctor appointment.) "He's in critical condition at Flushing Hospital."

FINAL EXAM, PART II

A few hours after Halmoni's phone call, I'm back in Kitchen Classroom. Cameras everywhere. Lights beating down. Six weeks ago, I first stood in this studio, blinking under all the spotlights, trembling to my core. I should feel nervous now, but I don't.

It's not something corny like, *This kitchen feels like a second home to me!* But when I first started the show, so much was riding on my winning. Or so I thought. Now, that "so muchness" feels small, silly. Haraboji was *attacked*. He is in the hospital, fighting for his life. And I thought the world would end if my soufflé had failed to achieve a perfect rise?

The stakes feel different now.

"You don't have to compete," Umma said. "We'll forfeit and jump on the next plane home. It's too much for you to be on national TV right now, Jackie."

Six weeks ago, Umma never would have said it's okay to quit. She'd say:

(a) I'm reneging my responsibilities, and people were re-
   lying on me. *Is this the kind of person you want to be in
   society?*

and

(b) Mediocre people do the "comfortable" and "compla-
   cent" thing. If you want to be extraordinary, you have
   to keep pushing yourself.

But maybe Umma's changed, too.

Umma went on, pleading: "You need to *take care* of yourself, Jackie."

But H&H never took self-care days. Sick or tired or sick
and tired, it didn't matter. Each day without fail, they got up
before the crack of dawn to work.

"Haraboji wouldn't want me to quit," I say finally.

I can't explain it exactly. But I just have this feeling that if I
walk away now, it'd mean everything he and Halmoni worked
so hard for was for nothing.

And even though she just told me I could walk away from
it all, Umma nods. Because deep down, she believes what I've
said, too.

HOST DENNIS BEGINS THE INTRO. River has his arms crossed
over his chest like he owns this. He looks confident and well
rested. Unlike me, River must have gotten a full night of sleep.

I tossed and turned all night, replaying the horror reel of Haraboji's attack. Mostly empty train car. Haraboji minding his own business, playing a golf game on his phone. The attacker sneaks up on him and—

I squeeze my eyes shut.

If Haraboji hadn't taken the subway that day, then would someone else have gotten attacked?

Would that person also be Asian?

My fingers knot into fists. If I could get my hands on that sicko now—

I shake out my anger. *Not worth fighting.* Haraboji was always the peacemaker. It was Halmoni who would never back down from a fight—with customers, with family, with random jerks on the street.

My fists slowly unfurl. But it's so hard to tamp down the anger. Why do bad things always and only happen to the good people?

If this had happened to a *bad* person. A criminal—

I catch myself. Then what does that make Oppa?

"Jackie!" Host Dennis is suddenly shoving his mic in my face. "How are you feeling today?"

Like I want to punch someone's lights out. "Like I'm ready to win!" I say, putting on my brightest, tightest, fakest smile.

"Tell the judges about your tasting menu!"

On my first day in Kitchen Classroom, Host Dennis asked me, *What's your story?* I was completely tongue-tied on national television. At Melty's, we cooked what the people wanted. Which was completely different from how we cooked in Bayside—immigrant mishmash. Which was again different from all my classical cookbooks about French techniques—the fancier and fussier, the better.

I thought my three "food journeys" had to be in three separate boxes. If I code-switched between them, it'd be like cross-contamination.

But we all contain multitudes—culinarily speaking, too. So why can't all three of my cooking selves exist within the one Jackie Oh?

"Well, H.D., judges, I'm a third generation New Yorker. So I make New York food. That's my quote-unquote schtick. People come to New York with nothing, like my grandparents. But if you can make it here, you can make it anywhere, right? So I take humble ingredients and transform them into that *something,* paying homage to different migrant groups that had to make a new home for themselves in New York. It's their native food, mixed with New York influences, retold through my point of view—like a big mash-up. Each dish will represent a fusion of different cultures that have uprooted to New York—from Asia to Latin America to the Caribbeans and back.

"This tasting menu is my love letter, warts and all, to the city that made me and my family. I call it 'America, According to Jackie Oh.'"

"Wow, Jackie." Host Dennis looks . . . moved? I don't think he's faking it. "That's quite a journey. And it sounds like an ambitious project! What inspired you to come up with this menu?"

"Besides failing history class?"

That gets a big laugh. (They don't know I'm not joking.)

"Well, H.D., I grew up cooking with my grandparents, my Haraboji, especially. And it's inspired by him—"

My throat catches. I gulp for air.

Host Dennis asks, "You okay, Jackie?"

"I . . ." I blink and blink and blink. If I say one more word, *I am going to lose it.* I look away from the camera and breathe hard. *In, out.* I hope they edit this part out of the final taping. "I'm fine."

Host Dennis looks at me intently. His eyes cloud over with concern. He whispers, so low the mic can't pick it up, "Hang in there, Jackie. A few more hours and this will all be over."

"The show must go on, right?" I whisper.

"The show must go on," he whispers back.

Then Host Dennis fixes his face for the camera, breaking into his signature toothy smile.

Maybe Host Dennis contains multitudes, too.

HOST DENNIS MOVES ON TO River, who shares his spiel about his "Scandinavian Meets Pacific Northwest Farm-to-Table Haute" menu.

"It's all about starting with the highest quality ingredients," River says. "My clients deserve only the finest."

In other words, untransformed. When you start with really expensive ingredients, then what's left to do to them? The labor is minimal.

Sounds like we're taking the exact opposite approach.

Jackie from day one would have been completely intimidated by River's menu. But I know better now. Let River Waters do River Waters.

Only I can do Jackie Oh.

APPA CALLED TO WISH ME good luck this morning. He was on his way to the hospital to meet Halmoni, to help her navigate Scary and Intimidating Medical English. Unlike Umma, he didn't tell me I could walk away.

"This is what we do, Jackie. We put one foot in front of the other. When it's hot, treat it like it's cold—"

Then his phone reception cut out and I lost Appa somewhere over the Fifty-Ninth Street Bridge.

But I think I understand what he meant. I remember Appa's face in the rearview mirror when we left Placid Falls. Keep on keeping on. That's what us Ohs do.

HOST DENNIS ANNOUNCES THE RULES for the Final Exam. River and I will each serve our courses in staggered start times. River goes first, and I'll start ten minutes behind him. At each of our one-hour marks, we present our first course: hors d'oeuvres. Then, in thirty-minute intervals, our appetizers, entrées, desserts. It's the quadrathlon of cooking competitions.

The staggered start times are so our food won't be judged cold. It also means I won't know what feedback the judges will be giving to River or vice versa. It's like cooking in a black box.

The producers have timed things down to the last minute, so they eke out the full workday for us, without violating child labor laws. The key is for me to use the first hour wisely, so I'm prepped for all of the subsequent courses.

I force my brain to focus on my mental spreadsheet with a rundown of my to-do list, down to the last minute. Umma had drilled me on the schedule on the plane. My thoughts keep threatening to go to negative, angry places. It takes all my willpower to shut out the darkness.

Hang in there, Jackie. A few more hours and this will all be over.

Host Dennis wraps up. And for what will be the final time, he says to us: "So cook off or—"

Trained monkeys that we are, we all scream,

"Burn Off!"

I. Hors D'oeuvres

River

"Enticement"

Toast points three ways:

Sous vide pork belly with hot honey and black truffle essence.

Bluefin crudo with sturgeon pearls.

Seared foie gras with tarragon onion gelée.

Jackie

"Just *Dough* It!"

NYC dough three ways:

"Egg & Cheese on an Everything" Sunny-side up quail egg and NY cave-aged cheddar served on a hand-rolled bagel chip dusted with "everything bagel" seasoning of black and white sesame, gochugaru salt, Szechuan pepper, and seaweed crystals, with gochujang aioli schmear.

"Slice Joint Pizza with a Side of Kimchi, What" Wood-burning-stove-baked mini pizza with hand-pulled Mozzarella di Bufala, tomato schmear, spicy cabbage pizza, and basil gochujang chili oil, served with fresh cucumber kimchi "al caballo" (on top).

"Korean Empanada" Mandu filling meets Argentine pasty: ground beef, japchae, hard-boiled egg whites, and parsley, deep-fried, with minari chimichurri dipping sauce.

Served with a dill pickle.

"Very playful," Judge Johnny says, taking a bite of the bagel hors d'oeuvres. "Ace move with the New York water! LA bagels are awful." He glances at Host Dennis. "No offense."

"Offense taken," Host Dennis says, and everyone laughs.

"You made these bagels yourself?" Judge Kelly asks. I nod. She lifts a bagel chip and points to the side, at the thin sliver of crust. "How did you achieve the shine on the bagel?"

"After boiling the bagels, I brushed them with a mixture of baking soda and water," I say. "I actually learned that tip from Gus. He was an excellent chef. I wish he'd made it to the finals."

River, at his station, seems to flinch as I say that.

Judge Stone says, "Your presentation is very neat. But I do feel for the carbophobes in our midst. This is *very* dough-forward, Jacqueline."

I wonder if he said the same thing to River's toast pointes.

"And what's with the pickle?" Judge Johnny waves a spear in the air, flopping it about.

"That's how Haraboji eats pizza." I say it like, *You got a problem with that?*

Just before I'm dismissed, Judge Johnny adds, "Not bad, Jackie-o, not bad! You keep this up, and we might have a winner on our hands."

II. Appetizers

River

"Serenity"

Green tea–smoked foraged mushrooms with tweezered microgreens, served with maple gochujang brown butter foam.

Jackie

"Midtown Salad Bar Power Lunch"

Ssam lettuce cups served with your choice of three proteins:

"Steakhouse style": soy-glazed short rib in iceberg lettuce cup.

"Halal cart" chicken: cumin, curry, turmeric, paprika, allspice, served over bed of spinach.

"Knish" potato croquette on steamed cabbage leaf.

Choose up to 3 ingredients to add to your cup: carrots, cherry tomatoes, mushrooms, snow peas, shredded scallions, red peppers, bagel-garlic croutons, blanched asparagus, avocado, edamame, sautéed kimchi.

Choice of dressing: buttermilk blue cheese, yogurt tahini, soy ginger, balsamic reduction, gochujang schmear.

Prepared table-side.

*Cash only. Leave the Amex at home.

"It's like a Choose Your Own Adventure!" Judge Johnny says as I take their orders. "I'll have one of each protein, dealer's choice on the sides and dressings."

"Why is this served à la minute?" Judge Stone asks, like it's a trick question.

"Because I didn't want the lettuce to wilt," I say, preparing the dishes.

"This one's a play on the steakhouse salad. Like an iceberg wedge salad," Judge Kelly says, biting into her wrap. She took it classic, with buttermilk blue cheese, tomato, and (to my surprise) kimchi.

"Exactly!" I say. "That one's an expense account lunch. And for the days you can't charge it to the corporation"— I point to the other two wraps—"you can go to the street carts."

But I've lost Judge Stone. "I'm both overwhelmed and *under*whelmed, if that paradoxical Schrödingerian feline state is even possible. We're halfway into your tasting menu, Jacqueline, and is *this* the best you can do? Halal cart?"

He pushes his plate away, like my chicken is so beneath him.

"If this were one of our Ten Dollar and Under challenges, that'd be one thing. But . . . this was your time to *bring it,* Jacqueline. There were no cash limits here."

He fixes his eyes at me. They're flat and cold. It's weird how blue eyes can manifest so differently in white people. On Host Dennis, they're like round and friendly marbles; on Stone, they're slants of chipped ice.

"Jacqueline," Judge Stone continues, "where's the *wow* factor?"

So what does that mean—only people who can afford the fanciest and freshest ingredients deserve a tasting menu? I think of KT's rice 'n' beans. What about those with food insecurity?

And suddenly I find myself blurting those words out loud.

Which Stone does *not* appreciate.

Judge Kelly's next. I pre-wince, in anticipation of the pile-on: *It's too all over the place. Bokjaphae. Low-class.*

But she says, "Stone, I'd beg to differ. Jacqueline did the work of not one but *three* different appetizers. There's a lot of behind-the-scenes prep that went into this course. And the flavors themselves are quite elevated."

Stone waves her off, like she's talking nonsense.

"Give me one stunning dish—a beautifully seared duck, a veal tenderloin, some gorgeous mushrooms. In the words of Coco Chanel, which your namesake donned on the regular: 'less is more.' *This* is a case of more is less."

Judge Stone says it with finality.

Judge Kelly crosses her arms over her chest. "Then you and I will just have to agree to disagree."

That's that, and I'm sent back to Kitchen Classroom to prep the next course.

III. Entrée

River

"Nascence"

Milk-fed veal tenderloin with a bourbon gastrique and late-summer smoked new potatoes, in a glass cloche.

Jackie

"KFC & Waffles"

Korean fried chicken: twice-fried chicken drumettes in red chili rub, coated in bagel crouton breadcrumbs, served with scallion waffles jerked with NYC-soda water. Served with banchan of soy-braised black beans, beet kkakdugi kimchi, and a slaw of pickled red and green cabbage.

We're halfway through the Final Exam, and I wish it would hurry up and be over already. It kind of kills my spirit to cook my food for people who aren't jazzed about it. Thankfully, the judges like the flavors of my chicken and waffles, and they nod as I talk about the origin of the dish, and my twist on the classic. Most sources point to chicken and waffles being invented in Harlem's jazz clubs. I talk about paying homage to southern Black Americans who migrated North to escape Jim Crow—as if that's escapable—and for better job opportunities. I talk about the rumored origins of KFC, and how some say the Black GIs stationed in Korea during the Korean War taught the local cooks about breaded and fried chicken. And KFC grew into its own food tradition, using Korean flavors—hello, Bonchon Chicken on Northern Boulevard—until they met in a harmonious smothering in New York.

And I talk about how you need all the banchan—accompaniments—to make this feel like a rounded meal—like a symphony.

But as I explain, my thoughts keep returning to Haraboji. Is he still alive? Will he make it? He can't not—he's my haraboji! My breathing becomes shallow.

Now Business Time, Jackie-ya. Haraboji needs me to stay focused.

Even though it's the hardest thing I've ever had to do.

IV. Dessert

River

"Luminescence"

Liquid nitrogen caramel and shishito pepper *iced* cream essence with cookie dirt, served with Chantilly whipped cream foam and gold leaf.

Jackie

"Cawfee Regular and a Black & White"

Classic New York black-and-white cookie, with vanilla and lemon cake base. Coffee regular (i.e., with milk and two sugars) syrup, poured over shaved ice bingsu affogato shooter.

My dessert service is held up because the crew have to clean up after River's "canister malfunction" sent white foam gushing everywhere. I'm worried about my dessert melting, but the producers keep my dish on dry ice before it's served.

Judge Johnny holds up my black-and-white cookie. "It's the key to 'racial harmony'!" He looks around, as if expecting thunderous applause. "What, no Seinfeld fans here? Get it? Because it's black and white? In harmony?"

Yeah, under an invisible yellow cake base.

"The yin and yang design is cute, but it's not Asian enough. Where's the Asian element here?" Stone demands.

"My Asian hands touched it," I blurt out. "Does *that* count?"

Judge Kelly bursts out laughing. Host Dennis . . . slow claps.

I know H&H would be disappointed that I'd said that because it's disrespectful of authority. But Stone was being so ridiculous. Do we all have to be so matchy-matchy Asian like that? Am I *only* allowed to cook Asian things because I have Asian skin, eyes, hair, and body? And did Stone ever question whether River's pheasant sausage was "white enough"?

Judge Johnny shakes his head, like I've committed a big no-no. And Judge Stone glares back at me with a look like, *You'll never work in this town again.*

So, yeah. Judge Stone is officially no longer my food hero. I'll live.

NOW THAT MY LAST COURSE has been served, the judges recap.

"You're giving me breakfast, you're giving me lunch. You're

taking me to Harlem, then to the Lower East Side . . ." Judge Johnny stares up at me in confusion. "What is this, Jacqueline? If I'm eating Italian, I'm eating Italian. I'm eating Jewish, I'm going to my nana's. You're all over the map! What's the focus here? I gotta say, it's obvious you can cook your *tail* off. But at the end of the day . . . I got to ask myself, am I willing to pay three hundred dollars for this meal?"

"I'll hook you up," I quip. "Seventy-five percent discount."

Seriously, though. Three hundred dollars? For *food*? That's outrageous.

"That being said, your KFC was . . ." Judge Johnny smacks his fingers to his lips in a chef's kiss. "I'd eat that all day long."

Judge Kelly says, "I just want to take a moment to recognize the *sheer amount of labor* that went into each of Jackie's dishes. And the attention to detail—"

"But are we talking quantity or quality?" Judge Stone interrupts. "I'll grant Jacqueline's dishes were precise and well executed, and plentiful, like a Lunar New Year banquet at Nai-nai's. But the fact of the matter remains: This tasting menu was glorified street food. Jacqueline, your food is *unrefined*."

Not going to lie—it stings.

All of the comments Judge Stone had for me before— *technical, precise, workhorse*—was it ever really praise?

"With all respect, Stone, you've never actually worked in a restaurant. You're just a food critic," Judge Kelly shoots back. "I know you appreciate thought experiments, but at a certain point, chefs have to be *practical* in addressing the needs of their diners."

"Kelly, you *went* there!" Judge Johnny laughs.

Judge Stone is struggling to keep it tight, but anger flares across his face.

"The use of *all* the parts of the product, reinterpreted across multiple dishes, in stocks, sauces, sides, and so forth, not only builds layers upon layers of flavor"—Judge Kelly ticks off her fingers—"but it's also economical and sustainable—an issue our industry isn't addressing with the urgency it deserves. In my estimation, this chef is already thinking like a restauranteur in managing costs and food waste. Plus, Jackie's menu was fun, it's in your face, it's expertly executed. . . . This is a menu that has attitude and doesn't care what you think." She looks up at me. "This is *you*, Jackie Oh."

My mouth drops. Did Judge Kelly really just say that? Through the whole competition, her only feedback was all the ways I've failed to measure up. Ways I was half empty, instead of half full. Going into the finals, I was sure she'd be the one to burn me. Not Stone.

Judge Kelly reminds me . . . of Umma? Tough love, all the way.

It's all starting to make sense.

"There's no cohesion, no *harmony*! What's the singular narrative of your tasting menu? There are way too many storylines going on . . ."

Judge Stone and Judge Kelly argue over each other, and Judge Johnny jumps back and forth between the two, pointing out my goods—"The marinade on that short rib!"—and my bads—"I could pop over to Zabar's right now and get the same black-and-white!" The Judges' Table devolves into chaos—

Just like the city itself.

Let your work do the talking. My food speaks for itself. It doesn't need me to jump in and get its back.

Before this competition, I'd spend my whole paycheck at Murray's on the fanciest meat and cheese and dairy. Just as I didn't think about sustainability—using the whole part of the product, instead of the best bits and discarding the rest.

I know you're always supposed to cook with the best quality ingredients. I'm all for that—*if* you can afford it. But what if you can't? Does that still mean you can't be a chef? Isn't the true sign of a chef someone who can make something from nothing?

Food insecurity is something the food world hasn't given enough thought to. When it should.

The way I grew up, there *is* no harmony. There's no one homogenous, cohesive, meat 'n' potatoes on a plate meal. Because that's not New York. The second you step outside, the city, five boroughs and all, is in your face; it's abrasive and fresh and coming at you hot. It's *unrefined*. In the time it takes you to sit down and lift your fork, a million and one sights/smells/tastes have gone by.

> **ME:**
> They told me to bring the heat.
> I brought the heat. If they can't
> take it, then . . . (shrugging)
> they can get the hell out of
> my kitchen.

VALEDICTORIAN

We're sent off to the Library, where River and I make awkward small talk and pretend to congratulate each other, even though it's obvious he thinks he's the superior chef, and I think he's a hack.

"You'll probably win," he says. "Because, you know, your kind of food is 'trending.'"

River brushes back his hair as he says it. His hands are soft and white, like Gus's bread loaves. No burn, cuts, calluses—nothing.

"Do you say things like that just to make yourself feel better for losing?" I say. When River doesn't answer, I continue, "Your liquid nitrogen and foams are just smoke and mirrors, hiding the fact that you have nothing meaningful to say. On the plate," I add. "Bottom line: You can't cook for bleep."

I don't actually say "bleep."

***

WHEN THEY CALL ME IN for my OTF, I can't remember a single word I say, only that I don't give a crap. We return to Kitchen Classroom. Host Dennis is back to his toga-fied self, which clashes with the classroom and chalkboard setup, but I guess the producers were like, whatever. They even brought in the gladiator Viking horn guy.

I can read the verdict all over the judges' faces—I know who's won.

Host Dennis raises his arms for his usual spiel. "Ladies, gentlemen, country*people*! Lend me your ears! Twelve teens battled it out in Kitchen Classroom. Only two teens remain! And now, our judges will weigh in on the winning tasting menu."

Judge Stone begins. "I see a lot of myself in this young chef. They're creative and determined. They give a brand-new definition to 'playing with food.' The tasting menu they presented for us was elegant and refined. My colleague Johnny said he'd gladly pay three hundred fifty dollars for that meal. I'd top that with four hundred dollars.

"It is my privilege, and my honor, to present to you the chef I believe represents the future of food. Not its past, or its stagnant present . . ."

I cooked my best today. I made a meal that was 100 percent Jackie Oh. I cooked my food, and maybe someday, other people will see *their* food journey in my dishes. Because isn't that how we achieve the universal? It's through the specific story.

"Jackie Oh!" Host Dennis says.

I look up, stunned. Did I totally miscall it?

"I'm afraid you've been *burnt*. Please exit Kitchen Class-room."

His eyes flood with sympathy, and sadness. But the show must go on.

"Which means the Valedictorian of BOH, the first-ever teen to win on this show, is . . . from Portland, Oregon: River Waters!"

As soon as the cameras stop rolling, the show will stop. I can leave this stage—we'll rush to LAX to JFK to Haraboji's bed-side at Flushing Hospital, praying to God he'll pull through.

But in this moment, as the studio fills with cheers, the bal-loons sail down and the spotlight shuts off me and swings to River, literally casting me in the shadows, I know there's one person smiling biggest and brightest in the audience, holding her arms wide open to me because—I know now—she's as proud that I'm her daughter as I am that she's my

Umma.

STOP
AAPI
HATE

Caption: Justice for Eun-Suk

TW: Violence, anti-AAPI hate, trauma

Friends, listen up. You remember my friend and Burnee Jackie Oh (hello everything bagels! 🥯 Check NYT for her recipe!!) Jackie's grandpa, Eun-Suk (은석) was attacked on the NYC subway. Eun-Suk (which Google tells me is Korean for Kind-Rock!) was just minding his own biz, heading super-early to his deli, Melty's (their Madison Ave sandwiches are 🔥!) One witness said the attacker called Eun-Suk, "F-g ch-k!" But the NYPD are NOT labeling this a hate crime. The attacker remains at large. Nothing was caught on tape.

Eun-Suk now has permanent brain damage. He is a mental vegetable for life.

Y'all know how much I love vegetables, but only in my SALADS not in my fellow humans.

This is a call to STOP ASIAN HATE.

100,000+ likes

@AsianAlltheWayThey keep doing this to us! Are we invisible?

@PerkyAF OMG Baja what color is your nail polish? LOVE

@ProwdBoyz GO HOME CH**KS

1,000+ likes

@RWB_Stripes 💯

@Trmp2024 And take ur China Flu w u!

@ALM U mean KUNG FLU lol

@Very_Azn We need to center AAPI stories!

@sunnydae We don't have it as bad as them. We will NEVER have it as bad as them.

@moon424 Since when is it a contest?

@jessmyth We are hurting with you. We stand with you.

@AmbrosiaLee Justice for Eun-Suk.

@powerhouseboy666 STFU, FAT GIRL! STFU FAT GIRL! ITS CALLED A TREADMILL. USE IT.

@ladiezman Love me a THICC Girl, I want to—

This comment has been flagged for deletion.

@Karensway You should think about your health . . .

@bodyposityvette Stop bodyshaming AMBROSIAS A QUEEN!!!

@joemassapeq Eun-Suk had it coming. His grandson Justin Oh is in JAIL for beating up innocent ppl! [link to Bayside Ledger article TK]

@RiteMakesMite KARMAS A B****

@SpanishLvr baja ur so hot I want to put my

> This comment is hidden due to explicit language.

@burnee439Still #teamjackie! Check out her interview in Bon Appetit!

@jackieo_fangirl58 💯

@rivermaniac69 💯 wrong. #teamriver

@TheNextRBG_LGW You can donate to these AAPI non-profits: KAFSC, KACF, Stop AAPI Hate. They're worthy causes that—

@AllLives Shut up Libtard!

> 500+ likes

@stephen_minfinity Jackie Oh's offline. She asked me to post this: "Haraboji's been discharged from the hospital. Our family is navigating the new normal. Thank you for all your support in this difficult time."

> 20,000 likes including @thekellysharpe

> **@SaraSeasFood** Is he ok???

> **@GusChi-town** Did Jackie get my care package?

> **@stephen_minfinity** Lets all give Jackie & her fam some space!

@AleVK Stop Asian hate

> liked by **@BDiaz @C_Dvrx @DocC @Mikedrop**

@JaneRQns Stop Asian hate

    liked by **@MaryRCutie @George_Is_Jacked**

@aDORAble Stop Asian hate

@ColinO_Congress AAPI + BLM Solidarity

@user40124793: The statistical likelihood of getting attacked on the subway is 1 in 1 million, versus the one in 8,000 chance of getting into a car accident.

@Jerr_e_lee: Not if ur azian, dude

@mandarinvenus: it's not always about race

@QueensReader Say their names: Michelle Go. Christina Yuna Lee. Yao Pan Ma. Hoa Nguyen. GuiYing Ma. Vincent Chin.

@GusChi-town Stop AAPI hate

    liked by **@Mei**

@SaraSeasFood Stop AAPI hate

@burnee444: Omg they leaked Calvin's audition tape! He's making Victoria sponge and it looks 😖

@FeeldaBurn I was today year's old when I learned Staten Island Calvin was a PASTRY CHEF 👀 😱

@cawfeeregular Did anyone see Calvins public apology to Jackie?? #imnotcrying #urcrying

@kevng1: Notice how the news NEVER mentioned the race of the attacker? Hmm . . .

@**BSC_QuakerO**: We stand with our Asian brothers and sisters #blasiansolidarity

@**OhEuniverse** Read this: NYT Op-Ed "I'm Done Being Your Model Minority" https://www.nytimes.com/2022/03/10/opinion/asian-american-hate-crimes.html

Appendix A

Korean Empanadas

A fast and loose recipe. Trial and error is the only way to get the portions right.

Ingredients

-Ground beef

-Diced onion

-Korean japchae (cellophane noodles), boiled, cooled, and chopped

-Hardboiled egg whites, chopped (Bingsu will snack on the yolks)

-Spanish or pimiento-stuffed olives, chopped

-Parsley, chopped

-Empanada wrappers for frying (Goya brand or homemade)

-Salt, pepper, and seasonings of choice (experiment!)

-Oil for deep frying, such as canola

Steps

1. **DEFROST** empanada wrappers at room temp.

2. **HEAT** oil in deep and shallow pan.

3. **COOK** ground beef and onions with seasonings over medium–high heat.

4. **ASSEMBLE** all filling ingredients. Experiment with the proportions (some people like their empanada filling more meat-forward, others more noodley). Now is the time to adjust seasonings.

5. **LET** filling cool so your wrappers don't turn gummy.

6. HOLDING an empanada wrapper in your open palm, heap a couple spoonfuls onto the wrapper and fold the wrapper over.

7. CRIMP using your fingers or the tines of a fork. You may want to use a little water to help seal the ends.

8. THE oil must be hot to achieve a proper fry; otherwise, the dumplings will turn soggy. You can test the oil by throwing a little salt into the oil—if it bubbles, it's ready. (*Caution: NEVER THROW WATER into hot oil!)

9. GENTLY place each empanada into the pan of hot oil and fry a few minutes on each side until golden brown. (Careful it doesn't turn black!)

10. USE a slotted spoon and remove empanadas from oil. Place on plate lined with paper towels to drain.

11. ENJOY!

> It's always better to have too much filling than not enough. You can serve the leftover filling over rice for an impromptu leftovers lunch. If you *do* end up with too many empanada wrappers, you can freeze for a later use.

Haraboji's Budae Jjigae aka "Army Stew"

INGREDIENTS

-Shin instant ramyun noodles

-Onion, thinly sliced

-Spam, hot dogs, or Vienna sausages in a can, sliced

-Egg

-Heap of gochjujang (red pepper paste)

-Heap of gochugaru (red pepper flakes)

-Garlic, minced

-Water

-Soy sauce

-Sugar

-Any veggies or meat scraps in the fridge

-Scallions, chopped

-Toasted sesame seeds

-Rice

-*Opt.* Broth seasonings, including a square or two of dashima (dried kelp) or a few myulchi (dried anchovies), guts and heads removed

-*Opt.* Odeng (fried fish cakes), cut into squares

-*Opt.* Dduk (sticky rice cakes), chopped

-*Opt.* Spoonfuls of kimchi

-*Opt.* Slice of American cheese

-*Mandatory* Dill pickles

STEPS

1. FILL a pot with water, all vegetables, all meat, dduk, fish cakes, broth seasonings (if using). Set to medium. Boil.

2. WHEN broth is boiling, add ramen noodles and flavor packets.

3. WHEN noodles get chewy (approx. 4 min), taste broth and adjust seasoning. Add to taste: gochujang (the spicier the better!), gochugaru, soy sauce, and sugar to balance heat. Add kimchi, if using. Stir.

4. CRACK raw egg into the broth. If you like whole eggs, leave to simmer undisturbed. If you like them more scrambled, then stir into the broth.

5. CAREFUL! Don't let ramen noodles get bloated or jjigae will be ruined!

6. TAKE off heat and sprinkle scallions, sesame seeds, and (if using) American cheese.

7. SERVE with Kosher dill pickles.

"Cawfee" Regular

Ingredients

-Coffee from a hot pot
-Milk (full fat, none of that fancy nut or oat stuff)
-Two sugars

Steps

1. **GO** to your nearest bodega.

2. **ORDER** a "cawfee" regular (never, for the love of God, a "regular coffee").

3. **ENJOY!**

Stephen Min's "Corporate Sell-Out" Oatmeal Juk Breakfast

Let's cut straight to the steps, no BS:

1. **COOK** steel-cut oats 1:4 ratio (oats: H_2O), with a pinch of salt, overnight in a slow cooker, 8 hours on low.

> If you cheat with any of that instant Quaker stuff, YOU'RE the one who has to live with yourself.

2. **GET** your toppings bar/mise en place ready: gim flakes, sesame seeds, frizzle up with garlic slivers and sprinkle in sugar, fried myulchi, whatever your little heart desires.

3. **SOFT-BOIL** an egg. You're aiming for jammy yolks. *Bon Appétit* has a good recipe. Hard-boiled eggs with tennis ball yolks are for amateurs.

4. **LADLE** up some oatmeal in a bowl. Top with desired toppings. Split the jammy egg in half and add on top.

5. **DRIZZLE** sesame seed oil, gochujang to taste.

6. **MASH** it up. Wolf it down.

Gus's Under 20 Minutes Flatbread*

Ingredients:

1 cup all-purpose flour**

1.5 teaspoons baking powder

Pinch of salt

1 cup Greek yogurt, plain, preferably whole milk

2 tablespoons olive oil, plus more for pan

-Optional 2 teaspoons of dried herbs (oregano, rosemary, carraway seeds, any of your favorites)

Toppings of your choice

Equipment:

Cast iron skillet

Heat-proof tongs

Mixing bowl

Flat surface

Rolling pin

Method:

1. **HEAT** cast iron skillet on high

2. **SIFT** the flour, baking powder, salt, and herbs (if using) in a bowl.

3. **ADD** yogurt and olive oil. Mix well.★★★

4. **FORM** dough into a ball with your hands and divide into 4.

5. **ROLL** out each dough part into as flat and round a shape as you can. Or get creative and experiment with oblong or other shapes.

6. ADD oil to the pan.

7. HEAT each bread in the skillet until the inside dough is cooked and the bottoms are golden brown (2–4min per side).

8. ADD toppings of your choice.

Disclaimers:

*This recipe is highly dependent based on the humidity levels and other variables of your cooking environment. You may have to experiment with measurements and/or other cooking methods. You can also want to experiment with portion sizes. Practice makes perfect!

**The biggest mistake people make is measuring their flour incorrectly, depending on how tightly they pack it down in a measuring cup. The best measure for flour is by weight. But since most people don't have a food scale, you can also use the spoon and butter knife method, which you can research. Exercise your best judgment.

***But not too well that you overwork the glutens in the flour. It will make the dough tough.

Appendix B

From *McMann's Authoritative Cookery series, Foundations of Good Cookery*

CHAPTER 2:
Holy, Thy Name Art Mirepoix

> so much depends
> upon
> a humble
> trio
> sweat–glazed onions
> carrots celery
> beneath the silver
> cloche

Mire *(holy)* poix *(trinity)* is the ultimate behind-the-scenes work-horse, wallflower, the unsung hero of the culinary landscape—like so much of the undocumented underbelly churning out the finest feasts from SoHo to Sonoma. This humble triumvirate of onions, carrots, and celery forms the backbone of most

French soups, stews, and sauces. Spaniards and the Latin Americans who hate them have their *sofrito:* onions, peppers, and tomatoes. Just as the Italians posit their *soffritto è superiore.* But to the Francophiles among us, the mirepoix is where it's at.

Any sous-chef worth his Himalayan sea salt will have the mirepoix as part of his mise en place at the ready, lest he risk the wrath of Chef on a Saturday night before service.

Imagine the indignation of being relegated to supporting cast, while the protein has the audacity to take main stage! But the mirepoix never tries to pull a Tanya to the protein's Nancy; it doth protest not; it does not go gently into that good night. Yet we must acknowledge that sans this humble holy trinity, the best, bougiest beef would be for not (*see p. 289 for the recipe*). Ratatouille would scurry off, tail tucked between its legs (*see also: Ratatouille à la McMann, p. 461*). Onions-carrots-celery are sautéed to the point of melting away, sacrificing their structural dignity for the greater good: flavor, and lots of it.

True to its name, the mirepoix is the ultimate culinary martyr.

For recipes featuring the mirepoix, see also

ACKNOWLEDGMENTS

I'm so grateful to the people who shared their time, talents, and energy to help make *What's Eating Jackie Oh?* the best book it could be.

I'd like to thank: Susan Kim and family, and all the Toasties of 51st and Madison team. Ustedes son los héroes.

For sharing your food TV expertise: Ashley Archer, Roen Guerin, Aimee Householder, Jon Luton, and Tigre McMullan.

To all the teachers and students I met with at my alma mater, Bronx Science, including Eleanor Coufos; Assistant Principal of English, Alessandra Zullo Casale; and Assistant Principal of Social Studies, David Colchamiro.

Thank you to Sarah Burnes and the whole Gernert team. Thank you to Jean Kwok, Meggie Miao, and Claudia Pak. To my colleagues and students at American University. To filmmakers Julie Ha and Eugene Yi and their heartbreaking documentary, *Free Chol Soo Lee*.

Any inaccuracies, simplifications, or omissions are my own

and/or for the sake of novelistic compression. I humbly beg forgiveness.

There are two turns of phrases in the book that I wish to credit: "anxious gargoyle" is from George Saunders's 2018 essay "Process & Spirit," in *The Writer's Chronicle*. I could not *unsee* this image, and nothing else I came up with had quite the same ring. *When it's cold, write it like it's hot; when it's hot, write it like it's cold* was wonderful advice Min Jin Lee gave to one of my American University students when she was our visiting writer in 2019. It is advice I continue to share with my students today.

This book wouldn't be without Phoebe Yeh. Thank you and Daniela Cortes for shepherding this work. Thank you to Barbara Marcus, Judith Haut, Mallory Loehr, Kris Kam, Adrienne Waintraub, trade + digital marketer tk, Erica Henegen, Sarah Pierre, Melinda Ackell, Ray Shappell, Michelle Crowe, Tisha Paul, CJ Han, Denise Morales Soto, Genevieve Kim, and all the wonderful folks in sales, marketing, and publicity at Random House Children's. Thanks to Jessica Cruickshank for her beautiful artwork. Thank you to all the librarians, educators, and booksellers for championing *Imposter Syndrome and Other Confessions of Alejandra Kim* and for fighting the good fight.

To all of my family. I'd especially like to thank my nephews Gage and Lucas, to whom this book is dedicated. I want a better world for you. It means everything that you can proudly bring your Korean lunches to school—progress I never dreamed was possible.

This novel was inspired by two things: my love of cooking with leftovers, and the fears and frustrations those in my community have faced over anti-AAPI hate. I've spoken with many students across the country like Jackie, who don't understand why they and their family are being targeted. Who, like Jackie, cannot make sense of this moment and are *done* being "model minorities." To my fellow Asians in America, who are tired of being pushed around (literally, metaphorically)—I also dedicate this book to you.